i

Eric McFarlane

First published 2024 by Eric McFarlane

ISBN 9798699048182

Copyright ©**Eric McFarlane** 2024

The right of **Eric McFarlane** to be identified as the author of this work has been asserted by the author in accordance with the Copyright, Designs and Patents Act 1988.

One

'GOOD MORNING, PROFESSOR. WHAT a beautiful day.'

Daniel Dreghorn knew that his voice sounded bright and confident because he felt confident. The sun shone from a cloudless sky, at least it did in the square outside the professor's university office. He had an offer of a new job and, after two months of togetherness, Lorraine still poured milk on his morning cereal. Yes, life was definitely worth living.

In contrast, professor Quentin Farquharson, Daniel's boss and Dean of Coatdyke University, slumped in his swivel chair and looked unnaturally down. The lines that had always creased his forehead below the fuzz of wispy white hair were crisscrossed by yet more and deeper lines. Papers and disposable coffee cups cluttered his desk, indeed some papers had been used to mop up the contents of the cups. He gave no response to the cheery greeting.

'Professor?' Daniel fingered the resignation letter in his pocket. How to proceed? He was used to Farquharson's day-to-day mood swings, which usually related to whether he had struck lucky the previous night. At an indeterminate seventy-plus he appeared to have no difficulty in finding an inexhaustible supply of lovers to service his palaeolithic plonker. The lovers' gender or species assignment seemed to cause him little concern.

'Professor, I came to give you—'

1

'Daniel, the very man!' He jerked into life as if someone had tugged a string. 'It's you I need.'

Daniel took a step away from the desk. 'No, really, I couldn't, thanks all the same. You see, I've brought my let—'

'I'm in terrible trouble, my fair friend. I need a saviour. You are my saviour, Daniel, my rock. Now I know I was right to keep you on.'

'No, wait. That's not quite—'

'I refer to our understanding, Daniel, our little arrangement.' He gave an exaggerated wink that twisted one side of his face into a ghastly leer. 'I had hoped to have no further need of your expert services, but you have turned out to be a worthwhile insurance policy.'

'I don't... understand.'

But he had a ghastly feeling that he did understand Farquharson's wittering. Well, if the old fool tried any funny business, it wouldn't work.

'It's been a few months now since you took on the position of chief technician after the sudden resignation of dear Mr Peabrose. Oh, and do sit down, my boy.'

Daniel perched on the hard-backed chair in front of the professor's desk and took a deep breath. 'Actually, it's been more than a year and I've decided on a change.' He reached into his pocket. 'Look, I have a let—'

'A year? Well, well, time flies does it not? A year, eh? And you have enjoyed your time in post?'

'Enjoyed? Well, yes. I'm happy enough, it's just—'

'Happiness is a strange phenomenon. Ephemeral, one might say. I too was happy until very recently. That is until the tides of darkness washed up on my shore.'

'Tides?'

'Of darkness, yes. A poetic phrase. Too poetic for what has befallen me.'

2

Daniel felt his face redden. His teeth clenched hard. He had to take control here. 'Professor. I'm sorry about your problems, but I've decided to go. To leave. Another job. I have a let—'

'Leave.' The professor looked as if he had been hit by a very large object travelling very fast, possibly a meteorite of the type that had done for the dinos. 'No, no, quite impossible. Not at this moment. Oh my goodness no.'

Daniel reached into his pocket. 'Professor, I'm sorry, but my mind is made up. I've been offered a job, and I'd like to give you my let—'

'Stop.' Farquharson boomed, raising his hand. Daniel stopped. 'We need to discuss a number of things. Things pertaining to your employment.' He rose and made his way slowly around the desk until he stood behind Daniel's chair.

Daniel flinched as a cadaverous hand rested on his shoulder.

'Now, I'm sure you will agree that I myself was instrumental in obtaining your current position for you.'

It was true. He nodded as skinny fingers worked their way around his neck.

'That without my recommendation you would not be employed at this university.'

He cringed as skeleton digits massaged his shoulder – those same fingers rumoured to have wormed into many an unsavoury place.

'You will remember that as part of that, we came to a little agreement.'

'Well—'

'An unofficial agreement. No signatures, witnesses, or anything of that sort. Just two gentlemen agreeing. Agreeing that one gentleman would help the other gentleman should that second gentleman ever have need of his services.'

'Yes, professor, I remember. But that's why I came here to tell you I have another job offer, and to give you my let—'

'So, my boy, I have need of your services. Urgently.' The fingers squeezed and then let go. Farquharson returned to his place behind the desk. 'A simple little job, that is all, and then you may retire to pastures new.'

Daniel rubbed his forehead hard. The old loony wasn't going to get away with this. Before he could come up with a reply, Farquharson continued.

'Of course, should you have any difficulty with this proposition we might have to consider where we stand vis-à-vis certain events. I refer to the sad, sad death of my dear wife, Jemima.'

Daniel wanted to scream. Instead, he farted, involuntarily and rather loudly. The professor turned around as if confused as to where the sound had come from.

'Professor, that's all in the past.'

To Daniel, it was in the past. Far from being *dear Jemima,* the man had very much wanted his wife dead. Unfortunately, her completely accidental fall from a great height had been linked by Farquharson to Daniel. This had resulted in undying thanks, a bundle of used banknotes and his current situation.

'Professor, I'd love to help, but—'

'Excellent, Daniel, welcome aboard.'

'No, no I meant—'

'And of course, we shall say no more of the little matter of the evidence inadvertently withheld from the police all those months ago.'

'What?'

'Yes, the little matter of the photographs linking you and my dear wife, Jemima. The photographs of your assignation.'

'Photographs?'

'But those must be destroyed. It wouldn't do for them to fall into the wrong hands, would it now? Oh dear no.'

He closed his eyes, breathed deeply, and tried to slow his thumping heart.

'And they will be destroyed when you fly the nest, eventually. As soon as I have the time. Meanwhile, there is this little matter. Can you help me?'

Daniel sat back in the chair. He'd been well and truly whacked. A distant voice said, 'You'd better tell me about it.'

Two

REYNOLDS IS HIS NAME and I just need to know what he is up to, my boy, that's all, were the professor's last words. *It's very simple. The man is visiting his solicitor this morning; you only have to follow him.*

So, that morning, Daniel had left Lorraine's snores and headed to town. Now here he was, hanging about outside the offices of Crummey and Worsted, solicitors, feeling conspicuously inconspicuous.

The offices were upstairs through a single door flanked by high-street shops. He tried walking backwards and forwards along the street a few times but, while walking towards the office door was OK, as soon as he turned his back on it, he had to fight the urge to glance over his shoulder. This wasn't helped by the increasing pedestrian traffic as morning wore on. He solved this problem by crossing the road and pretending to stare into a shop window. The reflection allowed him a good view of the office entrance. Perfect.

Much to his annoyance, a group of teenage girls passed, giggling and laughing and pointing at him. What was so funny? But he forgot all about them as the solicitor's door opened. He focussed on the man who appeared: young, long hair, hoodie. No way did that match the description, so he continued his vigil at the window.

'Daniel?' A female voice.

He turned to find Lorraine frowning at him. He really didn't want to meet her right now, in the middle of his mission as he had begun to think of it.

'Oh hi, I was...' the solicitor's door opened again.

'What are you doing here?'

'I was only...' He turned back to the window. Grey hair, tall, slightly stooped, it had to be his quarry, and then his eyes refocused behind the glass of the shop window. The first thing he noticed was that the display was extremely pink in hue. The second was that it contained rather a lot of lacy stuff, and the third was a large sign proclaiming that the randy rabbit would ride again. Realisation hit as he turned to see his quarry striding along the pavement much faster than was decent for a slightly stooped man with grey hair.

'Lorraine, sorry.' He started along the pavement. 'I have to go.'

'Daniel, why were you looking in that shop?'

His target was way ahead. He quickened his pace. Lorraine followed.

'Just... window shopping for a present. You weren't meant to see.'

'Daniel! You must know I don't do that sort of thing. It's disgusting. And will you stand still while we're talking?'

'No, no, it wasn't for you.'

'What?'

'Look, I'll explain later. I really must go.'

He sprinted up the road to where he had seen the grey-haired man turn a corner, leaving Lorraine, hands on hips, staring after him.

If only he could have waited a moment longer, he would have observed the solicitor's door open once more and a tall man with slicked-back, silver hair emerge. The man glanced right and left, then set off at a fast pace.

Daniel skidded around the corner in time to see his quarry enter the front cab of a taxi rank. The cab moved off as he sprinted to the top of the queue. An elderly woman with a stick and a hat had her hand on the door of the next taxi. Daniel barged past her.

'Excuse me, emergency. My wife.' He threw himself into the vehicle and slammed the door.

'Arsehole,' the woman screamed and stuck her middle finger in the air.

Daniel shrank away from the window as the vehicle pulled into traffic.

'Where to, squire?' the driver grunted.

Where to? Daniel peered through the windscreen. The taxi ahead had stopped at a red light. 'Just start off and I'll give you directions.'

The cab pulled out and joined the queue at the lights as they turned to green.

'Go right here.'

There was only one car between pursued and pursuer. 'Straight on now... no left.'

The driver gave Daniel a wary glance in the mirror.

'Are we following that cab in front?'

'No, no.'

'We are, aren't we? Don't worry. I know how to do this. MI5 is it?'

'No. Well not exactly.'

'Thought so. Don't you worry, squire. I'm on it. Know how to keep my mouth shut.'

Daniel sat back in his seat. At least he didn't have to give the driver directions. They were on the bypass now, with a safe distance between cars.

'So, doing much recruiting these days?' the driver asked.

'What, at the university?'

'Yeah, nice one. The university, I like that.' He paused. 'So, are you recruiting?'

'Oh yes, all the time, we're always taking people on.'

'Think I could fill a gap?'

The car in front had speeded up. Daniel leant forward anxiously.

'You can always apply.'

'Could you put a word in for me?'

'Sure, sure. Look, I think they're getting away.'

The cab accelerated so rapidly that Daniel slammed back into his seat.

'Don't worry, squire, they'll not lose me.'

Both cars turned off the bypass and drew to a halt at traffic lights by a roundabout.

'So how do I apply then?'

Daniel had just noticed the passenger in the cab they were following turn and glance behind. He ducked out of sight.

'You can ask for a form, or there's one on the website.'

'The website? As easy as that?'

'Yeah, University of Coatdyke.'

'A front, eh?'

'Sometimes I think so, but look, the lights are at...'

Tyres screeched as the taxi accelerated away.

A few minutes later, they were in the wasteland of an industrial estate. Some units were occupied, others seemed to have been abandoned years ago. Daniel's taxi pulled into the side of the road. Up ahead, he watched his quarry pay the fare and head towards the driveway of a large two-story unit. Whatever Reynolds' reason for being here, it wasn't where he lived. What should he do now?

'This is you, squire.' The driver lowered his voice. 'There going to be any rough stuff?'

'What?'

'Sorry, sorry. None of my business. You'll be getting out then?'

'Um… I guess. What do I owe you?'

The driver waved his hand. 'Forget it, squire. This has been an education. Look, here's my card. Beezer's the name. Beezer the geezer the lad's call me. Get it? Yeah?'

'Yes, sure, thanks.' Daniel pushed the cab door open.

'You'll put a good word in for me, eh? When my application comes through?'

'Application? Oh yeah, of course. There are always vacancies. In services and so on.'

Beezer whirled away in a cloud of dust and a shout of 'Yes!' leaving Daniel hesitating by the low brick wall that surrounded the drab, two-story unit. There was nothing to show what company occupied it, but it looked in decent condition, unlike some of its neighbours. Well, the least he could do was find out more about it.

Biting his thumbnail, he hesitated by the path leading to the entrance door. The building had no number, no sign emblazoned with a company name. He didn't even know what street this was. He checked his phone, but it seemed to be on strike. There had been a map near the entrance to the estate. OK, first, enquire inside at the reception desk, then walk back to the road, find the…

'Come on, don't hang about here,' a voice whispered urgently. A hand on his back pushed him forwards.

Heart thumping, Daniel turned around. A man in his thirties, a peaked cap pulled low on his forehead. 'What? I'm not—'

'Move it. Don't draw attention.'

The man grabbed his elbow and all but forced him down the path, through the unlocked entrance and into a spacious but dimly lit hallway.

A burly man with a shaven head and leather jacket stood, rock-like, in the centre of the hall. Legs apart and arms folded, he stared at them with fishlike eyes. After a few seconds appraisal, he stepped aside and motioned them upstairs with a nod of his head.

'Excuse me...' Daniel began.

'Come on will you? We're late. You know what he's like. Follow me.'

Daniel turned at the foot of the stairs. Shaven head watched him, head tilted to one side, hands in the pockets of his leather jacket. Daniel headed upstairs.

His companion stood outside a door on the left of the landing, listening. He ran a hand over his hair and cleared his throat. 'Don't worry, he's not started.'

'Look, really,' Daniel whispered. 'There's been a mistake, a terrible mistake.'

'Raise it at the meeting then, come on.' The man pushed the door open, and Daniel followed him inside.

The large room contained perhaps twenty-five people seated at a series of small tables, all facing away from the door and towards a dais at the front. Each table had a carafe of water and four glasses. No one was drinking. Two clones of shaven-head stood on either side of the dais staring at the audience. A conversational murmur filled the room.

Daniel joined his companion at an empty table. There seemed little else to do. He picked up a carafe and started to pour himself a glass of water but suddenly, horribly, became aware that voices had stopped. A pin might have been heard had it clattered to the floor. Instead, the only sound was the glug of water pouring from a full carafe. Glancing up, he saw a grey-haired, slightly stooped man stride towards the dais. Enthusiastic applause broke out as Daniel's glass overflowed and a torrent of water rushed for the table's edge. He put the carafe down, relieved to see the spillage absorbed by the thick cloth covering the table. The water's meniscus, however, winked at him mischievously over the top of his glass. Bending down, he put his lips to the glass and sucked at the very moment when applause broke suddenly to silence. The resulting noise, rather like a sink plunger working overtime on a Friday evening, reverberated around the room. Several heads turned in his direction, but the grey-haired man was speaking. It was Reynolds, the man he had followed from the solicitor's office.

'Friends, comrades.' The man raised his hands as if to quell the expected rapturous applause. 'Welcome to this, our second meeting. The Western Allotment Society is now in session.' A ripple of laughter jumped from table to table. 'And now, before I continue, our Chairman will read the minutes of our inaugural meeting.' He gestured towards a dark-haired, forty-something man in the front row.

Daniel put his elbows on the table and rested his chin in his hands. It was some sort of crappy gardening club. This would be a long morning. As the Chairman droned on, Daniel attempted to shut his brain down. He should go. Stand up and march from the room. It was rude, but he owed these gardeners nothing. A glance over his shoulder showed that another bulgy-muscled leather-jacket stood by the door, arms folded, head scanning left and right over the audience. Weird or what? He would have to make his excuses to that man, something that didn't appeal. There would be an argument. Sometimes it was best to keep your head down and let events take their course. He was suddenly aware that the Chairman had stopped talking, and that Reynolds was once again speaking.

'Most of you I know, some of you I don't but will very soon.'

For a moment, Daniel thought the man stared intently towards him as he tried to slip further into his seat.

'You are, however, all here by invitation, by personal introduction. We are a group of trusted friends, and that's how it will remain during the coming months as our great task nears completion.'

Our great task. That was weird. Could this really be the man Farquharson was after?

The man paused, cleared his throat and took a sip of water. 'You have all individually made your contribution, some in small ways, some in greater and some comrades have already paid the ultimate price of their lives, but this they were glad to do. Let us remember them.'

Daniel gazed around at bowed heads. This allotment business was a more serious one than he had realised. Heart attacks due to over vigorous digging most likely. He glanced at his companion who had his head obediently lowered and refused to meet his eye. He looked back towards the dais to find himself transfixed by the two hawk-like eyes of the speaker.

'Perhaps someone from the floor would like to say a few words at this point? Perhaps from among our newer recruits?'

Gimlet eyes bored into Daniel. Should he look away or stare in return? Heads swivelled towards him. Voices murmured. His companion gestured with an inclined head, advising him to get to his feet. He got to them. But what to say? Procrastinating, he lifted the glass of water and took a slow sip.

'Um...,' he said. *Good start, Daniel*, a little voice whispered from somewhere to the left of his hippocampus. He pulled his shoulders back. 'Gardening... can be a hazardous business.'

The grey-haired man's mouth formed what might have been a smile. His one-hundred-watt eyes dipped to perhaps eighty.

Encouraged, Daniel searched his mind for gardening lore. There wasn't much. 'Take weeds for instance. They're bad. We want to get rid of weeds.'

'Root them out,' a voice murmured.

'Destroy them,' came another. Voices rose in agreement.

It seemed he had latched onto the right subject. 'Yes, weeds are evil. They should be stopped. They strangle and kill the good guys. They should be exterminated by any means. Pull them out if we can, fine, but if other methods are needed, chemicals for instance, then so be it. They've asked for it.'

The audience applauded vigorously. 'Let them burn in hell,' came a shout from his left. 'Kill their children,' came from the right. 'Bomb the bastards.'

'Eh well...' Daniel began, but the raised hands of the leader saved him from further comment.

'Our young friend here has the right stuff, if I may borrow an expression. I would like a word after the meeting please, my friend.'

Daniel nodded cautiously. A shake of the head seemed inappropriate at that point.

'Any other comments?' The grey-haired man's eyes probed the room.

As Daniel sat down, his companion murmured, 'Well done,' and shook his hand vigorously. 'Good impression you've made.'

Daniel leant forward. 'Who is he?' he asked, gesturing towards the stage.

His friend pulled back, brow creasing into a frown. 'You mean you don't know?' There was an incredulous tone in the voice that indicated not only that he should know, but it was of vital importance to his safety and well-being that he did know.

'Oh yes, of course, I know *who* he is. What I meant was, who *is* he? You know who is he really?'

'That, as you well know, we never discuss here,' the man hissed. He continued to stare at Daniel with a look that inconsiderate motorists reserved for traffic wardens. 'And who introduced you here?'

That was enough. A glance behind him showed the exit firmly shut, a leather jacket in place. There seemed no other way out. 'It was... he's just over there.' Daniel gestured to the far side of the room. 'On the second table. We can all have a chat later. That would be nice. Wouldn't it?' His companion continued to frown. 'Over a coffee or something... maybe.'

At the front of the room, the grey-haired man was on his mobile, his lips set in a hard line. He raised a hand. 'Friends, our contact tells me that police are on their way. Institute emergency evacuation. You will all be contacted with date and time of next meeting.'

A shocked silence, then everyone rose to their feet, surging forward. On the left, a curtain was pulled back to reveal another door, and the crowd swept through, pulling Daniel in its slipstream. There was a crash from below that sounded like an entryway being reduced to matchwood and a muffled shout of, 'Police, police.' Then the door slammed shut behind them, cutting off the noise of splintering wood. He was carried along by the press of bodies as they hurried down cement steps and then along a dusty corridor. One of many doors opened on the right to many more descending steps and a rough, damp, and smelly, brick-lined tunnel, perhaps part of an old sewage system. Torches flashed in the darkness. No one spoke a word; it was as if they were following a well-rehearsed plan. Up more steps and then the group stopped. At the front of the long queue, Daniel saw a flash of sunlight as a door opened. They filed out rapidly. Waiting at the door was the grey-haired man.

'Venue C. You will be notified.' He smiled and shook Daniel's hand. For a moment, he held the grip and eyes that did not match the smile on his lips locked with Daniel's, but several people were pressing forward and he was released.

The door opened onto an alleyway leading to a busy road. Hurrying to the top, he looked right and left but recognised no one from the meeting. The Western Allotment Society had evaporated.

Three

DESPITE THAT TRULY WEIRD encounter, Lorraine was the next problem Daniel faced: how to explain his apparent preoccupation with the contents of a sex-shop window. It wasn't that she had no interest in sex, just that she was so straightforward about it. Randy rabbits and frilly underwear didn't figure and, being honest with himself, he was quite happy about that. The highly original solution came to Daniel's male brain as he walked past 23 Leonard Street: flowers, and lots of them. This may have been because 23 Leonard Street was occupied by Gentle and Hawksley, florists of renown.

He entered the shop tentatively. Previous purchases of flowers had been made in the anonymity of Tesco's bogof offers. It was certainly a florist: blooms floor to ceiling and a cloying stench of everything sweet.

'Good afternoon, sir.'

Daniel looked around and then down at the bald head of a tiny Asian-featured man with an intense expression.

'How may I be of assistance?'

'Are you Gentle?' Daniel asked, only realising how stupid that sounded as the words left his mouth. He coughed to disguise his embarrassment.

'No, sir. Mr Gentle passed away some years ago. I am Ahmed Shazar, the owner of this establishment. It is my endeavour to continue the ethos of the Gentle and Hawksley years. How may I assist?'

Daniel had rather been hoping he could pick something up. You didn't get assisted in Tesco. 'Well, I'm looking for some flowers.'

'Sir?' The man continued to look at him hopefully.

'Something... well... nice, you know?'

The man nodded as if he did indeed know.

'For my girlfriend.'

'Ah yes,' Shazar beamed. 'Roses, sir. You cannot go wrong with roses for the ladies.'

'Yes, roses would be just the thing, thank you.'

'Of course, it's a bit early, not the season here. We deal only with British-grown blooms, sir. Not the type that arrives from many parts of the world in frozen transport. So at certain times, there is much scarcity.' He turned to a display and started removing blood-red blooms. 'I could do a lovely bunch of these for forty-five pounds. Perhaps a few pink as well. Sir?'

Daniel realised he must have made some sort of sound. Forty-five pounds? Oh, what the hell. It was then that he remembered he had left his cards with Lorraine while she sorted a problem with her bank. So that left him with only – he fumbled in his pocket. 'Four pounds sixty-five!'

'Sorry, sir?'

'I said they're beautiful. But... I'm a little short at the moment. Could I have a few less, you know, cheaper?'

'Of course, sir. Anything you like.' He removed a few blooms. 'I'm sure you'll agree that's still very attractive for thirty-two.'

Daniel closed his eyes and took a deep breath. 'Have you anything less than four pounds sixty-five?'

The man made momentary eye contact then looked away. There was a pink spot on his cheek. He glanced around.

'I could do a single rose if sir could raise the limit very slightly.'

Daniel smiled and shook his head.

'Well, there are always daffodils. I'm sure you could afford...' A telephone trilled somewhere at the back of the shop. The man apologised and disappeared behind a screen. The ringing stopped.

Daffodils wouldn't do. They had daffodils in a window box at home. The yellow weeds were everywhere. In a bad mood, Lorraine would accuse him of stealing them from the park. No. Roses it must be, but what could he do? He could go home for his cards, but if she was there, they would have their confrontation without the flowers.

Later, he told himself that he acted without thinking, but, in reality, the plan had formed the moment he had found his lack of money. Credit. OK, he had no card, but he could take the flowers and pay later. He would pay, he knew that. He was an honest man and sometimes gave to charities. The owner wouldn't know, but that was the way of it. He looked around for paper – he would leave a note for Mr Shazar. No paper to be seen. A pen? No pen to be seen. Oh well. Behind the screen, Shazar was still talking. Right, go for it. A last check behind and he crossed to the display, grabbed a large bunch of roses and headed for the exit. Then he was out, racing down the street, shedding the occasional leaf and listening for a shout which never came. Only as he turned the first corner, breathless and sweating, did his visual processor catch up with his brain to dump the clear picture of a sign reading, *these premises are protected by CCTV*.

He had to get home. It was all getting too much. At a newsagent he bought a large sheet of wrapping paper for the flowers, checking first to see if it cost less than four sixty-five.

On the landing below his own, he stopped to wrap the flowers in the paper. Breathless and dishevelled, he burst into his flat.

'Daniel!' Lorraine shot to her feet, a small glass of sherry in her hand. She never drank on her own. 'Daniel I...' Whatever she had been going to say, she didn't.

'I've brought you some flowers, Lorraine.' He pushed the roughly wrapped bundle towards her.

She shook her head as if a bee was trapped in her hair. 'I don't understand, Daniel, these flowers.'

'I know, I know. I don't understand Daniel either sometimes. It's just to say sorry for everything. Well, this morning especially, and so on.'

'But they're roses, Daniel. How did you... how could you?'

'Because they're for you,' he said.

Logically, when you so often say the wrong thing, it stands to reason that by the law of averages you must occasionally say the right thing or so Daniel thought as Lorraine's lips pressed on his, her arms snaked around him and her tongue explored the results of Mr Fisher's first-class root-canal work.

Sometime later, with Lorraine in the bathroom *putting herself back together*, Daniel picked the flowers from the floor where they had been dropped so hurriedly and looked for something to put them in but found nothing suitable. It was an enormous bunch he had grabbed. He counted them, then he counted them again, then he sat down. Sixty-five separate stems. Sixty-five beautiful roses. How much had they been for each? He hadn't been given a price, but 4.65 was not enough. If they were five pounds, then that meant... Bloody hell, that meant almost four hundred quid. Four hundred. He couldn't spend that on flowers. He would have to take them back. But... Oh hell.

Lorraine appeared at the bathroom door, hair covered by a towel.

'You'll need more than one vase, Daniel.'

He smiled feebly.

'It was such a lovely thought. No one has ever been so nice to me before.' Her eyes were moist. She moved behind him, and her arms circled his neck. 'I've got to go out in a little while, Daniel, but you know I believe I'm beginning to understand men.'

'You are?'

'Yes, at least I'm beginning to understand what they want. Maybe not why, but what? Yes, I'm beginning to understand that.'

This statement left Daniel both confused and slightly alarmed.

'So, what but not why then?'

'That's it, and don't worry. I'm going to put things right for you.' She patted him on the head.

If she had waited, Daniel might have told her that things were just fine as they were, at least in what he thought she was talking about, but she waltzed into the bedroom humming to herself and shut the door leaving him with many, many red roses.

Four

DANIEL ROSE EARLY THE next morning after a disturbed night. Lorraine's snores, combined with alarming dreams of pursuit by strange men waving bunches of flowers, led to the bloodshot eyes that stared back at him from the bathroom mirror. The cloying stink of roses was everywhere. It permeated the flat, adhering to everything. He opened the windows to let the traffic fumes blow it away. The scent was only another chemical after all, and no chemical at that concentration could be healthy.

He munched joylessly through a bowl of cereal while staring at the mass of flowers distributed around the room in a variety of makeshift vases. What was he going to do? Pay for them. No question about it. But there wouldn't be enough cash until next month's salary arrived. He didn't even know what the exact cost would be. He could hardly return to the shop and ask. His face was probably on a poster behind the counter. Perhaps he could get someone to enquire for him, Alex might do it. Just to go in and say, *how much would sixty-five roses be?* There could be a discount for quantity. He only wanted to pay what he was due and maybe send a note of apology. And now he was on video. Caught in the act. The owner would have shown it to the police, and he would be marked out.

No, that wasn't right. He didn't have a police record. They couldn't go through their files and find him. In the bedroom, he heard Lorraine stir and yawn. Time to leave for work. Shit.

There was that business last year – with the professor's wife. The police had interviewed him then. What would be on file? That idiot, Inspector Dick, believed he had murdered the woman and had made a fool of himself. But Dick would be long gone, retired, probably in the loony bin. All right, keep your head down, Daniel, find the money for the flowers. Everything's fine. With those happy thoughts, he closed the door behind him and headed for the university.

On the way, he mulled over what he would tell Farquharson. It had been a very strange encounter with the Allotment Society, and why the hell would they be raided – using illegal weedkiller, pulling up endangered weeds? And yet perhaps he shouldn't be too surprised. It all fitted with Farquharson, the weirdest bird that Daniel had ever flown with.

The old university building rose in front of him. An imposing edifice with crenulated what-nots and architraved do-dahs, as a guide book might have described it. Or, as Daniel thought of it, a mouldering, damp-infested heap of crappy stones that should have been pulled down fifty years ago. The chemistry department was housed in one of the many flat-roofed, sixties blocks that leaked around the old dear.

The doorman glanced up and grunted as Daniel entered. He grunted back Politeness cost nothing, as his mother used to say in her sober moments.

His office was large and roomy. He was the chief technician after all, but his desk was bare. His promotion and pay rise last year as a thank you from the prof had been very welcome, but he had soon found that he was not expected to do much and terminal boredom had settled in. He grabbed a cup of plastic coffee from the machine and sat down with a crossword to wait for the morning meeting.

'Hello, excuse me.'

Damn, he had fallen asleep. Rose bushes had been closing in on him, scratching, tearing, his blood everywhere and behind them, the mad gardener gibbering and salivating, secateurs in hand.

'Sandra, yes good,' he tried to smile. 'Always first, eh?'

'I thought you were ill.'

'I'm fine.'

'You look pale.' She stared at him with intense eyes.

'Honestly, I'm fine. Nothing that the kiss of life wouldn't cure.'

She continued her unblinking stare. Sandra was the teaching labs' temp, paid a pittance for doing most of the work, which she did with a zeal and commitment that almost made him ashamed. But she lacked any sense of humour. The type of person to whom you couldn't be nasty but sometimes disliked intensely. One week of her contract to go and his feelings about losing her were ambiguous.

Alex wandered in a few minutes later.

'Hi, how's it going?' Daniel said, trying for light and bright. Alex scowled at the floor and dropped into an empty seat.

He took a deep breath. 'OK, guys, a busy day today. You know we have to set up the second-year experiments while their lab's being refurbished.'

'Yes,' said Sandra. 'You told us yesterday.'

Daniel tried hard to relax the tension in his jaw muscles.

'Well, where are we going to set them up?' Alex grunted.

'At the back. All the first-years will have to crowd up a bit.'

'They won't like it.'

'Well, Alex, you'll have to talk nicely to them. Can you do that?'

They were both irritating him this morning. Pressure was building in his emotional boiler. The phone rang. He grabbed it eagerly.

'Professor? Yes, of course. I'll be right up. Problems? Well not really. Perhaps a bit. I'll tell you.' He hung up.

'I've to see the prof so—'

'You don't say,' Alex interrupted. 'We thought it was your mother.'

'Alex... look just get on with it, both of you. I'll be back soon.'

Daniel left the chemistry block and made his way towards the old building. Alex's attitude was getting worse. Difficult to believe they had been buddies at one time. He knew what the problem was – his promotion. He had expected Alex to take it on board, but things had not improved in recent weeks. They would have to talk it through.

He headed through the pretentiously grand entrance and into the quadrangle. A few students wandered about. Even the odd tourist was visible snapping away at what they mistakenly believed was part of the nation's cultural heritage.

Daniel plodded upstairs to Farquharson's first-floor office, not at all sure what he would say to the old codger. He knocked on the office door and slipped in. A woman he had not seen before, presumably Farquharson's latest secretary, sat behind a desk. She looked up sharply. Deep frown lines etched her forehead. 'Can I help you?'

He stared at a large and formidable woman, perhaps fifty-five going on some more, not at all the professor's normal taste in secretaries which tended to the young and curvy. Chunky sausage fingers attached to a pair of meaty forearms linked in front of her as her lower lip pushed out.

'It's Daniel Dreghorn. To see the professor.'

'Have you an appointment?' she snapped. Her tone of voice indicated that those who did not have appointments had better move smartly while still in possession of all their credentials.

'Well, no actually, but I'm sure he'll see me. He phoned. Asked me to come up.'

The woman breathed in sharply, air rattling through seriously congested nasal passages. 'You wait there.' She pointed to an upright chair in the corner of the room. 'I'll enquire. And don't you touch anything.'

Daniel raised his hands in surrender as she bustled into the professor's office and shut the door behind her. She reappeared after several minutes and glared at him.

'Professor Farquharson will see you, but be quick. He's a very busy man.'

'Thank you. You're very kind.' He smiled at her, and she scowled back.

Inside the office, Farquharson stood by the large window staring into the courtyard below, shoulders slumped forward, his entire body bowed. He looked every one of his indeterminate number of years.

'Daniel.' He turned. 'I hope this is good news. Mission accomplished?' It sounded like of late all news had been bad.

'Yes, professor. Mission accomplished. I have an address although it's all a little strange.'

'Hah, I knew it. It fits the pattern. Sit down, my boy. Tell all.'

They sat facing each other, the professor gazing eagerly at Daniel as he described his encounter with the Western Allotment Society and the police. Farquharson sat in silence for a long moment, tapping his pencil on the desk.

'Well, well, indeed curious. There's nothing wrong with allotments, although they are sadly scarce these days. My cousin's sister used to have one, I believe. It is a tradition worth upholding in this day and age when so many traditions dwindle and rot on the vine of commerce.' His eyes focussed on a spot near his nose, and there was a lengthy silence.

Daniel crossed and uncrossed his legs several times while he waited for more.

'But why the police raid?' Farquharson continued abruptly.

'That's what I don't understand. What's so special about gardens?' Even as he said the words, last year's business with the greenhouse of cannabis came to mind. Could that be it? If so, his involvement would end right now.

'Curious, indeed.' Farquharson pressed his fingertips together and his eyelids flickered shut. A sure indication of retreat into the parallel universe he inhabited.

Daniel stood. 'Well, professor, whatever the reason, I've done my bit. I'd like you to accept my let—'

'Oh no, no, no, no.' Farquharson wagged a finger.

'But... you said...' He sighed as he sat down.

'You will recall, Daniel, that I asked you for an address.'

'I got you an address.'

'An address where a certain gentleman lived. You have given me an address where this man chaired a very unusual meeting. That is interesting in itself, but I need his home address for reasons which we don't have to go into.'

Daniel clenched his fists tightly together. 'How on earth am I supposed to find that?'

'Unfortunately, my boy, I have no knowledge of his further movements, but someone with your contacts? Well, it should not be too much of a problem.'

'My contacts?' Something told him to stop. Best not to say anything to the professor about his non-existent contacts for the moment. 'Wait, surely the office will have a record of his address?'

'Hah!' Farquharson raised his index finger and waved it in Daniel's direction. 'False. He has given a false address. Suspicious, eh?'

'I'll see what I can do,' he sighed, thinking it much more likely that the man had moved house or that university administration had simply cocked up again.

'Great stuff, that man. A real trooper. I knew you were reliable.'

Daniel searched the professor's face for traces of irony, but the man stood up and began to water the cacti on his windowsill with a small green watering can.

'Well, I'll be going now, professor.' He paused with his hand on the door knob.

Farquharson continued to water his pots. 'Some people swear by Rebutias, but I've always preferred the Mammillarias myself.'

'I'd never have guessed,' Daniel muttered as he left the professor's study. Ahead of him, the bulky secretary reared, hands on hips, like a colossus of antiquity, firmly blocking his way.

'You've been ten minutes,' her voice rumbled.

He stared up at her for a moment, then slowly pulled his sleeve back and looked at his watch. 'Gosh, you're right. Doesn't life pass quickly? I blame global warming.'

She gazed at him through slitted eyes as her lower lip worked threateningly against the upper. Then she took a step forward and he took a step backwards. Now she stood between him and his goal, the exit. A podgy finger prodded him in the chest.

'Think you're smart, eh? I know your kind, sonny. Just because you've got letters after your name, you think you're above the rest of us. Well, I've got news for you lot. You're not.'

Daniel shook his head. The woman was barking, not in control, face bright pink. Her body language said attack and, alarmingly, her right hand gripped a pair of pointed scissors.

to. Could he just get dressed and walk out? Would twenty-four hours make any difference to his health?

He heaved himself out of bed, slipped on a dressing gown and headed for the door leading to the two toilets shared with the general ward next door. A minute later, he was about to return to his room when something made him hesitate. A shadow had crossed the frosted glass panel set into the door. There was someone there. A nurse? They seemed constitutionally unable to enter the ward quietly. Perhaps Lorraine had returned, but surely she would have called out. He listened. Complete silence from behind the glass, but then he saw a silhouette cross towards the toilet. He turned the door lock and stood perfectly still, holding his breath, knowing that locked or not, a hard push would see the door open.

There was a knock – oh so polite. 'Mr Dreghorn?' A male voice, silky smooth.

Daniel reversed. The door behind him led to the general ward.

'Mr Dreghorn? We'd like a little chat.'

We? That decided it for Daniel. He turned about, opened the door to the other ward and slipped out as his unseen seeker rattled the handle.

There were six beds in the ward, all currently occupied, and a low murmur of conversation. It was visiting time, and no one paid him any attention. He pulled the dressing gown tight around him, aware that underneath he wore only boxer shorts.

A faint creaking came from the bathroom area. The door beyond was being forced open. He sped to the top of the ward and peered to the right up the corridor towards the entrance to his room. A man, clad in a black leather jacket, stood outside Daniel's door, currently looking away from him. To the left, the corridor stretched for what seemed like miles. He had no choice. He had to take a chance.

'Look, I think you've got the wrong idea.'

She ignored him. 'If I find you've been wasting the professor's time...'

What unspeakable torments awaited him on wasting the professor's time were left unsaid as she continued her advance around the desk.

Daniel retreated until his back was to the wall, caught between window and filing cabinet. 'Look this is silly.'

'Oh, silly am I now is it? Do you know that no one's ever called me silly before? Not in my hearing.' Specks of spittle projected from her mouth.

'No, honestly, I didn't mean that. Please...' The window – the only way. It was beside him – open. Blue sky beckoned. He hoisted himself onto the sill.

'No, you come back here!'

There was a long drop below, but a two-foot-wide ledge headed off in both directions. Making an instant decision, he stepped out and onto the shelf. There was an indistinct shout behind him as he edged around the wall. The ledge was wide, but the edges looked crumbly and unsafe. He scrambled through the first open window he found and onto a polished table. It was the library, and an elderly man with a grey beard glanced up from the book he was reading near Daniel's feet.

'Good morning,' the man said. 'Sorry if I'm in your way.' He pushed a pile of papers aside so that Daniel could step from the table to a chair and jump to the floor.

'Oh, that's OK. I mean, no problem... fine,' Daniel said, adjusting his shirt in the waistband of his jeans. The man had returned to his book and seemed to take no further notice of events. Otherwise, the library was deserted so, as explanations were not required, Daniel left.

On the way back to the lab, he thought of the professor's crazy secretary. He tried to put the thought in a box and throw it far, far away, but there was something sticky on the outside and it wouldn't leave his fingers. He even found time for a fleeting pang of sympathy for the old man.

A siren echoed around the quadrangle as a fire engine screeched to a halt and disgorged a clump of firemen. A small crowd gathered. Daniel joined them. From the conversations going on it seemed that someone had reported a potential suicide, a madman preparing to jump from a window ledge. He detached himself from the crowd and headed rapidly for the relative safety of his office.

Five

THE MORTAR BOARD WAS busy and noisy, which was not how Daniel liked pubs, but he had little choice. He desperately wanted to sort things out with Alex and had persuaded him to meet after work for a drink. They had been friends for years, and he needed to talk to someone about what was going on in his job.

He stood by the bar for several minutes trying to get attention, but gave up. He looked around vaguely for a table, and saw Alex gesturing at him from the doorway. Together they scanned the area but there wasn't a seat to be had. Daniel poked Alex in the ribs and headed to a table occupied by three short-skirted brunettes. 'Excuse me,' he said, pulled up a chair, stuck two fingers down his throat and gagged. Alex joined him at the suddenly empty table.

'I have a way with women, Alex. Whenever they see me they want to get away.'

'So, what's this about then?' Alex looked like he was struggling to keep a straight face.

'I only want to apologise, mate, if I've done something you don't like.'

Alex squirmed in his seat. 'No, it's not that. Not exactly. It's just you changed when you... you know.'

'No, I didn't.'

'Yes, you did.'

'I had to change a bit. I had to boss you about, manage you, and for sure that's no picnic.'

'Well... Oh hell, OK.' Alex put a hand out. 'I suppose I've been jealous.'

They shook, and Alex headed to the scrum at the bar for their drinks.

Daniel idly glanced around the raucous collection of drunks and getting-drunks that pressed in on him. A face on its own behind a group of jiggling, fatty-forty girlies made him shift his gaze from bare flesh for a moment. Had he seen the man before? But when he looked again, there was no one.

Alex returned with two pints, and they both took a long drink. The noise level had increased.

'Alex, you know the prof's new secretary?'

'Know her? No, I don't.'

'I mean you've heard of her?'

'He changes secretaries as soon as he gets bored with their shorthand technique. It's one hundred a minute at his age or there's nothing on the page at all.'

Daniel spluttered into his beer. 'Well, that's it, see. His new one's a real old battle-axe, not like anyone he's had before.'

'So? It's healthier, isn't it? Fancying someone your own age. Perhaps he's growing up.'

'That's not it, Alex. She's mad. I really don't see them going at it.'

'You're just ageist, Dan.'

'Maybe, but I had a run-in with her. I'm sure she was going to kill me. I had to go out the window.'

'Dan,' Alex put his hand on Daniel's arm. 'Hate to tell you but you're always out the window.'

'What's that supposed to mean?' He pulled his arm away sharply.

'Nothing, nothing.' Alex flapped his palms in the air. 'I only mean you're a wee bit impulsive. Jump to conclusions. That sort of thing. You always did.'

Daniel puffed out his cheeks. 'Don't know about that, but things are sure going wrong for me right now.'

'Oh?'

'Yeah.' Should he tell Alex about the job Farquharson had blackmailed him into? Perhaps not. 'Well, you wouldn't think buying flowers would turn into a minefield, would you?'

'Flowers?'

Alex looked sceptical, so he explained his run-in with the mad florist.

'Dan, you could have a disaster buying a bus ticket.'

It was even noisier now. More and more people crushed in. Students, academics even a few normal members of the public. Daniel became aware of a rather shapely bottom rammed against his shoulder and was enjoying the experience. 'Excuse me,' he said tapping the back a decent distance above the bottom.

'What?' A bearded face looked down at him.

'Sorry, nothing.' He cringed as the man turned back to his companions.

'It's too busy, Alex. I'm getting out.'

'OK mate, see you.' Alex had his eye fixed on a group of flirty looking females at the next table.

Daniel stood up and attempted to push through the crowd in the general direction of the door. Perhaps he could shout *fire* and wait for the reaction, but it was unlikely he would be heard. Moving was difficult and involved making swimming motions including quite a few breast strokes before he plunged into the cool evening air, took several deep breaths and set off for home.

The flat he shared with Lorraine was not in the most salubrious part of town, but it was home and he had grown attached to the place. It was in a quiet cul-de-sac off a busy road, and he was grateful for the drop in noise level as he reached his door. Lorraine would be home. She had promised to cook up something exciting tonight, and he was starving.

As he approached the entrance steps, fumbling for the key, a small, dark-clad figure detached from the shadows of the doorway and headed down, brushing Daniel's shoulder rather forcibly. 'Sorry,' he said, automatically.

The man didn't speak but stopped a few paces along the road, staring in the direction Daniel had come from as if waiting for someone. 'Don't mind me, wanker,' Daniel muttered under his breath.

He closed the main door behind him and strolled upstairs to his flat. Inside, it was silent, and the lights were all out. Strange.

'Lorraine,' he called, clicking the light switch several times with no effect

'Hello,' he shouted, pushing open the bedroom door, but it too was in darkness. He turned.

A strong arm grabbed him around the neck, another around the middle. 'Gotcha,' a husky voice hissed into his ear.

He tried to call out, but words wouldn't come. He struggled for breath. There was an aching pain in his chest. Hands released their grip, and he staggered back against the table, turned and slumped into a chair.

'Hello, Daniel. I hope you're ready,' said a voice, a female voice, Lorraine.

'Lor...' was all he could manage. She was dressed in a tiny black bra, lacy pants, fishnet tights. Pain was growing. An elephant had sat on his chest.

'It's all ready for you, lover boy, just for you. Just the way you like it. I hope you're up for it.'

She crossed to the table, straddled him where he sat slumped back in the chair and started to unbutton his shirt. The pain was unbearable. He couldn't speak. He couldn't breathe.

'Daniel, are you all right?' were the last words he heard.

Six

DANIEL LAY BACK AGAINST the plumped-up pillows and pulled the white sheets around his shoulders.

Heart attacks at your age are most unusual, Mr Dreghorn, but there's no permanent damage I can see, Dr Pemberton had said. To Daniel, it was unfortunate that the doctor wore rather thick glasses. Perhaps there had been extreme stress, or genetic factors might have played a part. Daniel had a list of dos and don'ts, the latter outranking the former substantially. Apart from that and several bottles of pills, he could go home tomorrow.

Lorraine sat at his bedside with a basket of fruit and an anxious expression.

'I'm so sorry, Daniel. It's all my fault.'

'No, no. We went through this yesterday, Lorrie. It's not your fault.'

'It is my fault. I should never have been so stupid, getting dressed up like a tart. Of course it would affect you.'

'No, it wasn't that. It was...' He tried to think what it had been. It must have been the shock of an arm around his neck. Or was it coming on anyway? How could he know? 'It really wasn't that. You looked great. You'd make a great tart.'

'What?' Her face had lost its concerned look.

'No, I mean seeing you dressed up like that... It was like you meant it. It would have been totally fantastic... if I hadn't had a heart attack.'

'OK, we can try again sometime eh, Danny?'

'Yeah. Yeah, sure. But not right away. I mean the doc says I need to rest and anyway it seems these pills I'm taking...'

'What about them?'

'Well, they have side effects. I may not be as active as I used to be. Just for a few weeks that is.'

'So? You never did much jogging or sporty stuff.'

'No, that's not what I meant.' Thankfully, he was saved from going any further, as Lorraine lost interest. She removed the wrapping from the basket of fruit she had brought and popped a grape into her mouth.

'It's nice you're in a single room, Daniel.'

'This is the special care room, Lorrie.'

Her cheeks reddened slightly.

'But not to worry, they would have moved me onto general except there are no beds. So here I am in luxury, eh?'

She grimaced, and they sat for a moment while Lorraine munched an apple. 'Oh, I've just remembered. There was someone at the flat looking for you.'

'Who was that then?'

'He wouldn't give me his name. Tall with a moustache. A bit baldy. I've seen him hanging about earlier. He looked furtive. Wanted to know if he could speak to you.'

'Did you tell him where I was?'

'Of course not. I said you were in bed and didn't want to be disturbed so he wouldn't realise I was alone in the house.'

'Good thinking.' He tried to remember all the tall bald men with moustaches that he knew. There weren't many. Although the description would have fitted his old geography teacher, Miss Amazon Basin 2001.

'Why do you have all these weird friends, Daniel?'

'My friends aren't weird.'

'Well, what about that Farquharson?'

'OK, he's weird, but he's hardly a friend. He's my boss.'

'And that guy from the florists, the Asian man?'

'What.' Daniel sat up in bed. 'How do you know him?'

'That's where I got the fruit. He had your picture on his back wall. At the time I thought it strange. We started talking and when I said I was your girlfriend, he said he'd love to meet you again.'

'Lorraine.' Daniel coughed as something caught in his throat and his heart knocked on his ribs.

'It was sweet of him even though he seemed a little odd. I said he could come for coffee sometime.'

'You gave him our address?'

'Yes, why not?'

'Shit.'

'Daniel, please. Anyway, what's wrong? He must be an old friend. How long have you known him?'

Daniel thought, and thought once more, and then tried some extra thinking for the hell of it. The only strategy that seemed appropriate was a hand on his chest and...

'Feeling exhausted now, Lorrie. Been a strain. Need to close my eyes.'

'Of course, Daniel, sorry. I've kept you talking too long. The doctor says you'll be home tomorrow.'

He raised a hand, trying to indicate that would be wonderful, but at the moment he'd like to sleep. Lorraine kissed him on the forehead and busied out the door.

Shit. What sort of mess was he in now? He sat up. The bald man must be one of the Allotment Society weirdoes. Why on earth did he call at the flat? The guy from the florist's shop was more serious. With one thing following another thing without time for more things in between, he had not returned to pay for those flowers. He had meant to, but would the florist believe that? Would he fanny. He had to go around there and pay, pron-

Tiptoeing from the room, he started down the corridor then took a glance backwards. Leather Jacket's head turned in his direction. Daniel hurled himself sideways through the nearest open door. Another ward, a female ward, patients talking, visitors visiting. A few heads looked up momentarily, but no one was interested. Six beds, five occupied, one with curtains partly drawn but empty. Heavy footsteps from the corridor behind. He scampered for the empty bed, drew the curtains around it then dropped to his knees and squeezed underneath the bed.

Feet squeaked into the ward, and suddenly the curtain whipped back. He could see only a pair of black shoes. They moved until level with his head. Heart racing, he debated whether to crawl out the other side of the bed and run.

'Excuse me? What are you doing?'

It was one of the nurses, praise be. There was a brief silence, then the shoes turned away.

'Oh sorry, nurse. I'm trying to find Mrs... Brown.'

'There's no one of that name here. You must be in the wrong ward. You'll have to leave.'

'Yes, of course, nurse. Sorry to have disturbed you.' A smooth voice, unhurried, in control.

Daniel took a deep breath and concentrated on slowing his heart. This wasn't good for him. The nurse had closed the curtains. He edged towards the side of the bed, knowing he would be seen, but staying put wasn't an option.

'This way.'

He paused. It was the nurse speaking again.

'That's right, Mrs Anderson, you sit there.' The bed creaked above him as a heavy weight fell onto the side. Two slippered feet appeared beside his nose.

'I'll give you a hand, luv. That's right, swing your legs around.' The bed creaked ominously.

Hell. Trapped, with a pair of cheesy slippers by his nose.

'I'll leave the curtains closed, OK? Doctor's coming in a few moments.'

That was better. Perhaps he could get away unnoticed. The nurse left with a swish of curtains, then more bumps and creaks above as the bed's occupant turned and twisted. Surely the woman would go to sleep. But he mustn't wait too long or the doctor would be here. Give it three minutes. But space was so cramped that it was impossible to bring his watch up to his eyes. Rhythmic breathing came from above. OK, go for it.

Wriggling his feet, thighs and upper body out from under the bed as quietly as possible, he turned over to a kneeling position and cautiously raised his head above the level of the mattress. No more than a handspan away, two dark, lacklustre eyes stared back at him.

Daniel opened his mouth and shut it again. He thought of several things to say. None of them entirely appropriate. He stood up and backed away slowly, as one might from a fierce jungle creature whose pointed teeth were on display.

The woman pulled herself upright with much effort. 'Doctor?' she wheezed.

'Ah...' said Daniel. He fumbled for the belt of his dressing gown but couldn't find it. Like Adam in the Garden of Eden, he became aware of his nakedness. Had he fastened the button on his boxer shorts?

'Doctor?' the woman repeated. She was an enormous woman with a puffy face and a rattling chest.

Daniel shook his head, but she gestured for him to come closer and he moved cautiously towards the bed. He wanted nothing more than escape but didn't want this woman to start screaming. What explanation could he dream up? Perhaps a cleaner who spoke no English. Then, lightning-fast, the woman's hand shot out and grabbed his upper arm. He yelped as untrimmed finger-nails dug into muscle and tried to pull away but was inexorably dragged towards her like a ship docking at the quayside.

'Doctor?' Her black, piggy eyes stared at him, unblinking.

'No, I'm not a doctor. I've got to go, please.'

He was beside the bed now, and in an instant her free hand flashed forward and fastened on to his testicles through the thin fabric of his boxers. She squeezed. He screamed.

'Doctor? Examine me,' she wheezed.

Through a thin film of tears, he was aware of the curtain whipping back.

'Mr Dreghorn! What do you think you're doing?'

His testicles and arm were instantly released, and he staggered backwards. Behind him a nurse stood, hands on hips, face flushed.

'What are you doing to Mrs Anderson?'

His mouth opened and shut several times, but nothing came out.

Tuts and mutters of 'disgraceful' came from a few faces gathered behind the nurse. Mrs Anderson lay back on the bed, staring at the ceiling and rhythmically thumping her chest with the palm of her hand.

'I... nothing.' Daniel finally managed to croak.

'If I find you were molesting that poor lady...'

'Sorry, got to go,' he muttered, pushing his way through the crowd of well-wishers.

'I'll have to report this, Mr Dreghorn. Please go to your room.'

Pervert, locked up and *Doctor?* followed him out.

Back in his room, a quick check in the mirror showed no obvious damage, but whether the machinery was still in working order remained to be seen. He had no desire to test it out right now. He only wanted to get out of this madhouse.

Thankfully, his unwanted visitors had evaporated and Daniel threw on clothes, dropped his bits and pieces into a carry bag, and cautiously peered into a reassuringly empty corridor. He turned towards the stairs and trotted downwards, certain that once he left this floor no one would stop him. That proved to be the case, and he was soon among the crowd in the hospital foyer. What now? Well home, of course, probably.

Several taxis waited hopefully outside the entrance. The grunt and scowl Daniel received from the driver as he gave the man his destination did not sound like gratitude, and as he sat in the taxi, doubts crystallised. Lorraine would be there when he got home. He would have to explain his sudden departure from hospital. He might have to explain the reason for his intimate bruises. Which, when he came to think, was all rather unbelievable.

'Stupid bugger!'

Screech of brakes. For once Daniel was glad he had secured his seat belt. The driver had a window down, gesticulating at the backside of a bus which had apparently behaved inappropriately.

'Bastards need to take a test.' This snarled in Daniel's direction, as the cab surged forward in an attempt to mate with the bus in front.

Judging comment to be superfluous, Daniel nodded his head as the taxi surged past the bus and cut in.

'Bleeding darkie immigrants think they own this bleeding country.'

Daniel glanced through the rear window at the irate but very white face of the bus driver. Was he supposed to say something? 'Um,' he tried.

'S'pose you're one of them bleeding-hearted liberals?'

Daniel squirmed in his seat. That was a question. 'God no. Me? No way.' He had to escape. Could he ask the cab to stop?

But that would cut the journey and the fare short. His bleeding driver would be bleeding unhappy. But thankfully the man subsided into inaudible mutterings meant for his personal consumption, and Daniel relaxed – briefly. Relaxed until he slipped a hand into his jacket pocket and his heart reminded him that recently it had been rather poorly. He didn't have his wallet.

Lorraine had insisted he should not leave valuables in the hospital room and had taken it home. He had nothing. No money, no cards, not even any change. He took a cautious glance at the stubby bull-like neck in front of him, but telepathy did not seem to be one of the man's talents.

Nearly at the flat. Time to put plan A into operation: get the hell out of this miserable situation.

'Look, turn right here, could you? Please, thanks. Thanks muchly.' He scrambled out of the cab before it had fully stopped and took several steps away from the kerb.

'My girlfriend's got my wallet. Expect you hear that a lot, eh? In your work, taxi driving and so on. I live just around the corner. I'm going to get it.'

'What?' The driver's hand shot through the open window and tried to grab Daniel's arm. 'Oh no, no way.'

'Yes, honestly. It's just around here.' He stumbled backwards but managed to stay upright.

'Stop right there, arsehole.'

Daniel sprinted towards the junction. The taxi crashed into reverse and whined after him. He dashed around the corner. The taxi shot into the street and there was a worrying bang as it mounted the kerb on the far side and the driver yelled something incomprehensible.

Daniel raced towards his flat, only dimly aware of a figure standing beside a large black car a short distance ahead.

As he was about to pass by, the man stepped forward and the car door opened.

'This way, sir. We would like a word with you.'

'Err...' was all Daniel managed as strong hands fastened on to him and lifted him bodily into the back seat of the vehicle. A door slammed, the car did a U-turn and raced away.

'Wha...' He struggled on the seat, squashed between two black-suited figures. 'What's going on?' The two men stared straight ahead while Daniel tried desperately to get his head together.

'Look, if this is about the roses, I can explain. I'm going to pay. I need a little time to... I would have taken them back, but Lorraine...' He stopped. The men stared stonily ahead. The driver in front was also clad in black and behind a glass screen.

'It's not about roses, is it?' Silence. 'Well, whatever it's about it's a mistake. I shouldn't be here.' The last words were muffled by the hood pulled over his head and knotted too tightly around his neck.

After what seemed like an hour but was probably only ten minutes, the car drew to a halt and one of the men whipped the mask from his head. They had stopped outside a three-story Victorian mansion. The man on his right got out. The other pointed and Daniel followed. With the two flanking him closely, they crunched along a driveway past a pair of crumbling stone lions and up the front steps. One of them waved a card at a reader beside the bell and the door swung open.

Daniel stepped into a dark, wood-panelled hallway and stopped, but a hand pushed him onward and up a flight of carpeted stairs. At the top, a thick oak door opened, and he was in front of a broad desk, behind which Reynolds sat. Or was it Reynolds? He had serious doubts about that. The man, whoever he was, glanced up, smiled, then stood with hand extended. Daniel shook the hand gingerly.

'Good afternoon, my young friend. We meet again. Please sit. I must apologise for the method of bringing you here. Unfortunately, you are difficult to find. You have had some medical problems?'

'Yes, a little heart murmur.'

'All over now?'

'I hope so.'

'You know, I never got your name?' The man poured two large measures of something that smelled strong from a decanter.

'It's Daniel Dreghorn.'

'Of course, and I am known as Number One.'

'Number one?' Daniel took an eye-watering swallow from his glass. Surely this couldn't be Reynolds.

'Exactly. Good, good. Now, we simply want to speak to you. I know you can be an asset to us. We all found your speech inspiring.'

Daniel had come to a conclusion, but he had to make sure. 'Look, this isn't anything at all to do with roses, is it?'

Number One put his head back and guffawed. 'Roses? No, unless you mean the rose of England.'

'So, it's purely the allotment thing?'

'Indeed.'

'And you don't know Gentle and Hawksley?'

The man frowned for a moment. 'I don't recall the names. Good operators, are they?'

'By appointment, so they must be, I guess.'

Number One chortled. 'I like a man with a sense of humour. Anyway, to business.' He topped up Daniel's glass. 'I believe you can be a great asset to our group.'

Daniel had been dreading this. In reality, his knowledge of gardening was limited to a few furtive flowerbed fumbles, in his teens, with his neighbour's daughter. Thankfully, his seeds had fallen on stony ground.

'I don't think...'

'Please, please. False modesty is charming up to a point, but only up to a point.'

The smile had dropped a notch. Daniel nodded.

'So, I have a task for you. A special package will be delivered to you sometime this week, along with instructions for its terminal transmission. You will transport it on to its final destination.'

Daniel blinked.

'Well, my friend, what think you?'

'Is that all?'

'All! A man of metal indeed.'

Metal? He began to have doubts. 'And what's in this package?'

'Ah. You know very well what it is, but let's, for the moment, say fertiliser. Very special fertiliser.'

'Oh right, a special recipe.' Now things made a little more sense.

'Indeed. Very special. But for now.' He stood and offered his hand. They shook.

'Courage brother, our struggle is just beginning,' were Number One's rather puzzling parting words as Daniel was escorted back downstairs, pushed into the car and driven home in silence.

Seven

He was still thinking about it the next day as he strolled into the university square. That and Lorraine's muted reaction to his return. She had made him a cup of tea and retired to bed, seemingly uninterested in his nascent explanations for an early expulsion from hospital. When he left that morning, she had been asleep.

'In here.'

Daniel turned, searching for the source of the urgent call. It appeared to come from the entrance to the gents' toilets.

'Daniel, please.'

He recognised Farquharson's voice. What was the old reprobate up to now? He paused at the toilet doorway. The professor stood by a cubicle, gesturing urgently. Daniel glanced over his shoulder. The sun shone innocently, and a reassuring number of students and staff wandered around in their accustomed early morning daze. What could possibly happen? He entered the dark and smelly portals of the toilets.

Farquharson's first reaction was not at all reassuring. He pushed Daniel into the nearest cubicle and bolted the door behind him.

'This is urgent,' were Farquharson's first breathless words. Up close, and they were closer than he would have chosen to be, the professor looked even worse than he had at their last meeting. His pallor was grey, as grey as Daniel's kitchen wall should he have painted it with B&Q morning grey instead of its current bright fuchsia. Stubble covered the man's chin, and his eyes seemed not to have slept for some time.

'Could we find somewhere else, professor? It's not very comfortable here.' Daniel tried unsuccessfully to wriggle away from Farquharson, but couldn't escape. Various parts of their bodies continued to touch disturbingly.

'Believe me, my boy, privacy is hard to come by. I've tried.' He let out a long sigh. 'You've met my secretary, Melody, I suppose?'

'I've met her all right. She chased me out the window.'

The professor shook his head. 'Melody Thunderbone. A terrible woman, Daniel, truly awful. She follows and records my every movement.'

'Thunderbone?'

Farquharson nodded and rolled his eyes.

'Get rid of her then. You're the boss.'

'If only it were that simple.'

A long pause followed. The professor rubbed his jaw, scratched his head. Daniel finally felt forced to say, 'If only it were that simple?'

'Ah my boy, you never spoke a truer word. I'm afraid, you know, that I have not been strictly honest with you.'

'You haven't?' said Daniel, rolling his eyes upwards. 'I'm really, really surprised to hear that.'

'No, you see this gentleman I asked you to follow... no, we need to go further back. The university authorities have formed a committee.'

'I'm sure they're good at that.'

'Yes indeed. Well, this committee is charged with looking at certain events last year, including the death of my dear wife Jemima, the death of that man Sharp and various other occurrences which we don't need to discuss right now. Of course, I gave my full co-operation. Unfortunately, they strayed into areas outside of their competence and began to make moral judgements on certain individuals whose lifestyles they chose to misunderstand.'

'You mean you?'

Farquharson coughed. 'Well, let us say for sake of argument, for the purposes of this discussion, ah... yes. So, a sub-committee has been formed, the Committee on University Morals, to look at the moral state of this university and the example being set by staff. This man you are investigating, professor Reynolds, is the chairman of this sub-committee. My intention is to discover anything I can about him.'

'Dish the dirt you mean?'

'A strange expression but relevant, I suppose.' Farquharson shuffled himself around and sat down on the toilet seat.

Daniel thought of his meeting at the Allotment Society and his interview at the house. 'Professor, I'm not sure if...'

'And that brings me to my so-called secretary.' He spat the word out as if he didn't want it contaminating his mouth any longer than necessary.

'I don't suppose you have a picture of Reynolds, do you?' Daniel tried with little hope of success.

'This creature, this abominable female, has been appointed by the committee to keep an eye on me. Those were Reynolds' exact words. She takes her job very seriously. She is reporting on me, spying on my every movement. I can do nothing here without her knowing. At this very moment, she is likely to be prowling the grounds in search of my spoor.'

The door to the toilets creaked open. Daniel held his breath as ponderous footsteps dragged across the floor. Farquharson's grey pallor turned even greyer. He shrank back against the cistern, connected with the handle, and caused the toilet to flush loudly.

Daniel closed his eyes. Sweat dampened the back of his neck. Being found in a toilet cubicle cheek-by-cheek with a man of known flexible inclinations would not look good on his cv. The footsteps stopped. He heard a zipper unzipping and, moments later, a heartfelt wheeze of relief. The professor gave Daniel a thumbs-up and beckoned him nearer. He bent so his ear was by the professor's lips.

'Peterson,' Farquharson whispered.

Daniel nodded. professor Peterson was another wrinkly of similar age to Farquharson. After what seemed like an eternity, the footsteps dragged back to the door and were gone.

Farquharson grimaced. 'Disgusting. Didn't even wash his hands. So...' There was a pause.

'Yes, professor?'

'I had better return, work and so forth. I'll leave you to your ah... business.'

'You were explaining the problem with your secretary.'

'Ah yes. A monstrous woman. As mad as a teacake.'

'A teacake?'

'Precisely. How will I clear my name, my boy? How will I ever hold my head up again? I have lost my freedom with this woman constantly beside me. Do you know she follows me home at night? I have seen her outside my house. She never sleeps. It's impossible. I need to deal with Reynolds firmly. Did you find out anything more other than the venue for this strange meeting?'

Daniel wasn't sure he had found out even that. 'Not really, apart from the allotment thing.'

'Yes. An allotment. Lots of things can be done on an allotment, wouldn't you say?'

Daniel rubbed his sweating forehead. He didn't suffer from claustrophobia, but ten minutes within touching distance of Farquharson was trying him to the limit.

'Well, I don't know about that, but he does seem a little strange, assuming that—'

'Hah. Precisely. I knew it. I'm going to need your help, Daniel. I want a report on his movements, who he sees and so forth.'

'Professor, that's not what we agreed. I had to find out his address and—'

'Enough,' the professor raised his hand. 'Remember our arrangement. Do this for me and my gratitude shall be without bounds. And now you should go lest anyone else enters this place. We will leave separately.'

He unbolted the door, ushered Daniel out and closed it behind him. Daniel stood for a minute trying to clear his thoughts, then sighed deeply and made his way outside, blinking in the burst of sunlight. At the far side of the square, the formidable figure of Melody Thunderbone strode towards the toilet block, pulling up the sleeves of her woollen jumper. Briefly, he considered dashing back to warn the professor, but it was one of those moments in life that passes so quickly that it barely registers in the universe's grand scheme. Unless the woman had suddenly turned blind, she must have seen him. Would she guess he had been talking to Farquharson, and what did that mean for his future health? He hurried towards the science labs.

There were no classes in the lab that day, which made for a relaxing time for all concerned, even if catch-up housekeeping and preparation continued at a frantic pace. He caught up with Alex at break as they took their usual seats in the far corner of the canteen with coffee and buns.

'What's new then?' Daniel asked, noting that Alex seemed chirpier than the last time they had talked.

Alex shrugged, 'Not much, you?'

'Same here I suppose.' He poured the spilt coffee in the saucer back into his cup, thinking that, in reality, much was happening.

'Interesting lives we lead, Dan, eh?'

Daniel took a slow sip of coffee. 'Actually, I suppose stuff is happening.'

'Hey, yeah, you were going for another job. How did that go?'

'Well, I got it.'

'Fantastic, when d'you leave then?'

'That's it, I'm not exactly sure. Farquharson's given me a special project.'

'Wow. A special project. What's that then? Polishing his doofer?'

'I think I'll let him do that himself. No, it's strange... it's... well, strange.' Daniel paused. 'Oh, what the hell.' He outlined to Alex the bones of what he had been doing over the last few days.

Alex grimaced. 'So that's where you were. And here's us thinking you were having long lie-ins with the lovely Lorrie. You're quite right. It's odd.'

'So, what do you reckon?'

'Easy. Tell him to get stuffed and leave. Simple.'

'Yeah but...' He had not told Alex of the attempted blackmail by the professor. 'Well, I feel I owe him. After all, this hasn't been a bad job, until now.'

'Your lookout, mate.' Alex drained his cup and stood. 'Some of us have work to do.'

'Right. Have you seen Sandra?'

'Sandra?'

'Yeah, Sandra. You know, the girl that works with us?' Most days they formed a trio for coffee.

'Well... I guess she's still around or something. Probably working. Look, I'll see you later, Dan.'

Alex hurried for the exit, leaving Daniel with a frown. His friend was strangely worried, almost embarrassed, and now they were back on good terms, he was concerned. Oh well, he had more to think about at the moment. Next week's audit, for instance. There appeared to be several pieces of missing equipment. He must check.

He finished his coffee and headed for the lab. Neither Sandra nor Alex were around, but before starting on the audit, he pulled a telephone directory from the shelf and looked up Reynolds. There were several of them, but a quick check in the university directory gave the man's first name as Adrian, and there was only one A. Reynolds. He noted the address. Absolutely typical of Farquharson. Well, that was one job less.

After a couple of phone calls, he decided he would have to get on with the audit, grabbed a notebook, and headed for the department's basement. It was a service area for the most part, but with several large storage rooms, one of which held his own lab's surplus equipment. That was the first place to check.

He unlocked the door and pushed inside. He noticed several things in rapid succession. The first was that the lights were on. His brain was still absorbing that and being irritated at the waste of Earth's scarce natural resources when he noticed the second thing: Sandra, facing him, seated on the edge of a table, with a faraway look in her eyes and her skirt up to her midriff. The third thing was Alex, on his knees and not facing him. For a few seconds, time seemed to run into an immovable barrier. Alex, being preoccupied and with ears muffled, had obviously not heard him enter. He caught Sandra's eye. She smiled sweetly at him and winked. For an awful moment, he thought she might say *come and join us,* and felt his face redden. He moved backwards, closed the door as quietly as possible, and locked it. What now? Well, back to his office, there wasn't much alternative.

He was seated in his swivel chair, biting the end of his pen and staring at the audit form, when Alex and Sandra slipped into the lab. Alex turned his head away as they passed the office and dropped the spare key set into a drawer. Sandra gave him a beaming smile. He placed the audit form aside; it could wait for another day. Something had to be said. He had to speak to both of them, but not together. No, definitely not together. At the office door, he called, 'Sandra, can I see you for a moment?'

She came straight into the office and stood in front of his desk, smoothing her lab coat over her hips.

'Look, sit down, Sandra. I know you only have a week to go but... well, I just wanted to say...'

She sat and crossed her legs. Wide, guileless eyes stared at him.

What did he want to say? That was the question. 'I wanted to say... that certain things must be done in your own time.'

'I was on my tea break.' She tilted her head to one side.

'Yes, but that's not the point. There are some things you can't do during the working day... and... and that's one of them.'

'You mean sex?'

'Yes, that's what I mean. It's not... I mean in your own time, fine, but not here and... so on.' He knew his face was burning. The whole thing was ridiculous.

'Is it only with Alex I can't do it?'

'Yes. No, I mean not with anyone. Not during the working day.'

'Not even with you?' Her eyebrows rose.

'What? No, of course not. Absolutely not. That is, no. Anyway, you and Alex are obviously.. aren't you?' She was teasing him for certain. He was seeing an entirely different side to what he had thought of as a mousy character.

'Alex and I are just passing the time. Keeping boredom away. It's not good to be bored, is it? Are you bored?'

Was he bored? Frequently. He stared at Sandra. He saw her differently now. The down-turned eyes coquettish rather than shy, the movement of her skirt further and further up her thigh deliberate rather than accidental, the toss of the hair a come-on rather than a rearranging of unruly strands. Daniel well knew he was slow on the uptake and that nuanced conversation passed him by. But there was no nuance here. It was being offered to him on a plate, with added salt and sauce and a double helping of mushy peas. What was he going to do? He had a girlfriend. He loved Lorraine, didn't he? He couldn't cheat on her, could he?

He heard Sandra uncross and recross her legs with a swish of nylon-clad thighs. His head held itself high, noble of purpose and pure of morals; his hormones tugged him towards the gutter. Heart, liver, spleen and lungs crowded around shouting *fight, fight, fight*.

'Bored?' he said and paused as his mouth dried and his warring organs battled it out. He knew that his next few words might affect the course of his life. 'Bored? I haven't time to be bored. Busy, busy, you know. Big job this, you know, sitting here doing... stuff. You know.'

Sandra stood and shrugged her shoulders. 'Sure. I'll be going. I'll let you get on with your stuff.' At the door, she wiggled her fingers in farewell and, with a final wriggle of her bottom, was gone.

Daniel stared at the empty doorway, trying to conjure her back.

Told you so, said huffy hormones.

Well done, said head, *it is a far, far better thing I do than—*

'Oh bugger off,' said Daniel.

Eight

IT WAS SEVEN PM, and Lorraine had not returned from work. Daniel sat at his kitchen table, turning his mobile over and over in his hand. He had tried to call her several times, but her phone appeared to be switched off. Of course, she would be with a friend somewhere. There was no need for worry. His thoughts turned to Sandra, Alex, and the vagaries of warring body parts.

The knock on the door startled him. It was sharp, peremptory, a no-nonsense type of knock that indicated the knocker did not spend time hanging around street corners waiting for life to happen. With one foot behind the door, he inched it open and peered through the gap.

'Mr Daniel Dreghorn?'

A scur-faced, youngish man loomed threateningly close to him, holding a briefcase in one hand.

'This isn't anything to do with flowers, is it?' Daniel muttered.

'I have a delivery for you.' The man pushed roughly past him and strode into the sitting-room.

He thought of protesting but decided against it. Leaving the front door open, he followed his guest who talked and acted as if time-wasting was not on the agenda.

'This is for you.' The man placed the briefcase on the floor and dug into his pocket. 'You will also need this.' He produced what looked like a pocket calculator. 'The activation code is 1812. Have you got that?'

'Yes, but...'

'Further contact will be made with the delivery address.'

Much to Daniel's amazement, he then saluted and offered his hand.

'Good luck to you, sir. This may be a practise but it is important. Number One sends his regards.'

Taking the hand, Daniel shook it limply and was squeezed hard in return.

'Look, I'm not sure...'

But the man was. He trotted smartly downstairs. Daniel kicked the door shut after him. So that's what it was about, this idiotic Number One with his fertiliser recipes. What the hell was he supposed to do with a case of fertiliser? He stared at the large briefcase in the middle of the room. Almost an overnight bag. It was surprisingly heavy when he picked it up. He shook it and tried the catches, but they were locked. Some slight movement was discernible inside, nothing more. So, they expected him to wait until he was told what to do. Fine, he could cope with that. He kicked the case under the bed and threw the calculator in after it. Right now, Lorraine's disappearance concerned him more.

She often visited friends overnight. She had her own life; she could do what she pleased. He didn't mind that, well not very much, but she would always tell him where she was going. So what had happened? Perhaps an accident? Should he call the police? But he knew he would be laughed at, or worse, patronised. After several drinks, a late supper and three episodes of Frasier from a box set, he fell into bed and an uneasy sleep.

Despite the thoughts churning through his head, he woke late next morning and reasonably refreshed but so late that the idea of breakfast did not even peer over the horizon. He threw on some clothing, most of which seemed to be his own, and rescued the case from under his bed before setting out for work at a smart pace.

Lorraine would be in touch this evening, no question of it. There would be some explanation. They would kiss and he would say that was all right, not to worry. He swung the briefcase cheerily from side to side.

In the department cloakroom, he pulled his labcoat on and dropped the case into the foot of his locker. It could stay there until they told him what to do with the damned thing.

INTERMISSION

A Modern Fairy Tale

Somewhere in a land far, far away, which for the purposes of this story we shall call Bishopton, there stood a tall, tall glass tower. At the very top of this tower lived (at least during daylight hours) a beautiful young lady with the longest blonde hair you have ever seen. Rachel Anne Penelope Unzell, for that was she, was a laboratory technician in Global Outsourcing, a company used by Britain's NHS to improve patient services beyond all recognition and save money.

Rachel was an excellent and conscientious technician, but alas, even the greatest among us must beware of the snares set by cruel and malevolent fates. The previous night, Rachel had let her hair down. It had been a special night, and she had let it down further than ever before. She had, in fact, got plastered.

And so, as we join Rachel this morning, we see her in a twilight world of pain and fear, her own personal Gotterdammerung. As fate would have it, the first sample Rachel picked up that morning belonged to Mr D Dreghorn and the second to Mr T Lowther of Greenwich. As she loaded up the carousel on her auto-analyser, a particularly vicious lightning-bolt of pain stabbed through her head. Rachel closed her eyes for a moment and tragically managed to swap the positions of these two samples. And thus it was that Mr D Dreghorn was destined to receive some very bad news. To balance this, and always in life there is balance if we look hard enough, Thomas Lowther received some excellent news. But that is another story.

Ten

WHEN DANIEL GOT BACK to the flat that evening, his phone was ringing. Throwing down the white sliced and pint of semi-skimmed, he snatched up the handset, hoping to hear Lorraine.

'Mr Daniel Dreghorn?' A husky female voice.

'Yes, you're speaking to him.' It had to be a sales pitch for something. Why hadn't he checked the number before picking up?

'This is the receptionist at the Mariah Pembroke Medical Centre. Your results are back and Dr Culshaw would like you to make an appointment to discuss them.'

'An appointment?'

'Yes, when would be convenient?'

Daniel stared at the telephone, scratching his crotch with his free hand. 'I don't understand. What results?'

'Your results.' There was a note of something non-professional in the receptionist's voice.

'Yes, but... I mean I don't know anything about results.'

'Yes, Mr Dreghorn, that's why you have to—'

'No, that is, I don't know of any tests being done. When was this? Can you tell me?'

There was a pause. 'There was a blood sample taken when you were in hospital last week. I see you discharged yourself. Perhaps there wasn't time to discuss it.'

'Ah yes. Right.'

'Dr Culshaw can see you at nine AM tomorrow if that suits.'

'Tomorrow? That's very quick.'

'Yes, does it suit you?'

'Well, look there isn't anything wrong is there?'

'Dr Culshaw will discuss it with you.'

Daniel's heart rate rose. 'It? What do you mean it?'

'I mean your results.'

'But you said it. He would discuss *it*. Does that mean there is something wrong?'

'I'm sorry, Mr Dreghorn. Dr Culshaw will talk to you about it... that is about your results. I'll book the appointment for you.' She hung up.

Feeling distinctly queasy, Daniel sat down. Results. There must be something wrong. The surgery wouldn't have phoned him with such an early appointment if there wasn't something wrong. He stumbled through to the kitchen and went through the motions of making tea, then poured himself a tumbler of whisky. What could it be? Heart perhaps, but the doctor had reassured him on that, and he had felt fine since leaving hospital. They must have discovered something awful when that sample was tested, something he would have heard about if he hadn't left in such a hurry, chased out by those stupid allotment people, he reminded himself.

He put the empty glass down and poured another. If only Lorraine was here, he could have told her. She would have been sympathetic. Right now, sympathy would have been welcome. Perhaps later he might phone her father and probe him circumspectly about his daughter's whereabouts.

In the bathroom, he undressed slowly. He had been very tired today. Tired and sluggish, that would be a symptom. After stripping off all his clothes, he stared at himself in the mirror. Wasn't that a new spot on his upper arm? He rubbed it gently.

Yes, definitely raised and slightly itchy. Extremely itchy. That was a bad sign. He turned around and looked over his shoulder; more or less OK. But even standing on tiptoe the half-length mirror meant he couldn't see below waist level. He grabbed a dining chair from the lounge and dragged it into the bathroom. With the chair in front of the mirror, he balanced carefully on the soft surface. Yes. There was a mole just below his left buttock. Not that big yet, but it was another symptom: spots, moles, tiredness. Well, he would describe all that to the doctor. He pulled clothes back on and returned to the lounge.

After a search, he found the TV remote and tuned into the late news. The lead item concerned the huge rise in hospital-acquired infections. My god, perhaps that was it. Had he caught something in hospital? That was why they were so worried about it. He would sue them; they had no right to treat him like that with their filthy hands. That big nurse with the orange beard hadn't washed his hands once. Although, to be fair, he had only seen him once on the ward.

The remote in his hand acted as a reminder. He headed for the bedroom and retrieved the control pad the weirdo had left him. It should have gone in the locker with the case. Tomorrow he would take it in. What was the number the man gave him? 1912? Why had he not written it down? No, it was 1812, like the overture. That was it. He punched the numbers into the pad, and a red light flashed once at the end. Wow, spectacular. He threw it onto the table. OK, more important, a call to Lorraine's father.

Before he could change his mind, he grabbed the telephone and hit speed dial. It was answered almost immediately.

'Hello?' A female voice.

'Um. I was looking for Mr Power?'

'You are through to the Power residence. How may I assist?'

Lorraine's mother had died some years previously, and he had heard nothing of a new woman in her father's life. Perhaps she was a house-keeper.

'This is Daniel Dreghorn could I speak to Mr Power?'

'Oh Daniel, the live-in lover, we haven't met.'

Daniel felt his face colouring. 'Yes, well. Err...'

'Sampson is not here at present. I am his partner, Celia Power.'

'Yes, Mrs... Celia. I just wondered...' He had not planned what to say. Best not be too direct; he didn't want to worry them.

'Is Lorraine there?' Damn it, that wasn't what he'd meant to say.

'Lorraine? She's with you, isn't she?' Celia sounded puzzled.

'Well, not exactly. Not with me as such at this moment.'

'So when will she be with you as such, Daniel?' There was a tone in her voice that he couldn't quite place. But it didn't sound like worry.

He had no choice now. 'In fact, I haven't seen her since the day before yesterday.'

'The day before yesterday? I'm sure there's nothing to worry about. Little Lolly does strange things sometimes. Look, if she's still missing tomorrow, you come around here in the afternoon and we'll talk about it. Would that suit you?'

Little Lolly? 'Yes. Yes, of course. You're very kind... Celia. Bye.'

'Goodbye, Danny.'

He put the phone down and realised as he did so that Celia had not told him if Lorraine had been in contact with her, or when her father would return.

As he got ready for bed, he heard the wail of several emergency vehicles in the distance. That was all he needed, something else to keep him awake tonight.

Eleven

THE WAITING ROOM WOULD be dreary. Doctors' surgeries were always the same, so Daniel had come prepared for a siege, with a newspaper under his arm and a packet of mints in his pocket. The Mariah Pembroke Medical Centre was bright and new, with doors that opened automatically if you approached them from the right direction. Unfortunately, Daniel did not, and the door stayed stubbornly shut. Retreating a few steps, he tried again. Still no movement. He peered through the glass into the cavernous interior, but there was no one visible. Perhaps he had the first appointment. He gave the door a kick and knocked on the panel. Then, in frustration, drew back his foot and let fly. A very hard part of the door came into conjunction with a very soft part of his trainer, and pain like an electric shock shot up his leg. It was as if the leg was no longer there. He collapsed to the pavement, moaning as pain blotted out his senses. With that, the door swished open, and he crawled inside.

'Help,' he croaked. 'Please help me.'

A lady who had been approaching him did a double-take and retreated to reception, where she had a muttered conversation with the wide and meaty woman behind the desk. This woman stomped towards Daniel and stopped so close to him that he could see a sticky substance adhering to the toe of her right shoe, no doubt what remained of the last unfortunate to cross her path.

'No begging here, my man. You'll have to go.'

'No, you don't understand,' Daniel moaned. 'It's my foot. I think I've broken something.'

'You should have gone to casualty then, not come here.'

'No, I've got an appointment. I hurt my foot when I kicked the door.'

'What?' The woman stepped back, and for a moment, Daniel thought she was going to lash out with her sticky shoe. But if that was her impulse, she resisted. He uncurled and sat up. The pain in his leg had lessened slightly.

'What's your name?' she snapped.

'Daniel Dreghorn.' He squeezed his eyes shut and turned onto all fours. The pain was just about bearable. When he opened his eyes, the woman was behind the castle of her desk. He crawled towards it and hoisted himself onto one leg.

'All right, you do appear to have an appointment.' Her voice indicated that she would have preferred if he had not, for then she could be let loose with the instruments of torture waiting for those that tried to fool her. 'Wait through there.'

Daniel hopped along beside the desk, dragging his injured foot behind him, and managed to reach the nearest chair without collapsing on the floor. It took some time to recover. In fact, it took fifteen minutes, at which point a voice echoed from far away into his scrambled head.

'Mr Dreghorn?'

He hoisted himself up and staggered towards the source of the voice. The doctor, standing in the doorway of his office, was in his fifties with greying hair and a pair of wafer-thin spectacles.

'My dear chap.' He rushed to Daniel's side as soon as he hobbled into view. 'Please take my arm.'

He helped Daniel to a seat and closed the door.

'Right, let's have a look at that leg of yours.'

'Well, actually that's not...'

'Come, come, just roll your trouser leg up for the moment.'

Although his leg still ached, Daniel had now decided that he was suffering from nothing more than a bad sprain. He pulled the cuff of his jeans up and rested his leg on the doctor's lap. He winced as cold fingers probed and manipulated his calf and ankle.

'Hm, I would say nothing broken, but there is considerable swelling. Perhaps an X-ray is called for. How exactly did this happen?'

'Well... it happened at the surgery.'

'Oh. Please explain.'

Even Daniel noticed the note of caution that entered the doctor's voice. 'I kicked your door... actually.'

'You kicked the door? Actually? Why?'

'Well, I suppose I was annoyed that it didn't open.'

His foot dropped from the doctor's knee onto the floor and the man pushed his chair back a fraction.

'I see. Perhaps an X-ray isn't called for. We'll see how things develop. I'll give you a prescription for painkillers.'

'But...'

'Two twice a day, morning and night.'

'But...'

'Come back if there's any further problem. Enjoy your day.'

'Wait, please, there was something else.'

'Oh?' The doctor glanced at his watch.

'Yes, you asked me to call.'

'I don't think so.'

'Well, I mean not you yourself, but the surgery called. I was to discuss the results of some tests.'

'Ah.' The doctor swivelled around to his computer.

Now that the trauma of the previous thirty minutes was fading, Daniel found his intense worry over those results return.

The doctor frowned as he read the pages on the computer. There seemed to be a lot of them.

'Doctor?'

He held up his hand. 'One moment, please. I need to re-read this. Got to be sure.'

Daniel's mouth was as dry as a Farquharson lecture as his heart made a valiant attempt to break through his chest wall.

Finally the doctor said, 'I see,' and tapped his teeth with a pen.

'What is it,' Daniel croaked. 'Am I ill?'

'How do you feel?' There was a most worrying smile on the man's face.

'Well... OK, mostly. A bit tired. I've got a few moles.'

'Tired, eh?'

'Yes... there's nothing wrong with that.'

'Of course not. It's just a symptom.'

'Of what? What's it a symptom of?'

The doctor turned back to the computer screen. 'The results from your blood test are here.'

'And... what? What is it?'

'It looks like you may have contracted hepatitis.'

Hepatitis. Was that good or bad? He'd heard of it of course, but... 'So, what does that mean? Is it serious?'

'Well, it's the B form.'

'Is that bad?'

'B for bad that's what we always say.'

'Shit.'

'But don't worry, there are treatments. Lots of avenues before we hit the brick wall, eh?'

Daniel stared ahead, his mind frozen.

'Only thing is, there's a complication.'

'What?'

'Yes, some unusual results for a man of your age. Tell me, in total confidence of course, do you share needles?'

The concept embodied in that question was so alien to Daniel that for one moment all that came to mind was a picture of his grandmother sitting in her favourite chair with her knitting needles clacking rapidly.

'Oh, I don't use them myself.'

The doctor's eyebrows rose. 'But if you did need a needle, what would you do?'

Daniel thought for a second. 'My grandmother has plenty. I could borrow from her I suppose. But I don't—'

'Your grandmother? And how long has she been using?'

'Using them? Well, all her life I sometimes think.'

The doctor shook his head. 'We mustn't judge.'

'I think it's the way she was brought up. I mean, people did it more in those days, didn't they? I mean, there weren't computers and—'

'Not where I came from.' The doctor interrupted, unnecessarily sharply Daniel thought, and then continued, 'Well, that may be your answer.'

'But surely you can't catch hepatitis from...'

'I assure you, it's only too possible. Do you practise safe sex?'

Daniel's mind had been entirely focussed on homely pictures of his Granny, and Christmas presents of long knitted scarves.

'Well, yes. I mean, I think so, but I don't see the connection.'

The doctor sighed. 'Oh dear, there is still such ignorance even among the educated. I can assure you that each new piece of research backs up the connection. So, you are doubly at risk.'

Daniel began to sweat. 'Doubly? But I still don't see—'

'I want you to return for a confirmatory test in two days. Make an appointment with the nurse.'

A confirmatory test. Daniel grasped at the straw that had floated into view. 'Right, right, thank you.' He made his way to the door on shaky legs.

'The nurse will also provide details of our addiction clinic.'

'What?' Daniel stopped in the open doorway, but the doctor was typing on his computer.

'And information on our sexual health programme. Have a good day.'

Daniel turned from the door to a surprisingly hushed waiting room and a sea of interested faces.

Twelve

BY THE TIME HE arrived at the university, Daniel realised there was a BIG problem. A problem that kicked his own health worries down the back stairs. It might have been something to do with the smell of singed wood, which he noticed as soon as he turned the corner into Huntly Street. It could have been the large number of police cars, blue lights winking, which obstructed the road. It could have been the hundreds of students talking in worried groups. But mostly, he believed, it was the sight of the chemistry block with a pall of black smoke hovering over the sizeable hole that had appeared in its front wall.

He stood perfectly still, trying to take in what his eyes were transmitting to his brain and failing miserably.

'Hey, Dan. You're late. Look at this shambles.' Alex strode towards him, arms flapping at the mess surrounding them.

'Been to the doctor. What's... what's...' He gestured lamely at the scene of bedlam.

'God, it's awful. There's been an explosion.'

Daniel gazed at the acres of shattered glass that littered the area around the chemistry block, at the gaping hole in the lower wall and the mound of debris around it.

'An explosion. I don't understand. How could there be?'

Two of the four fire engines in front of the building had rolled up their hoses. The white-helmeted fire officer was talking to a police officer nearby. It looked like the worst was over.

'Well nobody knows yet, do they? They'll need to investigate. Probably in the research labs. One of the idiots left an experiment cooking overnight.'

Daniel frowned. 'But there are no labs there, Alex, where the hole is. That's the utility area.'

Alex shrugged. 'Well, gas or something. Who knows? We'll have to wait.' He turned away. 'Hey look out, here's the Prof.'

Daniel watched Farquharson hobble towards them faster than he had ever seen the man move.

'Daniel, Daniel. Tragedy, tragedy. A dreadful business.'

The professor paused for a moment, seemingly out of breath, then produced a large red handkerchief and dabbed at his eyes.

'I searched for you, Daniel,' he muttered from behind the handkerchief. Then he snapped it downwards. 'Where have you been?' His watery blue eyes were disconcertingly intense.

'I... I... at the doctor. The surgery, for some tests, well sort of results of tests, actually.'

'I see.' Farquharson's wavering gaze briefly held his. 'They say it happened at 11.30 last night. That's when the first emergency calls went through.'

Daniel stared over the professor's shoulder at the chaotic scene surrounding them. The enormity of it had begun to sink in. 'What are we going to do now?'

'The fire brigade inform me they are finished here. Now we will have an investigation, of course. Forensics, Health and Safety are arriving. Police have begun interviewing staff. Can you proceed to room 208 at...' Farquharson paused and consulted a notepad in his hand. 'At ten past one this afternoon.'

'What? They want to interview me?'

'Don't be alarmed, Daniel. Preliminary interviews, they say. I myself have been spoken to already. There will be an emergency meeting afterwards for staff in order to plan our own investigation. I'd like you to be there, Daniel.'

'Yes, of course.'

'We can only be thankful for the timing. Nobody was in the building so there are no casualties.'

'Thank god.'

'Yes, indeed we should. Two pm this afternoon, Daniel, in the large meeting room next to my office.' Farquharson swept off to join a group of senior staff huddled in a doorway, several of whom puffed frantically at cigarettes.

⋙ ⋘

Room 208. Daniel stared at the gold lettering on the tasteful wooden plaque fixed to the mahogany door. His heart thumped in his chest, hard and fast. Not good. Had he taken his pill that morning? Couldn't remember. Why was he so nervous? No need to be nervous. This was routine. But he had so much stuff happening right now with his health, with Lorraine and with stupid Farquharson and his vendetta against Reynolds. He had every right to be nervous. Standing up straight, he knocked confidently on the door.

A young, female police officer in uniform opened the door and smiled at him.

He returned the smile. 'Daniel Dreghorn, reporting for duty.'

She checked a list of names on a clipboard and ticked one of them. 'Thank you, Mr Dreghorn, please come in and take a seat.'

The room was furnished only with a desk and several chairs. A burly man wearing a tweed jacket stood by the single window with his back to Daniel. As he sat down, the man turned around and Daniel's heart rate, which had reduced to a comfortable simmer, shot up to boiling point. A full black beard, squashed boxer's nose, lacklustre eyes. He knew this man. More importantly, this man might know him.

'Mr Dreghorn, thanks for coming in. I'm Detective Sergeant Barnes. This won't take long.' He dropped, too heavily, into the cheap office chair, which offered a squeak of protest.

Barnes was the sidekick of Detective Inspector Dick, whom Daniel had come up against during his attempt to escape the shitpile of his last involvement with a Farquharson scheme. This couldn't be good, but just how bad was it?

'Now, sir, were you working here yesterday?'

To Daniel's relief, Barnes gave no indication of recognition.

'Yes. Yes, I was.'

'And you work where?'

'The undergraduate teaching labs.'

Barnes consulted what seemed to be a plan of the chemistry department's layout, sitting on the desk beside him. 'When did you leave your laboratory last night?'

'Must have been about four-thirty or so.'

'Did you notice anything unusual? Any noises, any unscheduled work or maintenance, any strangers in the building?'

Daniel thought for a moment. 'No, nothing at all,' and relaxed back into the chair. No need to worry. He sneaked a glance at his watch and was suddenly aware of silence. When he looked up, the policeman's gaze had fixed on him.

'Have we met before, sir?'

Flapping a hand in front of his face, Daniel mumbled, 'Don't think so, not that I can recall. I mean I wouldn't forget that, would I?' Sweat broke out on the back of his neck.

Barnes seemed about to comment but then nodded. 'Of course. Thank you. That will be all. If you remember anything that may assist us, please contact me on this number.' He produced a business card.

Daniel grabbed the card and leapt from his chair so fast it tumbled backwards. 'Sorry,' he stammered, pulling the chair upright. 'Sorry,' he said to the constable who opened the door for him. 'Sorry,' he said to Barnes who stood watching him, stroking his beard.

Well, that had gone OK, he thought, once the door had closed. It seemed Barnes didn't remember him. Now for another meeting.

⇶ ⫷

Daniel's head jerked upwards once again. Three o'clock, and the meeting had barely started on the preliminaries. A glance around the room showed that no one had noticed his descent into near coma. Over thirty staff had crammed into the meeting room, and they divided into two camps: those who wanted to have their say on every procedural who-ha and what-not and those, like Daniel, who were making heroic efforts to remain sentient.

Farquharson was talking. The meeting had moved on to the meat, or at least the Quorn, of its business.

'... establish the sequence of events which have led us to this sad situation. The time of the explosion is placed exactly at seven minutes past eleven yesterday evening.'

That must have been the emergency sirens he had heard last night, Daniel realised.

'The source of the explosion has been identified as the first-floor gents' locker-room.'

Oh well, he needed a new labcoat. And then he remembered the briefcase of samples, now nothing but vapour. Hell, it wasn't his fault, he only had to explain, although the idea of explaining anything to the man who had left the samples with him did not appeal. The professor was still talking.

'Initially, a gas explosion was thought to be the cause, but I have this moment spoken to the authorities and they now believe that an explosive device was the source. This information is in the strictest confidence and must not be repeated outside this room.' He paused as a ripple of disbelief circulated the room and those awake nudged their senseless colleagues.

'Yes, an explosive device. CCTV footage has been examined and nothing untoward was found. The explosion appears to have originated from inside a locker. The remains of this locker are now being examined to see if the owner can be identified.'

At this point, the rusty wheels of suspicion that had been grinding around in Daniel's head seemed to take a bath in machine oil. They meshed together disturbingly to produce an even more disturbing output.

Seven minutes past eleven, explosion, locker. What had he been doing at eleven-seven? It was all very clear. He'd been watching the news, picked up that control thing the man had left and pressed buttons. A few minutes later, there had been sirens in the distance. He felt hot and then cold and then hot again. Nausea grabbed his belly and gave it a shake.

The professor continued. 'Yes, ladies and gentlemen, an inside job as they say. We have a terrorist in our midst.'

Then everyone attempted to talk at once, trying to give an opinion, trying to be heard. Farquharson banged a stapler on the table, paused to remove a staple from his finger, and tried again. The hubbub reduced in volume.

'Daniel?'

He jumped. Farquharson's gaze had fastened onto him.

'This occurred in your section. Do you have any comments?'

He opened his mouth and then shut it. The entire room stared at him. What was a terrorist supposed to say?

'A... a locker did you say?'

'So I am informed.'

'It's... awful.'

'Are you all right, Daniel? You seem very pale.'

'Sorry. The shock. Realising it's so close. Might be someone we know or... or maybe there's a mistake... somehow.'

'Hanging's too good for the bastards.' This from Fullerton of ethics and moral philosophy.

Daniel flapped his hand. 'I think I might get a drink of water if you don't mind.' Halfway to his feet, he stared at the glass and untouched carafe of water in front of him. 'And a breath of fresh air. Not feeling great.'

'Of course, Daniel. Understood. Please take your time. We'll let you know about emergency arrangements.'

Daniel staggered to the door, sincerely hoping that nobody understood. In the toilet a short distance down the corridor, he locked himself into a cubicle. After emptying his stomach and bowels, thankfully in sequence and not in tandem, he sat on the pedestal and thought grim thoughts. There was no question now, those fertiliser samples had been some sort of exploding stuff, that remote was the trigger and he the patsy in the middle. Another wave of nausea swept over him. He might have pressed the switch at any time. People could have been killed. He could have been a murderer. At least that wasn't on his conscience. But the authorities did not look too kindly on individuals who went around blowing things up. Could he explain? Perhaps. Would he be believed? No, he would not, unless he could point the finger at those allotment idiots.

OK, first thing, dump that control gadget. Right now. He jumped up and exited from the cubicle so fast that he almost collided with Fullerton.

'Oh hello, sorry... meeting finished is it?' He sidled towards the door.

'Finished. Hah. My god, if I get my hands on the bastards. Castrate 'em and drown 'em in hot tar. That's too good for them, eh?' Fullerton had a wild look in his eye and sweat on his forehead.

'Yes, oh yes, absolutely. Must be going you know. Got to... you know how it is.'

'Hah,' was Fullerton's parting comment as the door closed.

Daniel headed across the square at a fast pace, but did not run. There were few people about as the entire campus had been closed for the day. He found his mind speculating feverishly. Would they find the bomb had been in his locker? Almost certainly, what with modern forensics, DNA, CSI. He didn't stand a chance. But if the locker had been destroyed, blown to atoms, surely that would remove all evidence? But they were so damn clever these days. Even so, results might be ambiguous? Right, he agreed with himself, that was why he had to get rid of the remote. There was nothing ambiguous about that. He quickened his pace for home.

He was about fifty metres from the entrance to his block of flats when he noticed a male figure loitering there. The figure strolled away from him, hands behind back, but looked as if at any moment he might turn around and walk towards Daniel. The man had a long stave of wood clutched in the hands clasped behind him. He turned. Damnation. It was the Asian man from the florists. Daniel threw himself into the nearest doorway. This was too much. It was ridiculous. A simple mistake, but the man looked like he meant serious business.

He was hidden in the shallow recess of the doorway to a block of flats and shuffled backwards as far as possible. Could he be seen here? He waited for a minute and then, steadying himself on the doorframe with one hand, squinted around the edge of the recess. Two things happened at once: realisation that the Asian man was striding towards him, clutching the stave of wood with both hands, and a voice crackled from the entry phone.

'Come on up, darling. You're late.'

His hand had pressed one of the entry buttons. The door lock buzzed. Daniel knew that in certain situations the element of choice was blissfully absent and so he tugged the door open, pushed inside and let it slam shut as his pursuer reached the bottom of the steps. There was a shout and a flurry of thumps on the door.

He was at the foot of the common stairs. To either side were the ground floor flats. Perhaps he could find a back way out. A few seconds proved to him he could, but it was firmly locked. Upstairs, a door opened.

Daniel took a cautious peek through the glass panel at the side of the entrance. The Asian man was on the bottom step, arms folded, makeshift club tucked under his armpit, glaring at the door. An older, slightly built man passed by and hesitated. Perhaps Daniel could attract his attention, ask for help. But no, after a double take, he hurried away.

'Up here, honey, top floor.' A female voice wafted down the stairwell.

Daniel climbed the stairs slowly. This woman obviously thought she knew him, but when she found that wasn't so, perhaps they might laugh at the mistake, have a short conversation, and then he could return downstairs to wait for the beast to depart.

The door of the top flat opened wide. A blonde woman stood there wearing a dressing gown that ended well above her knees.

'You're late,' she announced. 'Got cold feet, have we?'

'What? No, no. There must be a mistake. Look, I don't think I know you.'

'Ooh, haven't been introduced, have we?' she minced. 'Well, I'm Sammie and come on in. It's cold out here.'

He could see little alternative so followed the woman through a short hallway into a room dimly lit by a red globe in a central ceiling light. Thick curtains covered the window, and it was excessively hot. It penetrated Daniel's skull that something was very, very wrong. A king-sized bed and two chairs filled more than half the room. On the wall opposite was... was... Daniel stared. It was a large wooden contraption with several sets of what could only be handcuffs hanging from it. To one side, in an umbrella stand, stood a series of whips and canes of varying lengths and diameters.

'Er...'

'OK, the preliminaries,' said Sammie. 'It's eighty-five, and that's in advance. Cash or credit cards, but no cheques. That's straight mind. Anything fancy is extra.'

'No really, that's not... I mean. I just came to get away.'

'Don't they all love? Way of the world.'

'No, it's not like that. There's a man. I think he's after me.'

Sammie shrugged. 'Each to his own. Some wouldn't complain. You've come to the right place, love. Now, time's getting on, and my diaries full today. Is it cash?'

'No.' Daniel backed towards the door. 'Look there's been a mistake. I must have pressed the wrong button.'

Sammie's expression hardened. 'You wait there, china. You've wasted my bleeding time. Time wasters is fifty quid.'

Daniel had his back to the door. His hand fumbled behind him for the handle. 'I'm sorry, really sorry, but I don't have fifty quid.'

'You won't have any knackers either if you don't cough.' She lifted a mobile from the end of the bed. 'Towser, we got another one here.'

Daniel was already a flight of stairs down when the door of the next flat to Sammie's flew open, and a grotesquely huge man burst onto the landing.

'Hey you.'

The voice reminded Daniel of being too close to a large aeroplane taking off. His feet shifted very fast to remove himself from the runway. He was at the ground floor entrance in what seemed like two seconds. Man-mountain crashed downstairs, bellowing an assortment of curses. But there was still one problem. The flower-shop man. There again, it wasn't a problem. He would take his chance with flower-shop man. Daniel threw the street door wide and careered across the road. The flowery man had gone. Man-mountain stood in the doorway questioning the marital status of Daniel's parents, among other points of a more anatomical nature.

It took only seconds for Daniel to reach his door, but he paused before going further, making sure that Sammie's friend had not followed. He really didn't want that muscled ox to know where he lived. Left and right, up and down, muscle-man had gone, flower-shop man had gone. It was safe to enter.

As his flat door clicked shut, he stood immobile, suppressing the urge to scream in case any of the neighbours were at home. Instead, he took several deep breaths, pausing only when a small fly lodged in his throat precipitating a coughing fit. First the remote. He removed the batteries, dumped it in the kitchen waste sack and left it ready to take downstairs to the communal bin. Then he poured himself a very large vodka and collapsed onto the couch.

His life was going horribly wrong. Lorraine had still not returned. He checked the telephone – no messages. In many ways, this was his main worry, but the list of subsidiary worries was endless. Blowing up the university headed that subsidiary list. He knew very well it did NOT make a good career move, perhaps akin to Attila the Hun producing paper doilies at his kids' tea party. They would find the locker belonged to him. Nothing surer. And then what? Best not go there at the moment. Another long drink made his throat and larynx burn in a most satisfying manner.

On top of that, there was the minor matter of hepatitis. He must read up on it if he wasn't dead before he had time. Strangely, death didn't seem so worrying now. Then there was the assortment of villains pursuing him. He included the Asian flower-shop man in this, even though he was not a villain as such, just a paranoid psychopath.

The doorbell rang. Daniel groaned inwardly. Outwardly he said, 'Bugger, what now?' before easing the door open only enough to see who was there.

'Professor?'

Farquharson faced him wearing a raincoat with the collar turned up and a homburg hat in a caricature of Inspector Clouseau.

'May I come in, my boy? Thank you.'

Reluctantly, Daniel opened the door wider. 'What are you doing here?'

'If I could take a seat for a moment.' Farquharson dropped into Daniel's chair with a sigh. 'Thank you, that's better. As to what I'm doing here. Ah, could you take my hat? Thank you. I come here only reluctantly, given the need for us not associate other than in the working environment. However, it has proved very difficult of late to find an appropriate time to discuss matters with you, and I have taken precautions to avoid being followed.'

'Yes.' Daniel said.

'Well, to put it bluntly, in a word as it were. How are things progressing in your investigations, eh? In your information gathering capacity concerning my friend and colleague, the committee chairman.'

'Ah, of course.' Amid the chaos of the last few days, the thought he was on a commission for the professor had been far from Daniel's mind.

'So...?' The professor raised one eyebrow, followed a few seconds later by the other in a disconcerting manner.

What the hell could he tell the man? 'Yes, yes indeed. Ah... would you like a drink, professor?'

'Thank you, dear boy. Most hospitable. I'll have a sweet Martini with lemonade.'

Daniel paused halfway to the kitchen. 'A... sweet Martini?'

'With lemonade, thank you.'

'Right, actually I don't have any Martini, sorry.'

'Don't worry. What do you have then?'

'Well, there's vodka and... lager.'

'Oh, it will have to be vodka for me, Daniel. Lager's not quite my... what do they say? Scene, is it?'

'I believe so, professor.' Daniel busied himself pouring two vodkas and set them down on the table.

Farquharson took his glass and sat forward. 'So tell me, what further information?'

'Well, this man I've been following...'

'This Reynolds fellow.'

'Well, possibly. That's the problem. It's all very strange.'

'Hah.' Farquharson made a tell-me-more gesture with his finger.

'Well, Reynolds, at least the man I followed. I told you about his gardening fetish?'

'Yes, yes... and?'

'There's more than that. In fact, I think he may be mixed up in the explosion.'

The professor slapped his right fist into his left palm. 'I knew it. I knew he was up to no good. The man's a charlatan.'

Daniel took a large swig of vodka and coughed. 'The thing is, you see, I believe I may have...'

'No, no, no. Please say no more. You've played your part admirably. I had my suspicions about that explosion.'

'It's just that he gave me, well, indirectly at least...'

'Offered a bribe, no doubt, which you refused. There will be compensation for you. Now what we need is proof.' The professor rose to his feet, put his arms around Daniel, and hugged him disturbingly.

'You are my rock, Daniel. A few photographics would be useful.'

'Photos?'

'Yes. Showing what the man's up to and so on. Who are his friends? Can you do that?'

'Well—'

'Excellent. Well done, that man. Get them to me as soon as possible. No time to waste, eh?' He patted Daniel's arm and made his way to the door then turned and waved. '*Auf wiedersehen*, my friend,' then he was gone.

Daniel slumped back in his chair. That had gone well. For a mad moment, he had thought he might confess all to Farquharson regarding his inadvertent part in the explosion, but that opportunity had passed. It was Reynolds, or whoever he had been following, who was responsible, even if indirectly. He had at least got that point across. The chance of getting photographs seemed remote. None of the strange gardening people seemed likely candidates to pose for family snaps.

Thirteen

DANIEL STARED UPWARDS AT the array of windows on the first floor. The house was huge: a Georgian mansion, probably worth more than he would earn in a lifetime of drudgery at the University. He had been here once before, soon after moving in with Lorraine, to a rather strained dinner with her father, who had made no concession to small talk and several pointed references to marriage.

He rang the bell and waited. It was opened a few moments later by a woman he assumed to be Celia. Very tall and having the advantage of two steps, she towered above Daniel in an intimidating manner. Her greeting, however, could not have been friendlier.

'Daniel, how delightful. Do come in.' The smile was wide and sunny as she stepped aside. 'Into the lounge now. On the left, as I'm sure you remember,' she said, following him into the room.

'Thank you for seeing me, Mrs Power. I know you're busy.'

'Daniel,' she frowned and wagged her finger at him. 'We'll have no more formality. I'm Celia to my friends, and you'll be in big trouble if you forget again.' She made a boxing motion with her fists, and then the sunny smile returned. 'Now, what can I get you to drink?'

'Well, a lager would be fine, thanks.'

'Right. You make yourself comfortable here and I'll fix things up.'

He sank into the cream leather sofa facing the window and watched as she busied herself at the corner bar. Daniel never claimed to be an observant person and only now noticed that Mrs Power was disturbingly overdressed. She wore what he could only describe, in his limited experience, as a cocktail dress: a tight-fitting black number sparkling with sequins. It was split from floor to ceiling or at least to thigh and revealed an alarming area of Mrs Power both upstairs and down.

She returned with a half-pint of lager and something red in a tall glass. She sat near him, too near for a three-seat sofa, and handed him his drink.

'So, Daniel, you were asking after dear Lorraine?'

'Yes, that's it. She still hasn't come back. There's been no message. You haven't heard from her?'

'Not a dicky-bird. So, you're worried, are you?' She smiled at him over the rim of her glass as she sipped the noxious-looking contents.

'Well yes, I am, actually.' About Lorraine and a million other things.

'Really, I wouldn't be, Daniel.' She bent towards him, and he found himself staring at her prominently displayed cleavage. 'The little girly has always gone her own way. She's like a swan.'

'A swan? I don't...'

'Floating along calm and placid up top but paddling like hell underneath.'

'Ah, I see.'

'I hate to say it, Daniel, but I suspect she has moved on.'

'Moved on?'

'Yes, pastures new, you know?' She smiled as she straightened up, and Daniel tore his gaze away from her chest.

'I don't think so. She wouldn't do that.'

Mrs Power shook her head slowly, lamenting his gullibility.

Would Lorraine leave him? She might, but she wouldn't march away without a goodbye. She wasn't like that. There hadn't even been a note left behind. Besides... 'I haven't seen her around the university either.'

Celia leant over and patted his knee. 'It means she's avoiding you, darling. I'm sorry.' Her glass clinked onto the table and she stretched her arms upwards. 'I'm sure Sampson would tell you the same thing.'

Daniel blinked hard and tried to keep his eyes from the twin peaks jutting towards him. 'Mr Power?'

'Unfortunately, he won't be back until tomorrow. A business meeting... he says.' She lowered her arms. 'So, I'll be all alone this afternoon.' A lengthy pause followed before she added, 'and tonight.'

Even Daniel's slow and rather innocent mind had caught up with the situation by now and had decided that...

'I'd better go.'

'There's no rush, Daniel.' She crossed her legs and made a desultory attempt to pull the hem of the dress over her knee. 'We could have another drink and then I can put something together for you if you want. If you're hungry.'

'No really...'

'Do you prefer it hot or cold?'

'What?' Daniel's mind spiralled around this question.

'Would you prefer something hot or cold for dinner?' She slid closer to him.

'Ah, right, but no. I've got to go. Someone I have to see.'

'See someone?' Celia's smile lessened a fraction.

Lifting the glass, he drained the last few drops and tried to replace it on the table. He missed, and it tumbled onto the thick pile carpet.

'Oh god, sorry.' He dropped onto his knees and scrambled for the glass before any residual lager found its way onto that expensive carpet. It was also a welcome distraction from Celia. Unfortunately, as he did so, it seemed as if the edge of the coffee table came up to meet him. He saw it in high-resolution slow motion as it rushed for his forehead There was a sharp bang.

~~≫≫ ≪≪~

He woke with a stinging headache to find himself lying on his back. He opened his eyes one at a time, afraid that they might break, and found he was in bed. A dressing table, chairs, lemon-coloured curtains covered the window, and outside it was nearly dark. This wasn't his own bedroom, and it wasn't a hospital, so he must still be at Celia's. That thought caused considerable anguish, and he tried to struggle to a sitting position.

'Daniel.' A sharp voice from close by.

He screamed and pulled the bedclothes around him. There had appeared to be no one else in the room. But there was. Celia, lurking on a chair beside his head.

'I'm so glad you're better, Daniel. I was really worried about you. That was quite a bang you gave your head.'

'Yes...' He had to cough to clear his throat. 'Yes, sorry. My head still hurts.'

'Oh Daniel, how can you forgive me? The whole thing was my fault. I feel responsible for you '

She reached out to touch his hand, but he whipped it away.

'No, no, my fault. Completely my fault. Really, totally. But now I'm feeling...' *Better* he was about to say but stopped as he realised that his shoulders were alarmingly bare. Completely bare. He moved his legs around cautiously and found that they were bare too. In fact, his underpants seemed to be the only thing left.

89

Celia pulled her chair further forward. 'Yes, Daniel, what are you beginning to feel?'

He realised right then he must get his brain functioning – urgently. And something else – he was in a double bed. Now this may have had nothing to do with another thing – Celia wore a pink dressing gown embroidered with red dragons, or it might have had everything to do with it. Best to play safe.

'God, my heads throbbing.' He put his hands to his forehead and rubbed.

'Oh, my poor darling boy. Can I get you an aspirin? Would that help?'

'Yes, please. Yes, that would definitely help a lot.'

'Wait right there my little sweetmeat, and I'll get you what you need.'

She left the room, and when he heard a cupboard opening and water running, he leapt from the bed and over to the window. Curtains pulled aside, he stared out onto the Powers' front lawn. Damn, one floor up. He tried the windows, but they were both locked.

'Just coming, Daniel.'

He pulled the curtains back together and jumped into bed as the door opened.

'Here we are, dear, an aspirin especially for you.' She handed him three white tablets and a glass of milky-white liquid.

He took the tablets and stared at the glass. What was the woman up to?

'It's to help you sleep. You need to sleep.'

That was true; he did need to sleep. He didn't feel too great. At least sound asleep, there was no worry about the double bed or the pink dressing gown embroidered with red dragons. He swallowed the aspirins and gulped down the contents of the glass.

'There now. You lie back and you'll feel much better in the morning.' She patted his pillows, and he snuggled down under the covers.

She waved to him from the doorway. 'Happy dreams now.'

He lifted a hand in a sign of thanks as the door closed.

Thank god. Now he could relax. Trying to leave at the moment would be stupid. No point in antagonising the woman. Better to wait until morning then downstairs, have a bite to eat, announce a pressing engagement and walk out. She was after him. No doubt of that. So, what was the problem? Women rarely threw themselves at him Celia wasn't unattractive, in fact decidedly sexy in an older woman sort of way. But there was Lorraine. He couldn't jump into bed with her father's girlfriend. That might seriously affect a girl. He had read that somewhere. But what if Lorraine had left him? Celia seemed sure that was the case. If she had left without a word, without a note, for some other man, did it matter what he did? But from his memory of a previous meeting, he knew that Sampson Power was not a man to cross lightly. So many questions, so many problems, so many choices.

⟶⟫⟫⟫ ⟪⟪⟪⟵

Daniel watched with curiosity as two white rabbits copulated briskly in a corner of the bedroom. 'Daniel, come on Daniel,' one of them whispered as its whiskers trembled.

'No, no. I mustn't,' he heard himself say.

'Daniel.' The voice was louder. He forced his eyelids open. 'Daniel, it's me. Just wake up my darling. You need to take this.'

'What?' His eyelids had shut again. The rabbit's eyes had changed from pink to bright red.

'Here you are, Daniel.'

He felt himself being pulled upright. Celia was there with a little blue pill in her hand and a glass of water. She placed the pill between his lips, and he swallowed. She gave him a sip of water.

'Here you are. That's for your dreams, lover.'

He tried to say thank you. She was being very kind to him. Such a nice woman. He should be more charitable. The bunnies had gone, leaving behind a scuttling heap of woodlice.

Fourteen

DANIEL WOKE AND GROANED. The headache was still there, but a different headache, a thumping, pounding headache. A hangover headache. With an effort, he raised his head off the pillow. Beside the bed was a small table with a packet of aspirin, a carafe of water and a glass. How thoughtful of her. He popped a couple of tablets and lay back.

What was the time? Bright light filtered through the closed curtains, so definitely morning. He didn't have a watch. In fact, where were his clothes? A glance around the room showed nothing in sight. Must be in one of the cupboards. Only then did he realise something very, very strange. His underpants were gone. He was naked. Last night, before going to sleep, he had been wearing them. He knew for certain. And now they were absent. Which meant that someone, not himself, had removed them. While he slept, an underpants remover had been at work. The someone could only have been...

There was another thing. As the aspirin kicked in and his headache lessened, he became aware of something else. His hands wandered downwards. It was that feeling, the one you get in the morning when... But that was impossible. Insane.

He heard footsteps ascending the stairs, and dropped back onto the pillows, seriously puzzled. Celia pushed into the room, dressed in a long flowing skirt and tight, white sweater and carrying a tray in front of her.

'Daniel, you're awake. How lovely. I've brought you break-fast in bed.'

'What? No, you shouldn't have. I should get up.' He struggled forward but remembered in time that, under the bed-clothes, everything was on display.

'Relax, Daniel, and tuck into this.' She pulled back a tea towel to reveal a plate of bacon and fried eggs, a packet of cereal and a jug of milk. The fried bacon smelled exquisite and made him realise that his last meal had been some considerable time ago.

'OK, well, just this once,' he said.

She sat on the chair beside the bed and watched as he picked up knife and fork and started to eat.

'How is it, Daniel? Is the egg how you like it?'

'Yes, great.' He made a circle with his finger and thumb.

'We've got to keep up your strength.' She smiled. 'A young man like you needs to be strong and virile.'

'Sorry,' Daniel muttered as the fork slipped from his fingers onto the plate. Had she lingered overlong on the virile? He decided to ignore it.

'I'm so happy to have you here, Daniel.'

She looked different from last night. Her eyes sparkled, and there was a faint blush on her cheeks.

'Yes... well. I'm... it looks as if it will be a nice day.'

'Every day is going to be nice now you are here, Daniel.'

'Yeeees...'

'I hope you didn't mind me giving you that sleeping potion last night. It was for the best.'

'No, no. I'm fine with that.' It relieved him to get onto an-other subject, but then he remembered... 'What was the blue pill?'

Celia thought for a moment. 'Blue pill? I don't recall a blue pill, Daniel.'

'But you gave... I woke up, and you gave me this pill...' He stopped, confused, as a memory returned: a discussion some weeks ago in the canteen concerning blue pills. There had been a lot of joking. What was it? Aw crap.

'Oh, I remember now,' she said. 'It was an iron tablet. To keep your strength up.'

He stared at her. She looked back, guileless, sexy. Iron indeed. It wasn't his strength she was keeping up. He was ninety-nine per cent convinced she had fed him a Viagra pill. What the hell had happened last night? She couldn't have, surely? Not without him knowing. Was that possible? He thought about the feeling he'd noticed that morning and about the way she looked. And particularly about the absent underpants.

'Are you all right, Daniel? You've stopped eating.'

'No, no, all OK. Just full.'

'But you've only eaten one slice of bacon.'

'I'm a light eater. Oh well...' He put the tray aside and stretched. 'I feel so much better this morning after last night. After my sleep, I mean. My good night's rest. Oh yes, it was great, the sleep that is. Must be going now. If you could maybe get my clothes, that would be wonderful.'

Celia shook her head. 'Daniel, please don't rush things. Concussion can be a serious matter. You'd be much better staying another day... and night.'

'No,' he squeaked and then coughed. 'I'm fine. There's stuff to do. People to see about things. I lead a very busy life, you know.'

She tapped the side of her nose. 'Well, you're certainly good at the business, Daniel, but I think rest is the best prescription.'

He swallowed convulsively. 'Really, Celia, someone's coming around to my flat today. They'll be worried if I'm not there.'

She frowned. 'You wouldn't lie to me would you, Daniel?'

'God no, absolutely not. Not me. Look if I could please get my clothes.'

'Of course, Daniel. I'll get them right now. I'll take this tray away and be back up in a few minutes.' That smile again. He hated that smile. 'You relax and rest some more.'

'No. Really, I'm fine. I'll just go to the bathroom.'

'Lie down,' she barked.

Daniel lay back and watched her gather up the breakfast things. She closed the door, and he heard footsteps going downstairs. This had turned into a nightmare. He had to get out. Heaving his legs over the side of the bed, he pulled himself upright but staggered to one side. My god, perhaps he did have concussion, but no, it was more likely to be the after-effects of that sleeping stuff she'd fed him last night. He should never have taken it. Naked, he stumbled to the only cupboard and pulled it open. Nothing. Two hanging rails, both empty. Damn the woman. What had she done with his clothes? Beside the cupboard was a small chest with three drawers which yielded nothing but a dead moth and a one-pence coin.

He crossed to the window and drew the curtains apart. He tried the catch again in case it had magically unlocked itself. The houses to right and left, were out of sight. In front of the garden was the estate access road with open fields beyond. He should simply walk out, march downstairs, ignore Celia and leave. But not without clothes. He would be arrested. The bedsheets? It would be easy to make some sort of covering. No, best wait a little longer. He lay down on the bed again. She would be up with his clothes in a while, he was sure.

A frustrating hour or more later, he wasn't so sure. There had been no sound from downstairs. She had no right to do this. He wouldn't take any more of it, also he very much needed to find the toilet. Padding over to the door, he pulled it open a crack and peered out. 'Celia,' he shouted. 'Celia, you were going to bring me my clothes.' There was no reply.

He yanked the door wide and crossed to the head of the stairs. 'Hello. Is anybody there?'

'Daniel.' A soft voice behind him.

He yelped and turned to see Celia coming out of one of the other bedrooms.

'Daniel, I told you to wait.' She looked him up and down.

'I...' Both of his hands covered his crotch. 'I was looking...'

'I said I was going to bring your clothes. You men, always so impatient.' She advanced towards him.

He scuttled back into the bedroom, pushed the door partly shut and peered out. 'So when will I get them?' He tried to sound more insistent.

'I decided to wash them for you.'

'Wash?'

'Yes, wash, you know as in clean. They needed it.'

'But they didn't need washing. I didn't want them washed. You've no right...'

'Oooh Daniel, don't get angry. Little Celia was only trying to help,' she said in a baby voice.

'Well... how long will they be?'

She paused. 'Let me see now. They're still in the machine so I'll have to dry them, iron them. They should be ready sometime this afternoon. So, you get back to bed.' She advanced on the door and pushed hard.

Daniel let go, threw himself into bed and pulled the covers up to his chin.

From outside she cooed, 'That's right, my little darling. You rest now and I'll bring you up lunch later on. Something spicy perhaps?'

'No, no there's no need for lunch. Please, I'll wait.' But she had opened the door. 'Look perhaps... could I borrow some clothes?'

'Borrow? Not unless you want to get into my underwear.' She gave a huge wink.

Bloody hell. 'What about men's clothes? I mean Mr Power. His clothes?'

'They wouldn't fit you, Daniel. Absolutely not.'

'There must be something.' His voice was rising in pitch. Then he remembered. 'And Mr Power is back today. Best if I go before he arrives, I should think. Wouldn't you? I mean to prevent misunderstandings. Not that there's anything to misunderstand, naturally.'

Celia chuckled and riffled fingers through his hair. 'Don't you worry about Sampson. He's away on business. Won't be back for a week.'

Daniel sat up, heart beating faster than ever. 'What? But you told me he was due back today.'

'Did I? Can't remember. You're probably making it up, naughty boy. Anyway, it's no matter. Just you wait there and rest.' She retreated to the door. 'Bye, bye. See you soonikins.' Her fingers waved through the gap and the door shut.

Daniel massaged his forehead. There was a soft click. No. Surely not. He tumbled out of bed, listened at the door for a second then took the handle and turned. Locked! She'd locked him in. He shook the handle. Bugger her. He stamped his foot, returned to the bed and perched on the edge.

Locked in. Now his predicament registered fully. The woman was mad. Her partner was away for a week. No one knew he was here. Not only mad, she might be dangerous. She had probably raped him although he wasn't entirely sure on that, and if it came up (hah!) she would likely claim the opposite. She had stolen his clothes, locked him in. But why?

Some sort of sex slave? That was crazy. But she *was* crazy. It didn't matter why; he had to escape.

He had until lunchtime, whenever that was. What time was it? She had taken his watch and doubtless shoved it in the washing machine along with his clothes. But there was one matter important above all others at the moment. He glanced around the room again. Nothing, absolutely nothing. She'd even taken the glass away. Right, she only had herself to blame. He pulled out the bottom drawer of the chest, relieved himself into its interior and slammed it shut before the urine could drip out onto the carpet. That would teach the bitch.

If only he could catch someone's attention. At the window, nothing had changed. The road remained deserted. A splattering of rain coated the glass. It was a large window with a sill that barely came above his knees. It didn't seem that far to the ground. Get it open, then perhaps he could jump. There was grass in front, but the view immediately below was obscured. It might be a concrete patio.

He was about to turn away when he noticed a figure on the road: a middle-aged woman holding a toddler by the hand. She had stopped and was staring directly at him. Yes. He waved. After a moment, the woman raised a hand and waved back. *Help*, he mouthed, *please help*. There was no way she could understand that. If only he had something to write with. The child pointed at him. The woman moved on, tugging the toddler behind her. Daniel jumped up and down and waved his hands. The woman stopped and stared. In sudden realisation of how it must look, he froze and crossed his hands over his crotch. The woman put her left hand in the crook of her arm and raised a fist. Aw shit. He watched as she disappeared from view.

He turned away and slumped onto the bed. That woman would not come to his rescue and, not only that, it appeared that the sight of a naked man shaking his doolallies from behind a first-floor window didn't remotely bother her, so she was unlikely to report him to the police. And the mad witch of the west would be up soon ready to do who knew what. He was sure she had no intention of bringing his clothes. Oh Hell. He lay back. A strong odour of drying urine hung in the air. The hell with it.

He jumped off the bed. This nightmare had to end no matter what. There was a door and a window, both locked. OK, the window would be easier, so that was what it would be. He grabbed the bedside chair in both hands and advanced on the window. He swung the chair above his head but hesitated. Flying glass was bad at the best of times. In his exposed condition, it could result in rapid castration, which, while it might solve his current problem with Celia, was rather an extreme measure.

He put the chair down, tugged the sheet from the bed and draped it over himself until it covered him on all sides, then picked up the chair again. Aiming for the window, he swung it around once and hurled it with all the force he could find. It bounced off the glass and thumped him on the temple. Dizzy, he sat down on the floor and pulled the sheet from his head. Blood streaked it like a giant bandage removed from a deep wound. He explored his face and cranium carefully and found that his ear was bleeding. He stared at the completely unmarked window, looking as if only a butterfly had brushed against it. A dark rage filled his mind, directed at this Window of Satan. He grabbed the chair once more and, with teeth clenched, raised it high above his head. Then, from downstairs, a siren wailed.

'Daniel, Daniel.' She raced upstairs screaming his name hysterically.

He grabbed the bedsheet and wrapped it around himself in a makeshift toga. She was at the door, fumbling at the lock. 'Oh my god, oh my god. Wait, please.' The door burst open and he cowered backwards as she rushed him, mobile thrust forward.

100

'They want to speak to you. Christ. Do whatever they say. Please.' She threw the mobile onto the bed and sank to her knees sobbing.

Daniel picked up the phone between two fingers. If this was a double-glazing sales call, Celia was overreacting. He cleared his throat and held the phone a few centimetres from his ear. 'H... hello,' he said, unable to think of anything more appropriate for the circumstances.

'Good afternoon, Mr Dreghorn. Number one here.' The voice sounded cool and smooth and for a second, he was puzzled.

'Number one? Oh... Number One. Of course. Look I think there may have been a...'

'We know what happened, Mr Dreghorn, and we are not pleased with the outcome.'

'I never knew... it should never have been...'

'Indeed, we are rather displeased with your performance. That is why we have taken steps to ensure a better outcome next time.'

Daniel felt the blood rush to his face. 'Next time? Let me assure you, sir, that there will be no... Ah... what did you mean by taking steps?'

'We have a young lady in custody. Someone you know.'

'What?'

'In protective custody. I assure you she has not yet been harmed.'

'You mean...' Daniel stared at Celia who sat on the floor, head in hands. 'You mean Lorraine?'

'That is her name.'

'You've kidnapped Lorraine. What the hell... I don't understand.'

'You will be informed, Mr Dreghorn. Meanwhile, a package is on its way with proof of our good faith.'

'Good faith? I don't understand.'

'All will be explained. Good day.'

'But...' The line went dead.

Celia moaned. 'They've kidnapped our poor little girl. Sampson will say it's my fault.' Tears dripped onto her chin. 'They're going to kill her. What are we going to do, Daniel?'

'What? They didn't say anything about killing to me.'

She pulled herself upright by hanging on to his toga, almost causing it to come adrift. 'What else would kidnappers do, stupid? They kill people. They will murder that little girl and there's nothing we can do.'

Daniel struggled to take on board this change of circumstance. 'I wouldn't give up, you know. There might be ways of getting her back.'

'Oh Daniel, if only I could believe that. I'd do anything for help to get her back.' She advanced on him, both hands forward as if seeking an embrace.

He stepped back. 'No, no, I don't need a reward. She's my girlfriend. I'm desperate to help her too, remember.'

Celia paused. 'I suppose so. Well, you'd better get on with it, hadn't you?'

'What? Ah yes, so if you could just...'

'Clothes, yes of course. I'll get them.'

Daniel watched her dart from the bedroom and burst into the room opposite. She returned a few seconds later, and dumped a crumpled bundle onto the bed. He stared for a moment at the untidy heap. 'These are my clothes?'

She nodded.

'But I thought you'd washed them.'

She shrugged. 'Let's not waste time on details. Get dressed now and we can be underway. Quickly!' She crossed her arms and glared at him.

He felt cheated. He really believed she had washed his clothes, even though it was an obvious ploy to keep him here, and now here was his sweaty underwear waiting for him.

'Oh, all right, I suppose you're embarrassed. I'll leave you to change. I'll be downstairs.' She marched out and slammed the door behind her.

Slowly, he unwound the bedsheet toga and dressed in his sweat-scented clothes. Why was life so complex? He must get Lorraine back. He wanted to get Lorraine back. She meant a lot to him. As a result, it was almost certain he would have to do another job for the allotment terrorists. That was bad. He was convinced now that these people were not the ones Farquharson wanted. Somewhere lines had crossed so badly that there had been a major short circuit. That was bad. He had blown up his department and they might discover the fact. That was even worse and, Hell's teeth, he was sick: he had hepatitis. That was really bad. The only good thing was that all the cavorting around kept his mind from it. What else? Craps, that was enough for now. He pulled on his trainers and tottered downstairs.

Celia was waiting for him in the hall. 'Will you come on, for God's sake We have to move.' She headed for the door.

Daniel stopped. 'What? No wait, where are you going?'

'Going? I'm taking you home. The quicker you get there the quicker you can get in touch with these people and find little Lorraine.'

'Ah... well no really, there's no need. I can find my own way.'

'Yes? And how will you manage that?'

'Well, same way I came here, by bus.'

Her eyebrows drew together in a frown. 'Bus? You took a bus? How quaint. Well, there's no time for that nonsense. I'll drive you home. Come on.'

She grabbed his arm, threw the door open and pushed him towards the Range Rover already sitting in the drive. Daniel climbed into the passenger seat while Celia locked her front door. She joined him in the car and revved down the driveway scattering small stones and a group of small children about to cross her path.

Several scary minutes later, they pulled up outside Daniel's flat. He threw open the car door and staggered onto the pavement. 'Right, I'll be in touch. Let you know what happens.'

Ignoring this, Celia locked the Range Rover and headed directly for him, mouth set in a tight line. 'Come on. Let's go. We need to discuss tactics.' She was already beside the door, staring at him, arms folded, foot tapping. 'You're very slow,' she said.

He opened the main door, and they made their way upstairs. Outside his flat, Celia's disgust at the peeling orange paint and the faint odour of cat was obvious. Inside the flat, he knew immediately that something was wrong. A strange smell pervaded the air. Not strong and not horrible, but unfamiliar. He opened the sitting-room door and his heart rate hit the stratosphere as a figure rose from the couch and turned to greet him.

Fifteen

'AH, DANIEL, HOME AT last. I've been waiting for you. Would you like some tea?'

Daniel gaped at professor Farquharson, totally unable to understand what was happening. 'Professor, what are you... how are you...'

'I'm moderately well thank you, Daniel, considering the circum...' Farquharson paused as Celia pushed past Daniel and into the lounge. A huge smile cracked his face, and his hand extended towards her. 'And you must introduce me to your bewitching young girlfriend, Daniel?'

'This is...' Daniel began, but Celia giggled.

'I'm Celia, Celia Power, and I'm not his girlfriend, I assure you.'

'Celia, Celia, what a beautiful name.'

They were still holding hands Daniel rolled his eyes heavenwards. 'Professor, I don't understand what...'

Celia beamed. 'And you are?'

'Farquharson, my dear, but it's Quentin to all my close friends. Oh, and please sit down, my dear. Daniel, tea would be nice. And how do you like it, Celia? Tea, I mean.'

A coarse guffaw came from Celia. Daniel glared at Farquharson. He could feel fingernails biting into his palms and a knot of tension at the back of his neck.

'Professor. What... are... you... doing... in... my... flat?'

The professor glanced away from Celia for a moment and raised an eyebrow. 'Doing? I was waiting for you, my boy, but I'll explain later.' He turned back to Celia.

'Now!' Daniel's forceful voice surprised even himself.

'What?'

'I want to know why you are in my flat, and I want to know right now.'

Farquharson frowned. 'Oh, if we must.' To Celia, he said, 'Excuse me a moment, my dear. This won't interest you.' He paused and stared somewhere to the left of Daniel's right ear. 'I needed peace, Daniel. I needed to get away from that awful woman. I needed sanctuary from the ugly rumour machine of the committee. So, I thought of you, my saviour in times past. Perhaps once more you might come to the rescue of a failing old man.'

Celia hooted. 'Not failing, Quentin. Anyone can see you are not failing.'

The professor nodded, acknowledging that he knew everyone was acquainted with the fact that he was not failing. 'Anyway, Daniel, I came here, but you were not at home.' His head drooped and shook slowly from side to side, the pain of being so grievously let down by his trusted friend easy to see in his eyes.

Celia frowned at him and Daniel was on the point of apologising for his absence when the biggest puzzle of all came back to him. 'But you're here.'

'Yes, Daniel, that is so.'

'But how did you get in? The door was locked. There's no way... I don't understand.'

'Ah. There are ways you know.' The professor looked shifty.

'And those would be?'

Celia grabbed Farquharson's arm. 'Daniel, leave this poor man alone. The way you're talking anyone would think he's done something wrong.'

Farquharson took her hand and stroked it with his index finger. 'Don't you worry, my dear. These barbs are like the proverbial duck with water on its back to me. Like a match in Hades, they are as nothing.'

Daniel felt his head growing bigger. So big it might explode and leave a mess all over the new carpet that Lorraine had chosen so carefully. He hit his forehead several times with the heel of his left hand. The lovebirds stared at him as if he had finally lost it.

'How did you get into my flat?' He stared hard at the professor, ignoring the beginning of another protest from Celia.

'To my shame, I broke in, my boy. What else?'

'You broke in... but how? The door's not broken.'

Farquharson sat back and placed his hands behind his head. 'A confession is in order to you both. In our lives, most of us occasionally do things we are not proud of, things that we would prefer to forget. Well, I have not always been the upright, God-fearing citizen you see before you today.' He paused. 'Celia, my dear, perhaps you could fetch Daniel a glass of water, as he seems to be in some distress.'

Once Daniel's coughing fit had subsided, and he had sipped sufficient water, the professor continued. 'Among my many shameful accomplishments is the ability to enter a locked room without undue difficulty. I had lessons from a master and still retain a good set of tools, so I am afraid that your door presented little difficulty, Daniel, to my great shame.'

He bent forward, elbows on knees, and rubbed his eyes. 'Oh dear, oh dear. What have I done?'

Celia patted his thigh. 'There, there, don't distress yourself. We're all tempted by things we shouldn't do.' She glared at Daniel. 'You've upset him. The poor man couldn't help himself. You've no right.'

Daniel let his mouth open but found that no words he could think of expressed his feelings at that moment. 'I'll get your tea,' he muttered, and headed into the kitchen, slamming the door in what would have been a very satisfying manner if it hadn't resulted in two wine glasses toppling from their place at the edge of the cupboard shelf and smashing on the floor. He kicked the pieces to the side, grabbed the kettle and turned the water full on, splashing the floor and himself as well as filling the kettle. Calm down. This was not making things better. As the kettle sang, he attempted to think it through.

For no reason that Daniel could see, Farquharson had broken into his flat and made himself at home. He was now in the sitting-room making overtures to a woman who may have, probably had, almost certainly had, done something bad to Daniel only a few hours before. And now he was making them a cup of tea.

The kettle boiled. He made the tea and poured it. Celia, of course, knew nothing of Farquharson's sordid history of sexual exploits, and this gave Daniel great satisfaction. They were made for each other. It would serve her right if she caught brucellosis. He stared at the teacups. Some cyanide would have come in useful. With the cups on a tray, he picked three sugar-covered biscuits from a tin, and paused. Now that was a thought. Perhaps there was some left. A thorough inspection of the store cupboard turned up what he wanted, right at the back behind the instant mash – red chilli powder, best before July 2015; an excellent vintage. Taking one of the biscuits, he licked it and dipped it into the tin then sprinkled a heap of caster sugar on a plate and dipped the biscuit again. He repeated this with a second biscuit and replaced the third one in the biscuit tin. The result looked wonderful. With a tray carrying the three cups and two biscuits and wearing a broad smile, he pushed the kitchen door open and almost dropped the tray.

Farquharson and Celia were in a close clinch, lips pressed together. Celia's skirt was further up her thighs than Daniel wanted to see and her hand, although she whisked it away, had been inside the professor's shirt. It was a truly revolting spectacle. Even if wrinkly sex didn't stop at seventy or eighty or whatever age the the man was, he had no wish to see it, and certainly not in his front room. The two turkeys pulled apart and had the decency to look embarrassed.

'Daniel,' said Celia, tying the top two buttons on her blouse. 'Please knock before you come in. Quentin and I were discussing private things.'

Taking a deep breath, he forced a smile back on his lips. 'Sorry. Tea anyone?'

'You are a brick, Daniel.' The professor took a cup and turned towards Celia. 'We mustn't criticise, for this man is my rock and has saved my Titanic many times from the icebergs of life.'

Celia scowled at Daniel.

'Biscuit anyone?' He picked up the plate and offered it to Celia. 'Spiced cookies.'

They each took a biscuit while he sat down opposite them to watch. He didn't have long to wait.

Celia took a sip of tea, bit into her biscuit and turned to Farquharson. 'Quentin I...' She stopped. Her jaws worked for a few more seconds, then she took a long gulp of tea. Her mouth opened as if she were trying to speak.

'My dear, are you all right?' The professor reached for her hand, but she pulled away and pressed it to her throat. She staggered upright, face turning purple.

'Bathroom's through there,' Daniel pointed. 'Are you OK?'

She pushed past him, and the bathroom door slammed behind her.

The professor stared at the closed door. 'Extraordinary,' he muttered. 'Quite extraordinary.'

They sat in awkward silence for a few moments, listening to the sound of retching and running water.

Eventually, the professor asked, 'So how are you, Daniel?'

'Bloody awful. I've had a terrible time.'

'Capital, capital, and that young lady of yours?' He looked towards the bathroom door as another bought of coughing broke out.

'She's been kidnapped.'

'Yes, I believe it's becoming common these days. Look, Daniel, you've seen a bit of life. What do you think of Celia? Do you think she and I might be compatible?'

'I think you're perfect for each other.'

'Excellent. That's as I hoped. It seems she's attracted to me.'

'She's my girlfriend's father's partner, or ex-partner possibly.'

'Good heavens, what a remarkable coincidence.'

'Well not quite. They've kidnapped her.'

'What? But...' Farquharson turned to the bathroom, which for the moment was silent.

'No, my girlfriend has been kidnapped, Celia's... whatever.'

'Good heavens. How dreadful. We must do something. Poor Celia must be so upset.'

'She was before she met you,' Daniel muttered.

'What was that?' He cupped a hand around his ear.

'Perhaps we should go to the police.'

Farquharson rubbed his chin and met this suggestion with silence. They listened as a fresh bout of retching broke out in the bathroom.

'I'm never too sure about the police, my boy. They tend to stray from the point and poke their noses into other completely unimportant matters. Side issues of no relevance. It can be difficult.'

Daniel nodded. This matched his feelings exactly. After blowing up the chemistry department, he was not keen to get the police involved. But what else could they do?

The bathroom door inched open and Celia's pale face peered out. Farquharson was instantly on his feet and helped her to a chair. They muttered to each other while, without asking, Daniel swept up the remains of the biscuits and prepared some fresh tea in the kitchen. He returned to the sitting-room with three cups.

'Celia has told me all about the kidnap, Daniel. Something must be done. If only we knew who these people were.'

Celia remained ashen-faced, but a menacing glint had come back to her eye. Daniel dropped into the armchair. 'I may have an idea about that.'

They stared at him.

'Well. . you know the chairman of the committee, the man you wanted me to follow, well I think that somehow—'

'Hah. I might have known. Despicable man. But I never thought he would stoop to this.'

'No, no. That's not it. You see when I thought I was following him, it seems that somehow I got involved—'

'Daniel,' the professor raised a hand, stopping any further comment. 'I've always said you are a good man. That's what I've said, Celia.' He turned to her.

If Celia's eyes had belonged to the Peruvian eye-venom-spitting cobra, then those eyes would have spat venom at Daniel now.

'Unfortunately, good men have the problem that they see the best in others. They do not see past the glittering surface to the heart of darkness within where evil gathers in a lake of blackness only to bubble to the surface at the slightest provocation, the slightest hint of criticism of their methods, purely because a fellow is unconventional, has a lifestyle that differs from their own and chooses a different path—'

'Professor?'

'They think they can sink their teeth into his skin. They think they have the right to criticise when in fact—'

'Professor!'

'What? Sorry, sorry. Yes, well now we know who is responsible, we can take action.'

'No, that's not—'

'Celia. I believe I can deal with this man.' The professor pulled his shoulders back as far as they would go.

Celia's eyes opened wide. 'Oh Quentin, I would be so grateful.'

Oh Hell. Daniel sank back into his chair. Why did no one listen to him? Sometimes he had sensible things to say. Occasionally, he was right. So now what? Kick these two old turkeys out of his flat, that was what. He stood up. So did Farquharson.

'Well, my boy, you have been most hospitable. I appreciate the loan of your bed and I'm sure you have been very generous to Celia too, but I regret we can stay no longer. Celia has agreed to offer me refuge in her house for the moment. We shall have a council of war. I shall call you when we have decided what to do.'

He offered his hand and Daniel shook it. Celia did not offer hers. He blinked, and the pair were gone. Oh well, it had been that easy. He wished them well together, the weird and the weirder. Wait. What had Farquharson said? Something about the loan of his bed? It was true. In the bedroom, the rumpled bedclothes smelt of... stale professor. He stripped the bed and stuffed everything into the washing machine. No way was he sharing a bed with that man's hair and dead skin.

Breakfast in bed seemed an aeon ago, and he was ravenous, so prepared a lunch of tomato soup and a ham sandwich. Why was life full of problems? At least university classes had closed for a few days until the mess was sorted out. So, he had some days off. But of course, the mess was caused by... The doorbell played *Frere Jacques*. What now?

He paused at the door. If only he had got one of those spy things fitted. He slipped the chain into its slot and peered out. No one there, at least no one visible. They might be waiting out of sight on his blind side, ready to jump him. Then he glanced down at an oblong parcel sitting on the landing. He unhooked the chain, opened the door fully, grabbed the package and slammed the door behind him. The parcel was no bigger than his hand, neatly wrapped in brown paper and taped on all edges. There was no address.

On an impulse, he ran to the window in time to see a car turning out of the street and accelerating away. He grabbed a pair of scissors, returned to the parcel and snipped away the paper. Underneath was a plain box, also securely taped. He slit the tape, opened the box and emptied a white mass of polystyrene granules onto the floor to reveal a folded envelope and another smaller box.

He took the envelope and tore it open. A sheet of paper inside read: *You will be informed of your next move soon. This box contains evidence of our serious purpose. Don't have us deliver another one.*

Daniel shook the box. It weighed very little, but something rattled inside. Then he dropped it as if it had grown teeth and bitten him. It couldn't be. They wouldn't. But they might. He had seen it in films, seen it in the news. It happened. Kidnappers cutting bits of their victims to show... Oh god. Could it be Lorraine rattling around in there? At least it was a small box. There wasn't space for a hand or a foot. That was some comfort.

He would have to open it. With eyes half shut, he cut open the box, and holding it at arm's length, opened the lid. He let his breath out. It was a photograph, only a photograph. He squinted at it, not wanting to look too closely. A head peered over an opened newspaper; undoubtedly it would be yesterday's edition. Something was pointing at her head. It could have been a gun. OK, so they had her, but he had never doubted that. It left him no worse off. He threw the photograph aside, glanced inside the box and screamed.

His chair clattered backwards. The box fell to the floor spilling the rest of its contents: a small plastic bag containing something. Something horrible. He approached the bag and poked it with the point of his shoe. Inside, a brown, bloody and horrible thing shifted. It would be a finger, no question of it. They had cut off her finger. He prodded the package again. Yes, that's what it was. His stomach wobbled as he squeezed his eyes shut and took several deep breaths.

What did it mean? It meant that whatever they wanted him to do, he would have to do it. It was all too much right now. Grabbing a palette knife from the kitchen drawer, he scooped up the plastic bag, popped it back in the box, closed the lid and placed the box in the fridge behind the bacon and a jar of expired onion chutney. What now?

Sixteen

HE HAD TO PRIORITISE. There was too much happening. Life shouldn't be like this, well not his life. Right now, he could do nothing for Lorraine as he had no idea where they had taken her. Of course, she might be in Number One's mansion if he could find his way back there, but that seemed impossible. No, he would have to wait until they contacted him. He poured himself a beer and switched on the TV to see the latest Reality-Cooking-Antique-Makeover show. Background noise was all he wanted – something to distract. Why couldn't you switch the picture off and leave the sound? A design flaw for sure.

So, next thing – health. The hepatitis business was worrying and he must find out more about it. Aw hell, he was supposed to be at the surgery this afternoon for another test. The appointment was for three-thirty. OK, enough time if he took a taxi. He pushed the part-finished beer aside and reached for his mobile.

Ten minutes later he stood, arms folded, on the bottom step. Five minutes they had said – nothing. Taxis were always the same. They lived in an alternate universe where time moved at half the speed it did here. That would be a good place to live. You'd get twice as much done.

This happy thought resulted in Daniel having a smile on his face when the black cab drew up.

'Medical centre,' he said to the driver, dropping into the back seat and checking his watch. It wouldn't take more than ten minutes even with traffic. Relax, there was plenty of time.

OK, so these nutters from the Allotment Society intended to contact him. That would be his chance to help Lorraine. Perhaps he should come up with a reason he had to see her or demand to see her as a condition of doing whatever they wanted him to do. No, demanding might not go down too well, subtlety was needed.

He glanced about. Traffic seemed light this morning. It shouldn't be long now. The street did not look at all familiar, but taxi drivers knew what they were doing. The man was likely taking a shortcut to avoid roadworks. Five minutes later, he wasn't so sure.

He rapped on the glass panel separating him from the driver. The panel slid back so quickly that Daniel's hand almost went through the gap.

'Excuse me, but you know I asked for the medical centre?'

There was a pause as the driver made a left turn. 'Medical centre? Oh yes, mate. You'll be going to the medical centre.' A croak that might have been a laugh followed this comment.

Daniel sat back. 'Good, it's just... I mean you know your job, I'm sure, but we are taking a long time to get there.'

'Yes, well, we're going to pay another call first, ain't we?'

Daniel lunged forward. 'Another call. I'm not paying for any other calls. I'm only paying for the medical centre.'

The driver let out a barrel-scraping laugh. 'Yeah, that's your problem. Not very good at paying, are you?'

Daniel shook his head, trying to tell himself this conversation wasn't happening. 'Look, this is ridiculous. I don't know what you're...' Then he looked at the driver. Looked at him closely, at the thick neck, the red face, the spiky hair. 'Oh hell... oh shit...'

'That's right, mate.' The glass partition slammed shut.

It was the taxi driver he had dodged outside his house. The one he hadn't paid. It seemed as if the incident had happened weeks ago, but it was only days. This madman was taking him somewhere. Wherever it was, it would not be somewhere he wanted to go.

'Excuse me.' He tried to open the partition, but it was impossible from the passenger side. He knocked on the glass.

A voice crackled from the speaker. 'Enjoy the ride. While you can.'

'It's a mistake,' Daniel shouted. 'I was going to pay, but things, stuff... happened. Look I'm sorry. I'll pay you now. Double if you want.' Speaker silent, the taxi sped on.

This was kidnap. He should try to attract attention. But by now they had left town streets behind, following a quiet country road without a pedestrian to be seen. It would have been a pleasant drive if he wasn't beginning to panic. What was the man up to? *Enjoy the ride while you can*? That didn't sound good. It sounded like a threat. But he couldn't mean actual harm, could he? Obviously not. Perhaps the idiot would abandon him miles from town and leave him to walk home. Inconvenient but... His head jerked upwards as the cab slowed. They turned left and bumped down a stony track thickly wooded on both sides. It had started to rain.

The vehicle came to a halt as it left the shelter of the trees and the engine rattled to silence. An eternity seemed to pass before the driver got out and stood, hands on hips, looking right and left. Then he lifted his face to the sky, took a deep breath, turned to stare at Daniel and fixed him with an expression like that of an alligator finding its first meal in months. There were red rims to his hooded eyes. He took each of the fingers of his right hand and popped the joints in turn with an audible crack. Daniel's desire for any kind of relationship with this guy had not increased. As the man spat on the ground and headed towards him, Daniel lunged for the door on the other side. It was locked.

Panic rose from somewhere around his bowels. Or was it heading the other way? This guy wished him harm, he was now certain of it. The driver popped the doors with his key fob and pulled open the one nearest him. He stepped back, bowed slightly and gestured to Daniel to come out. Daniel didn't feel like playing.

'This is a huge mistake. It's so stupid. I was going to pay you.'

The driver's smile evaporated like cat pee on a hotplate. 'What did you call me?'

'What? I didn't call you anything.' He tried to back further away.

'You called me stupid,' the driver snarled.

'No...'

'I don't like being called stupid.'

'No, of course. No one likes being called stupid.' Daniel's hand fumbled behind his back for the handle on the other door.

He pressed down as the man lunged for his leg. There was a shout. The door flew open and Daniel fell backwards out of the taxi, tumbling head over heels. He scrambled to his feet to see the driver leaning against the cab holding both hands over his face. Blood leaked from his nose. It looked like he had thumped his face on something hard.

The time for any logical discussion on the merits of the credit system in relation to taxi rides was over. Daniel ran. He had a few seconds start. He raced from the cab and the trees towards the open ground beyond. Then he skidded to a halt. The open ground wasn't – it was open space, and he was on the sharp rim of a quarry stretching away in an arc on either side. A glance back showed the driver wearing a manic grin and shaking his head. Daniel peered over the edge. Below, a vertical drop of at least fifty metres fell into a sea of angular blocks. To left and right bushes and tree roots bordered the quarry rim, passable but difficult. Behind him, his nemesis lumbered forward, a tyre lever in hand.

'Look, can we discuss this? It's ridiculous. It's so stupid to—' But what might have been his last words were cut off as madman let out a roar and charged towards him.

Daniel turned left and scrambled between the quarry rim and the bushes. The edge close on his right was of no concern as he barrelled along the perimeter. He slowed after a minute. No noise behind him. Good. He stopped and turned. Nothing visible. Was the idiot hiding in the bushes somewhere, waiting? Quite possible. Ahead, the vegetation grew denser: a mass of brambles and nettles, the occasional fallen tree jutting over the abyss. At least having come this far, he knew he could get back. But where was the damn psychopathic driver? Perhaps he had given up? Taken his taxi and returned to brighten some other fare's day.

Convincing himself of this, he turned about and teetered along the way he had come, much more aware now of the fatal drop on his left. He clung to bushes where it was possible and offered prayers where it was not, making many very rash promises about future behaviour if he should survive.

It was only as he returned safely to the clearing that he realised something was wrong. First thing, the taxi was still there. Second, there was no sign of the driver.

'Hello,' he called. 'Hello is there anyone there?' and then, 'Aw shit, no... couldn't be,' as he turned to face the quarry again.

Flat on his belly, he wriggled towards the cliff edge and poked his head into space, desperate not to see what he feared he might. But there it was. His gaze focused on the crumpled figure of the driver, on his back, spread-eagled over a knife-edged granite block. The man's head pointed downwards at a strange angle.

In fact, it looked as if it was only partially attached to his body. Daniel closed his eyes and shuffled away from the precipice.

He sat on his haunches and stayed that way, arms wrapped around his legs, chin resting on his knees, for several minutes. There was no hurry. Whatever he did, there was no hurry. The man was dead: as dead as it was possible to be and then add a bit. A broken back followed by decapitation couldn't get more final. OK, he mustn't panic, but what now?

He tottered to his feet and stumbled back to the taxi. First, he had to report the accident to the police. It was stupid crazy. He didn't want to be involved but there was no option. Someone had died. He fumbled for his mobile and thumbed 999. Nothing. The signal bar was at zero. His fists clenched hard. Why me? All right then, the situation required logic. Choices. He could walk out. They had passed through several villages, perhaps forty or fifty minutes to the nearest one, or there was the taxi itself.

He sat in the driver's seat, still warm from its now cooling occupant. The key dangled from below the steering wheel. Perhaps he could drive back. But he couldn't drive. How difficult could it be for a few miles? Or even to the edge of the forest. That would help. OK, file that for now, but there was the radio. All taxis had radios. That was the answer.

It was switched off, but he found the on-button easily; the one that had ON printed below, so he pressed it. A burst of static made him jump. A series of calls from a harassed operator followed. The call button was clear enough on the right of the display so all he had to do was press and speak. What to say? That was a problem. Perhaps something like:

He's fallen over the cliff.
Pardon?
The cliff, he's fallen over.
Who is this?

It's the driver, he's fallen over.

Who has fallen over, caller?

OK, the guy must have a name. It had to be written some-where inside. But he soon realised that it wasn't anywhere ob-vious. This was getting desperate; he had to do something. He glanced at his watch. Fifteen minutes since he'd first seen the driver's mangled body.

So, Mr Dreghorn, you waited fifteen minutes before reporting the finding of the body. Can you please tell the court why that was?

Well, err.

Why did you not call an ambulance immediately?

Well, he was dead. It didn't seem urgent.

Didn't seem urgent? Tell me, Mr Dreghorn, what are your medical qualifications?

Well, none.

And your long-range qualifications?

Sorry?

Your qualifications for telling that someone has deceased from a distance of fifty metres? (pause for ripple of laughter).

Well, err.

This was not good. To be precise, it looked bloody awful. He was bound to be suspected of doing away with the man. But only if... Daniel's brain throbbed into life. Who knew he was here? Possibly no one unless the taxi driver had discussed his plans with a colleague. It seemed unlikely he would do that. So, he simply had to leave. Walk out – without being seen of course. His fingerprints were all over the cab, but so must be those of a thousand other passengers, and it wasn't as if he was in any criminal database. And the idiot was dead. Totally dead. Noth-ing he could do would help him, so why complicate matters? He would save the police time and effort in questioning him. It was his public duty not to impede the investigation.

He stepped out of the taxi. This was the only sensible way. The police always got the wrong idea; he knew that from experience. But one last thing to do. Back in the driver's seat, he started up the engine. Then, leaving the door open and keeping one foot on the ground, grabbed the handbrake and eased it downwards. A gentle slope led towards the quarry rim, but the vehicle stayed put. He jumped out, stepped behind and, with both hands on the boot, shoved hard. The taxi rolled forward, slowly at first but with increasing speed. Standing back, he watched as it bounced almost silently over the rutted ground and crashed through a clump of bramble bushes as its speed built up. Momentum was too great now and nothing would stop it as it careered towards the edge. Daniel held his breath as the cab reached the quarry rim, shot into space, and disappeared. A few seconds of timeless silence passed before it hit bottom with a noise like a taxi hitting earth at ninety miles an hour. Then all was quiet and still.

Daniel ran towards the precipice, dropping to his knees for the last few metres. He wriggled forward on his belly until his head poked over the edge. Below, the wreckage was still recognisably taxi but looked as if a giant had ground his heel into it. As he watched, a wisp of smoke appeared from the mangled remains, closely followed by a rapidly expanding orange fireball.

The only sound that escaped him was 'sh...' as he rolled away and kept rolling, dimly aware of the *whump* of an explosion and a burning sensation on his head. Scrabbling among the undergrowth, he scooped up a handful of mud and slapped it onto his smouldering scalp.

He sat up and gingerly massaged his head. It seemed OK. If he was really burnt, it would be painful, wouldn't it? He stared at the rapidly crusting mud on his hands. He must be filthy. What now? Get the hell away, that was what. Someone might have heard the explosion.

On trembling legs, he staggered back to the treeline and headed down the track. Several miles to the village. Would he make it? Of course. His legs recovered and his spirits lifted as he left the carnage in the quarry behind.

Seventeen

IT WAS EARLY EVENING, and light was fading when Daniel paused at the village signpost. It had taken him an hour to walk this far and his legs and feet told him forcefully that pain and suffering would follow were he to continue. The road had been blessedly quiet apart from several police cars and an ambulance screaming in convoy towards the quarry. He had avoided these by falling down the embankment into a thicket of bramble bushes.

Ahead of him, a young girl of about ten emerged from the driveway of her house and turned in his direction. Engrossed with her mobile, she was only a few metres from him when she paused and looked up. She stopped dead and stared. Daniel slowed and smiled, thinking vaguely to ask her about the bed-and-breakfast situation in the village, but her face crumpled and she backed away from him, looking as if she might burst into tears at any moment. He raised a hand. She screamed and sprinted back to the drive, turned for one last look, then plunged inside the house and slammed the door.

What was going on here? He wandered on, glancing sideways as he passed the girl's house in time to see the curtains swished shut. This was a mystery, but he didn't dwell on it for a short way ahead was a detached house with a welcoming B&B sign outside and the even more welcoming *vacancies* below it. He marched up to the door and pressed the bell firmly. After a few seconds, a short, middle-aged lady opened it and stood perfectly still, staring up at him with wide eyes.

'Excuse me,' said Daniel. 'But I'm looking for bed-and-breakfast. Is it OK?'

She continued to stare at him and stand so rigidly that he wondered if she had turned to stone.

'Ah... bed-and-breakfast. I believe you do it. Your sign says vacancies. Can you tell me how much? I mean, it doesn't matter as such. I just need a bed.'

The monolith that was a small, middle-aged woman creaked into life. With eyes still fixed on Daniel's face, she ever so slowly raised a hand to the door and pushed it shut.

'No wait, please... bed-and-breakfast?' Daniel said, desperately. But only a tiny gap remained between door and frame through which an unblinking eye was visible. Then the door shut, and he heard the click of a lock turning and the rattle of a chain.

A string of expletives formed in his head, but he was too stunned to make use of them. Instead, he trudged to the top of the drive. There was something about this village. The village of the damned, that's what it was: full of damnably rude people.

But he still needed somewhere to stay the night. To cheer him up, a light drizzle began to fall. He slouched further down the road, cursing everything around him but paused at a spiked gate set into a high wall; *Bed and Breakfast* stencilled onto an irregular slab of chipboard nailed to it. All right, one last try. Pushing the gate open, he stepped through. It creaked closed behind him on very rusty hinges. Ahead, the house could have been an identikit picture of the earlier one, but not so well looked after—the grass to either side yellow and straggly, the trees mostly bare. A smell of damp and decay permeated the air: perhaps a compost heap. It was colder in here and darker.

Daniel shivered and hurried to the front door. No sign of a bell anywhere, so he knocked loudly.

His knock was answered almost immediately as the door swung open and a skinny man in an open-necked shirt and jeans stared out.

'I'm looking for a bed, that is bed-and-breakfast. Have you any vacancies?' he asked, trying for his firmest voice.

The man gazed at him. There was no expression on his thin face. For a moment Daniel thought he would get the village treatment, but after a second or two, the face cracked into what might have been a smile.

'Bed-and-breakfast? Yes, of course, sir. I have vacancies here. You are welcome. Please.' He stood aside and waved Daniel into a dark hallway. The door swung shut, cutting out what natural light there was.

'Oh dear, do excuse me.' The man brushed past Daniel and flicked a switch. Above them, a dim lightbulb stuttered into life, succeeding only in deepening the shadows in the hall.

'I try to save power, you know. Electricity is so expensive. Yes.' His head bobbed up and down. 'Everything is so expensive. Yes.'

Daniel wondered if he had chosen wisely in knocking on this door. But what was the alternative? To have another door slammed in his face? At least this man had invited him in and now he had a room for the night. The guy was a little eccentric, but eccentrics could be likeable.

The possibly likeable eccentric stood at the foot of the stairs. 'Your room's up here, sir. By the way, I'm Arnold, Arnold Finklebaum.' He raised an eyebrow.

Daniel offered his hand. 'Daniel Dreghorn.' Feeling something needed to be added he said, 'Pleased to meet you.'

'Yes, yes. The feeling is reciprocated.'

They shook hands. Arnold's palm was cold and slightly sticky.

'Your room's just up here at the top of the stairs. It's forty pounds for the night. A bargain, sir. Yes. It's not en soot but there's a bathroom beside it which is exclusively for the use of yourself.' His eyes flickered over Daniel. 'You might want to tidy up, or something.'

'Thank you, Mr... thank you, Arnold. I'll be going then.' Daniel started up the stairs.

'Oh and do come down for a chat. When you're ready that is, anytime. I'll be in the lounge.'

Daniel's shoulders drooped. A chat was the last thing he wanted. He turned and stared into Mr Finklebaum's labrador eyes. 'Possibly. OK, but only for a few minutes. I need an early night.'

Finklebaum nodded. 'Early night, oh my of course. Yes.'

Scanning his first-floor bedroom, Daniel decided that adequate was the word. The creaky-springed bed seemed to bear the imprint of many previous occupants, but the sheets appeared clean. He turned to the window. A single unwashed pane looked over the same soggy garden by which he had approached the house. A few twisted chestnut trees obscured any view of the road. He drew the curtains, crossed to the door, and flicked the light switch. Another dim energy-saver yawned and flickered into a state approaching life. He dropped into an armchair and sighed long and hard. OK, what now?

First thing, a good night's rest. He looked down at his dirt-caked jeans. No, first thing was a bath. Then – there was no alternative – speak to his landlord for the very briefest time that politeness required. So then, third, would be a good night's rest and, in the morning, back to his flat and begin to sort out the mess he was in. He had to find a way of rescuing Lorraine, keep Celia at bay, see the doctor, avoid questions about a dead taxi driver, keep Farquharson pacified... He slumped further into the chair. What a disaster. OK, at least get started.

In the bathroom, he switched on the light and stared into the mirror. He stared for a long moment, transfixed by the horrible vision that glowered back. To make sure it was real, he raised his hand and rubbed it over the top of his head. At the front, hair had been burnt away leaving a blackened frazzle. The rest of his hair stood up in bloody, mud-crusted spikes. Grey mud and great scratches where congealed blood had oozed streaked his soot-covered face. The effect was nightmarish in the extreme. He now thought back with much sympathy to the reaction of the young girl and of the landlady. But curiously, his host had shown little or no surprise. He turned on the taps and immersed his head in the basin.

After a soak in a tepid bath and the removal of large quantities of sludge from his hair, he felt much improved. The necessity of putting his filthy clothes back on was unfortunate, but unavoidable. Perhaps by morning, the mud would have dried and he could brush the worst of it away.

That taxi driver, that mental taxi driver. The man had intended to kill him, or at the least beat him to a jelly. There was no question. He could dredge up no sympathy for the man's death, but there might be big trouble ahead. Perhaps even now he should go to the police. The death had been an accident. He had been in shock. That was it. In shock and had wandered away not knowing what he was doing. That could work. It wasn't far from the truth. But he had tried to cover up, pushed the cab over the quarry edge and they would discover that. He watched all the crime dramas. They might realise that the driver had not tipped from the vehicle but had fallen over earlier. Idiot. What was he thinking?. Say nothing, that was the best plan and if they caught up with him, then shock, memory loss. That was it.

Mr Finklebaum sat in an easy chair in the corner of the lounge, eyes shut, TV sound set at a murmur. Daniel hesitated in the doorway. Was the man asleep?

'Come in. Please come in.' He was not. 'So good of you to come, sir. Yes, yes, so good. Please be seated.' He indicated the chair opposite him.

Daniel sat. 'I was on my way to bed, but I decided I'd call in for a moment because... well, as I said I would.'

Finklebaum nodded. 'So good of you to give up your time to keep an old man happy, and please call me Ambrose.'

Daniel said nothing for a few seconds as he mulled over these points. First, he had not thought of the man as being particularly old. A weird git, maybe, but old? Early middle age at most. Second, could he really call anyone Ambrose? And anyway, third, hadn't the man called himself Arnold earlier?

'Yes, OK,' he said.

'You missed the local news report,' said Mr Finklebaum. 'I recorded it for you.'

'That's very kind, but I must get to bed. Tired, you know.'

'Here it is. Just playing it now.'

Daniel sighed and sank back into his chair as a tiny television struggled into life.

Finklebaum shook his head and clicked his tongue as the newsreader started into the first item.

Local taxi driver Simon Makepeace died today in what may have been a freak accident. A reporter spoke from in front of a blue police tape stretched across a familiar entrance.

'Shit,' Daniel said. Which neatly summed up the situation.

'Dreadful business.' Finklebaum's head nodded back and forth.

The mangled remains of Thomas Makepeace's taxi-cab were located deep in this quarry. His body was found nearby. Police have refused to eliminate the possibility of foul play. Anyone who has seen or heard anything out of the ordinary is urged to contact the police.

'Dreadful business, yes. Absolutely dreadful, and so close too. Why I could walk there if it wasn't for my feet. I'm sure a fit chap like you could do it, walk there that is. Oh yes.'

Daniel geared his brain up for escape. 'Yes, it's a funny old world, isn't it? Or rather tragic. Not funny, just tragic. Murder isn't funny if it was murder and not some terrible accident like they said. What happened anyway? I must be going. Bed, you know. Tired.'

Finklebaum stared at him. 'It makes one wonder who could be in one's own house.'

Daniel jumped to his feet. 'Yes, that's true. Well, it's time I went. Got to be up early tomorrow.'

'They say there was lots of blood. The murderer must be covered in it.'

'Horrible, absolutely horrible.'

'Good that you managed to get cleaned up so quickly.'

Daniel closed his eyes for a moment. It was certain that this man knew or thought he knew about the quarry incident. He laughed or tried to. 'I was mucky, wasn't I? Fell in the ditch, you know. Terrible, all muddy and so on. Thank goodness I found somewhere I could have a bath. I'm very grateful.'

Finklebaum smiled, or rather a thin fissure opened across his granite-lined face. 'I like to help. I'm just a lonely old man, but I like to help.'

'Yes, you've certainly been a big help to me.' Daniel stared at the screen.

'They say the police want information. They are looking for witnesses who might have observed activity at the quarry or have seen anyone suspicious... suspiciously dirty.'

'Ah,' said Daniel.

'I am a law-abiding man, sir. If I saw such a person, I would have to comply with the request of the police, would I not?'

Daniel nodded his head slowly. One part of his brain continued to seek a way out while the other told him he was screwed. 'Have... have you seen this man. . at all?'

Finklebaum stroked his chin. 'Now, perhaps I have and perhaps I have not.'

Daniel waited. He was certain the bugger would ask him for money. Well, he could give him something. Enough to keep the man quiet and get himself out of the house. Finklebaum didn't know who he was, or how to find him. Thank god for that. Wait. Had he told him his name? He couldn't remember.

'I live on my own, you understand. Yes. I do indeed. It's a lonely life ' He stopped as if waiting for a reply.

'I suppose it must be.'

'Sometimes I wish I had company. Someone who might be nice to me.' Another smile shivered its way across his face, not daring to linger for long in such hostile territory.

In the deep recesses of Daniel's brain, a tiny alarm bell tinkled raucously. 'Oh,' he said.

'Yes indeed. A companion, an intimate companion.' He leant forwards, breathing hard, wafting the stink of vinegar and furniture polish in Daniel's direction.

'So,' he continued. 'Perhaps you should go to bed. Have an early night. That would be good – for both of us. Don't you think?'

Daniel's mouth was like cardboard. He knew exactly what this obnoxious man was suggesting. He had to get away. Just walk out? But this charade wasn't spur of the moment. It had been planned. The front door would be locked; he knew it.

'An early night,' Daniel paused and coughed, trying for a deeper voice. 'Yes, of course. Good idea.'

He rose on shaky legs and opened the door. Finklebaum was on his feet at once. 'You carry on, my dear sir. I'll switch things off down here. Oh yes.' A bony hand patted Daniel's shoulder and fingers ran lightly down his spine.

'OK, I'm away,' Daniel yelped and scampered for the stairway.

He raced up to his bedroom, slammed the door – no lock of course – and cast around helplessly. As options were non-existent, he dragged the metal-framed bed across the floorboards and forced it against the bedroom door. What now? The window.

'Daniel?' The door handle rattled.

'Please wait,' he shouted. 'I'm washing.'

Crossing to the window, he yanked the curtains back, took hold of the lower sash, and pulled. Nothing. He tried again. Useless. The frame had been nailed shut. Bugger.

'I'm ready for you.'

'Right, OK, just washing still. With you in a moment.'

He would have to break the window. It would be noisy. He could no longer claim he was washing. He picked up the chair, lined the back up with the glass and propelled it forward as hard as possible. The window exploded outwards, rotten frame and glass going together. An angry yell came from outside, and the bed scraped across the floor as the door was forced open.

Daniel put his leg out of the window and straddled the sill. It didn't appear too far down –but far enough to break your neck, son, his inner voice bleated. He turned back to the room. A hand appeared around the doorframe, closely followed by an arm and an outbreak of cursing. The hand held something that looked metallic and sharp. It had to be the window. He heaved his other leg over the sill, balanced for a few desperate seconds, took a deep breath, and jumped. As he sped earthwards, he would have liked to concentrate on landing on his feet, on flexing his legs to minimise damage, on dreaming up gruesome tortures to visit on Finklebaum in a parallel life. Unfortunately, three quarters of a second of flight allowed for none of these things and the earth smashed into him with a surprisingly undramatic thud. He lay still for several seconds, thinking death wasn't as bad as he'd been led to believe, then the pain started.

He pulled himself to a sitting position, barely able to breathe. His chest felt as if an elephant had rested on it, his back as if a herd of wildebeest with untrimmed toenails had decided en masse to begin an energetic mating ritual there. A figure at a window above sprayed invective at him, then stopped. Feet clattered downstairs. The lunatic was coming to get him.

Daniel crawled on all fours towards a tree and heaved himself upright by catching hold of a branch. One leg was OK, but the other seemed filled with ground glass. He hobbled for the gate, grabbed the handle and turned. Nothing. He shook it and questioned the marital status of the pig iron that had brought it into being. No result.

There was a screech from behind as Finklebaum burst from the front door. Daniel leapt for the top of the gate and curled his fingers around it. Somehow, he scrambled up and over the spikes and landed in a heap on the other side. His pursuer rattled the locked gate but could not open it. He hopped around, shaking his fists at Daniel like a demented pixie, incandescent with rage.

Daniel retreated to a safe distance and turned to see the man crouching on his haunches and apparently howling at the moon. He presented a finger and hobbled away as fast as his injured leg would allow.

Eighteen

IT WAS FOUR AM when Daniel inserted the key in his front door. Food, drink, bed – bliss. The journey home had been a tortured one. He had staggered another two miles before calling a taxi. The trip had cost him thirty-five pounds, but he had paid without argument. As the door swung shut, he noticed that the hall light was on, which was strange. It was off when he had left the flat. Despite everything, electricity bills still worried him as well as the ever-present problem of global penguin loss. His exhausted brain had cranked around to the conclusion that if he had turned it off, then someone else must have...

'Daniel.' The urgent whisper came from the sitting-room and he recognised the whisperer.

'Professor, why are you here?' He couldn't even summon up the energy to be surprised. Farquharson stood by the fireplace, alternately folding his arms and scratching his head. Daniel slumped into a chair and let out a contented sigh.

'Daniel, we've got problems.' Farquharson's eyes swivelled left then right.

'Professor, I know I've got problems, believe me.'

'No, you don't understand...'

'And what are you doing here? How did you get in?'

'Well, Celia and I were looking for somewhere private, some-where to... you know. Her own abode was inappropriate in the circumstances as her um… friend might return and I realised you were away, so we came here.'

'But…'

'Ah, the door. It was only a five-lever. I used my kit.'

'Your kit?' Daniel stared.

'Yes.' Farquharson adjusted his collar.

'You used your kit again and opened my door.' The man was worse than ever.

'Yes, I apologise but that's not important now. Events have overtaken us. Catastrophic events.'

'You've broken your lockpick?'

'What? No, don't be silly, Daniel. This is serious. *Deadly* serious.'

'OK, tell me all about it then.' He bent down and tugged off his shoes.

'Well as I say,' the professor coughed. 'We were in your flat indulging in a little… horseplay shall we say.'

'Christ, I suppose you were in my bed. I'll have to change the sheets yet again.'

The professor scratched his head. 'Yes… well… yes but the thing is you see things got a little out of hand. Celia grew quite… well… excited and indeed so did I as one does as I'm sure you understand.'

'Chance would be a fine thing,' Daniel muttered.

'What?'

'Nothing, nothing. Look, professor, do I need to know all this?'

'Yes, Daniel, you do.' Farquharson lowered his voice. 'You see, Celia was obviously more worked up than I was. Perhaps it's my age, I don't know, perhaps there was something wrong with her, something she didn't know about, or perhaps she did know about it. These things can be difficult to—'

'Professor!'

'Yes, yes sorry. Well, to cut a long story short, not that it's all that long you understand. Quite short you might say—'

'Professor,' Daniel yelled.

'Yes, yes, yes. Well, in summary... she died.'

Daniel sat silent for a moment. 'Oh my god.'

'Yes indeed.' The professor rubbed his hands together.

'Professor, I'm so sorry.' He reached forward and touched the leathery skin of Farquharson's hand. 'What a shock for you.'

'Yes.'

'You were quite close to Celia, weren't you?'

'Well, I was at the time, that's true,' Farquharson sighed.

'Terrible, just terrible. And this happened last night?'

'Yes.'

'Only a few hours ago?'

'Yes.'

'You must still be in shock. Look where...' Daniel gestured around the flat. 'I mean where have they taken her? That is, I'd like to go to the funeral. She and I didn't exactly see eye to... you know, eye, but...'

The professor stared straight ahead.

'I know it's too soon, of course... I mean she must have family... for arrangements and so on. Will it be a burial or...'

'I don't know, Daniel. I was hoping you could help.'

'Of course. Absolutely. If there's anything I can do. Anything at all.'

Farquharson remained silent.

'Did they take her to the funeral parlour or... I suppose there might be an autopsy?'

'No, they haven't and there won't.'

'So where exactly is she?'

'Exactly, Daniel, exactly.' The professor took a deep breath. 'Exactly, she is in your bath.'

Daniel stared at Farquharson, an expression of friendly concern frozen on his face. His mind churned around the varied meanings that could be attached to the collection of words the man had used. After a period of time, which may have been rather long, it came up with the most likely one.

'She's in my bath?'

The professor sighed. 'Yes, in your bath.'

'But, but... the doctor... surely...'

'I didn't call doctor or ambulance.'

'What? Why on earth not?' Daniel stood but felt woozy so sat down again.

'She was dead, my boy, believe me. A doctor would have done no good.'

Daniel clasped his hands to his head. 'That's not the point... you're supposed to... you can't just... what the hell are you...' He collapsed back into his chair. The room was rotating disconcertingly.

'Daniel, try to be calm. I understand how shocked you are. You must understand I have my position. I can't possibly get mixed up in this.'

'But...'

'I am completely blameless. Her heart must have given out due to extreme... provocation. Very regrettable.'

'Regrettable? Christ almighty, you have to report this. If you're blameless, there won't be a problem. Telephone ambulance or police or something.' He grabbed the phone.

'She's been dead eight hours, Daniel.'

'So? You still...'

'Why didn't you report it earlier? Questions will be asked.'

'Why didn't *I* report it?' Daniel gasped. 'Me... I... you...'

'She's in *your* bath,' Farquharson sniffed.

'But I wasn't here.'

'And where were you? Are there witnesses? I'm asking what you will be asked.'

'Of course there are witnesses.' He paused, thought about where he had been, thought about witnesses, at least one of whom had been last seen lying in the bottom of a quarry.

'But you can vouch that I wasn't...'

The professor inspected his fingernails. 'Daniel, I find myself in a very delicate situation.'

'Delicate?'

'Exactly so. That is why I need your help. This is what I have been paying you for this last year, to render assistance to me in my hour of greatest need. When the cumulonimbus gather and lightning strafes, that is when I am glad I have my rock.'

'Rock? You're off your *rocker*.' Daniel jumped to his feet. 'Christ, you can't leave dead bodies lying around.'

'Obviously not,' said the professor, mildly. 'But thankfully there is only one.'

'I'm going to be sick,' Daniel headed for the bathroom but stopped at the door. He prodded a finger forward, but it recoiled as if zapped by a science-fiction force field that had been erected there. 'Oh my god.'

'So, Daniel, I must leave you now.' The professor was on his feet.

Daniel whirled about. 'Oh no! You are not leaving me with a dead body in my bathroom.'

'I suppose I could help you move it to the bedroom if it would be of any help.'

'Professor, I feel I'm going mad. You must report this to the police. Dead bodies can't be left lying around like... like...'

'Daniel, please remain calm.' The professor placed an arm on Daniel's shoulder. 'I've tried to explain. My position at the university is a delicate one at the moment. The committee is investigating past... occurrences as you know. I can't afford to provide them with more ammunition. Celia has unfortunately died. The outcome for her is fixed. It is merely a matter of tidying up. So I have turned to you. With your contacts—'

'I haven't got any contacts, you idiot. None at all. It's all in your stupid mind.'

Farquharson touched a finger to the side of his nose. 'Of course, Daniel, I understand. However, I'm sure that these non-contacts will help you remove a body from the scene. A simple matter.'

Daniel sat down. The man was round the twist. Totally bonkers. He put his head in his hands and stared at the floor. The front door slammed. 'Professor... no...' He shot to his feet and stumbled to the door. But Farquharson had gone, foot-steps rapidly receding downstairs. 'Professor,' he hissed, but it was no use. The entrance banged shut with a resonant finality. He closed his own door quietly. Some serious thinking was required.

But first... He crossed to the bathroom, reached out a hand and turned the handle. He pulled the door towards him very slowly and peered around it. Everything seemed more or less normal apart from a few scuff marks on the floor. He couldn't see over the rim of the bath. Might it all be some wild lunacy on the professor's part? A feeble hope sputtered into life.

He slipped inside and tiptoed towards the bathtub as if he might wake its occupant, and there his newly minted hope gut-tered and died. Celia lay full-length inside the bath. Her face was pale, and a faint smile shimmered around her lips. She looked as if she would rise at any moment complaining about how hard the beds were here. His dressing-gown covered her, but he did not try to move it, unsure of what lay below.

Closing the bathroom door as quietly as he had opened it, he plodded to the kitchen and filled the kettle. He returned to his chair while the water hissed. What was he going to do?

His nutcase of a boss had landed him in it up to the eyeballs, that was for sure. A dead body in his bath. Worse, a body whose house he had spent considerable time in, he realised. But even now he should make a statement to the police. It would be difficult, but surely he could explain. Farquharson would have to be brought into the story and would deny everything. And then there was the quarry incident. It had been on TV; it would be in the papers. And there was Lorraine. He couldn't afford to spend weeks arguing about this, possibly in custody. He had to rescue her from these allotment psychos. So that meant... OK, how *do* you dispose of a body?

Nineteen

DANIEL WOKE WITH A headache. He hadn't slept well, waking several times through the night from dreams he couldn't recall, but they had not featured Father Christmas or the Good Fairy. At six AM he had given into aquatic pressure and tiptoed into the bathroom to relieve himself. He tried not to look at the still-smiling Celia, but his eyes wandered as he peed and his stomach churned.

A substantial breakfast later and he felt better, or at least able to think clearly. He thought about books he had read and films seen where people disposed of bodies. It never appeared to be too difficult. There was the acid method, but that would need even more acid than the chemistry department possessed. There was the chopping into little bits method, but he couldn't stomach that. Then there was disposal en masse, the only way he could deal with it. But how? And where? How long did he have before someone came looking for her?

All right, first, wherever she might end up, he had to get her out of the flat. But he couldn't drag a body downstairs. She had to be disguised, wrapped up in some fashion. A supply of plastic sheeting was needed.

Ten minutes later, behind Carpets-R-us, Daniel rummaged through a plastic-stuffed skip. Much of the content was ripped or in tatters, but he soon found what he wanted—several enormous bags that had enclosed wide rolls. He folded them as small as possible and checked that there was no one in sight. Right, back home quickly. But despite the desire to be safely in his flat, Daniel paused at a newsagent's window where a recognisable face stared out from a quarter-page photograph. *Taxi's last fare* read the headline. He bought a copy and scanned the article. Mental instability was mentioned. A former girlfriend had come forward to say the man had attacked her. Neighbours said he had been either depressed or very happy. The tone of the piece indicated that suicide was the obvious explanation, but the police had not confirmed. Well, it wasn't good, but neither was it bad. He dumped the paper and hurried home.

By the time he got back, he was already sweating. None of his neighbours had seen him, as far as he could judge, but dozens of people must have passed him on the street as he carried an unwieldy jumble of plastic home. But now he was committed.

He threw down the bundle and poured himself a large whisky. It helped. A refill glugged into the glass. OK, to work. At the bathroom, he took a deep breath and pulled the door open. Why wouldn't she stop smiling? What was so bloody funny? He removed his dressing gown from her and was much relieved to find the corpse fully clothed. He grabbed a cold arm and tugged. Nothing—Celia refused to budge. Back in the kitchen, he finished the second whisky then, with much heaving and sweating, managed to pull her from the bath and dump her onto the bathmat. He grabbed the mat, dragged the body through to the sitting-room and collapsed onto a chair.

Another whisky later, he retrieved two black bin bags from the kitchen and slid her feet into one and her upper body into the other. A liberal application of parcel tape secured the two together. With a great deal of effort, he crammed the package into the largest of the carpet sacks he had retrieved and tied off the end with nylon rope. He paused and peered at the wrapped body before him. Celia, dead or alive, seemed far less intimidating when you couldn't see her. He prepared a chicken sandwich as his mind wandered over the *what next* question. For a wild moment, he thought of the postal system. What did it cost to send seventy kilogrammes *poste restante* to a post office somewhere in the Badlands of Mongolia or Borneo? Surely he could afford it. It would require a large and sturdy box. One of the many courier firms would collect from him. But that was the problem: someone would know he had sent it. And he would have to pay with a traceable credit card. Another plan began to form.

⟫⟫⟫ ⟪⟪⟪

Midnight had passed more than an hour ago; it was time to act. Daniel dragged the wrapped Celia towards the front door, but he was panting when he got there. Not practical. He wouldn't make it down three flights of stairs and around to the back of the flats. Hell, he would end up beside Celia inside the package. Anyway, it was too noisy and therefore risky. If anyone woke and came to investigate, it would all be over. OK, there was another, faster way.

He opened his front door, stepped outside and locked the door behind him. He padded downstairs to the rear of the tenement block and peered up towards his third-floor kitchen window. Good. All the windows above were dark apart from his own. The area immediately below the window was a patch of soft muddy earth and grass—perfect. Back upstairs, he struggled through to the kitchen with Celia, turned the light off and opened the window. Pulling a table towards the gap, he heaved the plastic-wrapped body onto it with much sweating and cursing. A careful check both underneath the window and on the visible section of pavement showed no midnight marauders. He slid the body from table to work-surface and from there partway

143

through the open window. Nearly done. He paused to wipe away the sweat that had run into his eyes, then yelped as gravity took over. Thinking about it later, he could have sworn that Celia wriggled her shoulders and, with a whoosh, the package had gone. A heavy thump and a rattle came from below as it disturbed a metallic object.

Daniel drew in his breath and held it. It seemed like an entire minute passed as he listened. In the distance a dog whined, a police siren wailed, below was silence. He had survived the first stage.

He threw on a jacket, pulled a woolly hat onto his head, raced downstairs and peered into the dark well of his backyard. Nothing to be heard. The flashlight on his mobile illuminated the scene. The package lay in a grotesque heap, but the plastic sheeting was unbroken. He didn't want to think of the condition of the contents, so he didn't. An array of black wheelie bins stood against the rear wall. Selecting one at random, he grabbed the lid and gagged as the putrid stench from it almost laid him low. Holding his breath, he pulled out several rubbish sacks and at least some of their contents and laid the bin on its side. Then he took the packaged Celia, dragged her to the bin and manoeuvred her inside.

That was the difficult bit over, now for the very difficult part. It was five minutes along open road before he reached the canal towpath. Not busy roads; he had walked the route earlier. Not the sort of roads frequented by police cars, the sort where they might actually see crimes being committed, but it was risky just the same. Pushing a wheelie bin along a road at two AM with a body on board was tricky to explain. But it must be done. With difficulty, he tipped up the bin and set off.

Very soon he realised that the bin was not a new one. It didn't move smoothly, and it squeaked. It squeaked with every revolution of the wheels. He stopped for a few seconds to rest his aching arms. Upstairs, in the house beside him, a light went on and a curtain twitched. He turned his head away and started off again. It wasn't much further, no more than a hundred metres, but ahead a dark figure slipped from the driveway of a house. Daniel hesitated. What could he do? The figure turned towards him and strode rapidly along the pavement. Retreating was not an option. Should he simply abandon the bin and run? But that was an invitation for the man to look inside. No, he would have to brazen it out.

The man drew level with him. He was dressed in a black turtle-neck and jeans and wore black gloves. Daniel searched desperately for something to explain himself. The man slowed, glanced at him, then half smiled, clicked his tongue twice and was gone. Daniel shook his head. What did that mean? Who cared? He tipped up his bin again and made a squeaky dash for the canal.

Bollards. After turning onto the towpath, he instantly met his first problem. To discourage the use of the canal by motor-bikers, the local council had erected a bollard in the middle of the path. There was no way the wheelie bin could get around it. He had to take a diversion into the bushes, and it took ten minutes to return to the towpath, scratched and breathless. Another couple of minutes and he was beside the pile of bricks he had stashed earlier in the day among the long grass. Tipping the bin over with a thump, he heaved out the contents, looped a length of nylon cord through four of the hollow centred bricks and secured them to one end of the package. He repeated the exercise at the other end. Now came the tricky bit. He couldn't judge, it was all down to luck.

With his knife, he made a series of small slits in the top, middle and bottom of the plastic. Then he rolled Celia across the path and into the water. The package floated as he hoped. A shove pushed it towards deeper water in the canal's centre.

He held his breath as Celia slowly pirouetted around and then escaped air reduced buoyancy and she sank sedately from sight to leave nothing but a trail of bubbles. He stood for a moment with the ridiculous feeling that he should say a prayer, perhaps sing a hymn, but contented himself with a muttered, 'Thank god.'

He grabbed the wheelie bin and squeaked back to his flat.

Twenty

DETECTIVE SERGEANT BARNES EASED his car to a halt beside the three-bedroom semi. Yet again, he wondered if this visit was wise. This was the home of his former boss, Detective Inspector Dick. He had no idea what arrangements had been put in place by HR after Dick's breakdown, but they had resulted in the man's permanent sick leave.

Barnes made up his mind, squeezed his bulky frame from behind the wheel and strolled down the short path to the front door. Dick's last case had involved some dubious goings on at the university and he was keen to discuss one of the suspects in that case with Dick. He knocked sharply on the door but had to knock a second time before it opened.

'What is it?' snapped the stooped, middle-aged man in the doorway.

'Dick. Hello. It's Barnes here. How are things with you?' He extended a hand cautiously, afraid it might be ignored.

'Barnes. Well, well. Been a long time. Thought I might have seen you before now.'

He cleared his throat. 'Yes, too long,' he said gruffly. 'Always meant to call, never quite made it. Pressure at work you know.' He attempted a sincere smile and managed at least half of it. The truth was he had never liked Dick and had been happy to see him go.

Dick drew himself up and gave an appraising stare. 'You'd better come in and tell me what you're after.'

Five minutes later, they sat squashed around a tiny table in the kitchen, cups of weak tea in hand.

Dick slurped a mouthful and emptied his saucer back into the cup. 'Dreghorn, you say?'

Barnes detected a narrowing of Dick's eyes and a straightening of his shoulders. 'You'll have heard about the taxi driver in the quarry? We don't know if it was an accident or murder, but there was someone in that cab and they haven't come forward.'

Dick nodded but said nothing.

'Well, we have a disappearance now. A middle-aged bag. No body but there are questions. And this Dreghorn was shacked up with the daughter of the guy she was dating. But nothing to connect him you understand.'

'Dreghorn,' Dick repeated, drawing out the word as if savouring a gourmet treat.

'It's just that after your run-in with this guy, I wondered if you might have any information or even any thoughts.'

'The bugger was never charged with anything.'

'Yes, but you always said he was—'

'Not a thing. Lily-white. That's how he came out of it.'

Barnes scowled. This wasn't what he wanted to hear. 'Yes, that's how he came out, but it's not what you believe, is it?'

'I'm a sick man, Barnes. What I think doesn't matter.'

He watched as Dick scribbled feverishly in a spiral-bound notebook he had produced. His pasty cheeks had taken on a pinker hue, and the ghost of a smile hovered on his lips.

'It does matter. I trust your instincts.' It took great effort to force the words out.

'My instincts are you're looking in the wrong place. The man's an incompetent wanker, that's all.' Dick gave a brief smile and finished the rest of his tea. 'Ignore him,' he added.

'That's your advice?'

'Absolutely.'

'Well, I'd better be going.' Barnes stood up. 'Thanks for your help.' He attempted and failed to avoid too much emphasis on *help*. But Dick appeared not to notice. *Thanks for nothing* he added under his breath.

After their goodbyes, Dick stood for a long time, rubbing his hands together vigorously and smiling to himself as if some hilarious joke had just crossed his mind.

Twenty-One

IT HAD BEEN ANOTHER disturbed night for Daniel with little sleep. When he did drop off, nightmare pictures of eyes circling his bed wakened him. What if he had been caught on video? Cameras were everywhere these days, although he had seen nothing.

He rose early and prepared toast and tea, not his usual breakfast, but his appetite had gone. As he poured a second cup, his phone rang. He picked it up with thumb and forefinger only, ready to drop it should some death ray zap from the thing.

'Daniel, how goes our little project?'

'God, it's you, professor.'

'Yes, that's correct. I'm anxious to know how our collaboration is proceeding if you get my drift.'

Daniel drew a deep sigh. 'Your project is complete,' *you asshole*, he muttered to himself.

'My aunt's what? Sorry, I don't understand you.'

'It's finished, done, complete, over with, OK?'

'Yes, yes Daniel, I get your meaning. There is no need to shout, although I do appreciate the stress involved even for someone of experience such as yourself. The appropriate arrangements will be made for your expenses.'

Too tired to argue, Daniel hung up without another word. Farquharson would pay him for his services. Well damn right. The man owed him, but it made the situation look even worse.

OK, at least now he had time to decide on the next move. The medical centre, that was it. He must do something about his blood test. Definitely no taxi; he would walk. Walking was good for your health. He downed his tepid tea, threw on a jacket and headed downstairs.

A crisp, bright morning beckoned, and Daniel paused on the front step to take several deep breaths. As he set off, he failed to notice the tall man with grey sunken cheeks who seemed to form from the shadows of the adjacent doorway, glance right and left, and move off in Daniel's footsteps. This man in his turn did not see – as far as we can tell – the tubby red-faced individual who heaved himself out of his parked car, stood for a moment with a puzzled expression on his face, then trotted after the pursuer and pursued.

It was only a fifteen-minute walk to the medical centre. If only, oh if only he hadn't hailed that taxi, he wouldn't have got involved in the quarry incident, then he would have been back at his flat to prevent Celia and her lover from having their fatal ding-dong and he would be free of all this nonsense. It was too much. How could fate be so cruel?

'What was that?' said a frowning receptionist.

'Oh sorry, I was miles away. My name's Daniel Dreghorn. I missed an appointment. It was for a test, an urgent test. Is it possible to—'

'Next appointment's Friday.'

'Friday? I can't wait until Friday.'

'Friday 2.30 do you want it?' The receptionist adjusted her glasses and sat up straighter.

'I... no .. I... It's not that I don't want it, but this is urgent. You see, I've got this thing.' Daniel glanced at the queue that had formed. He lowered his voice. 'This thing wrong with me. It's got to be confirmed, see. It's urgent.'

'What? What thing?' the receptionist cupped a hand over her ear.

'Hepatitis. They think I've got hepatitis. I need a test.'

'I told you Friday – oh just a minute,' she tapped on her computer. 'Dreghorn you said?'

'Yes.'

'Mum, what's Heparitus?' said a high-pitched voice behind him.

Daniel turned to see the woman at the head of the queue glaring at him, a small girl tugging at her skirt.

The receptionist had returned from her cyber explorations. 'It's a blood test you need.'

'Yes, I *know* that.'

'Well, you should have told me.'

'I did tell you, you...'

She frowned, raised her finger and pointed at a sign behind the counter that said in large print for the hard of hearing, WE TAKE A ZERO-TOLERANCE APPROACH TO THE ABUSE OF OUR STAFF.

'God's sake, I wasn't abusing you, I'm just saying that...'

'Anyway,' she cut in. 'The nurse can do that. Please have a seat.'

Daniel humphed through to the waiting area, half pleased and half irritated.

He was still fuming about justice and stupidity two minutes later when a tall, thin-faced man occupied the seat next to him. The man watched him in a way that did not put him at his ease.

'Mr Dreghorn?' The voice was low but authoritative, the type of voice that returned Daniel to his school desk and encouraged him to say – yes sir.

'Well... possibly,' he said.

'I have something for you.' The man was breathing hard through a constricted nose, and his upper body swayed in Daniel's direction.

Daniel swayed in the opposite direction and wondered when the nurse would call him.

The man produced a thin, brown envelope from an inside pocket and pushed it towards him.

He took the envelope. 'Well it's my lucky day,' he said, and then, 'Christ, are you from...'

The man shook his head.

'I mean are you one of the...'

The man raised his hand in a gesture of silence.

'You're the lot that...'

The man stood and offered a handshake. 'I must go now. I suspect we shall meet again.'

Daniel tentatively extended a few fingers, which were, as he feared, crushed in a robotic clamp.

You handled that well, he thought, as he tore open the envelope and pulled out a single sheet of A4.

If you want to see your girlfriend again do exactly as we say... were the first words he read.

'Mr Dreghorn?' The nurse, hovered at the edge of the waiting area. He stared at her, open-mouthed. What the hell was he going to do?

She coughed. 'Mr Dreghorn, can you come this way please?'

He followed her into her room, although cubicle was a better description of the claustrophobic box. Lorraine? What could he do?

'I'm Nurse Freesia, Mr Dreghorn. Now, you're here for a blood test, is that right?'

He had an impossible choice. What could he do except go through with it?

'Mr Dreghorn?'

'Oh sorry, what was it?'

'I said a blood test.'

'Yes, a blood test.'

'Right fine,' her voice sounded a little crisp to Daniel's ears. 'I'll just check your notes. Won't be a moment.'

Daniel looked at her for the first time, looked past the uniform, and then he looked again. She was remarkably like... Impossible of course, it couldn't be... could it?

'Celia?' he said.

'Syphilis?' she said.

'What?' they said together.

'I said Celia,' Daniel began and then, 'What do you mean syphilis? I don't understand.'

The nurse frowned. 'Why did you call me Celia?'

By now Daniel had decided that Celia had not risen from the dead. This woman bore only a slight resemblance to her. Perhaps he was hallucinating. 'No reason. You just look a bit like someone I used to know. I mean someone I do know. It's not that they are dead or anything. Still very much alive in fact... anyway syphilis, why did you say syphilis?'

'It says down here they're checking for syphilis.'

'What? No, that's rubbish. I don't have syphilis, never have.'

'Mr Dreghorn, I'm a professional, I assure you there is no need for embarrassment.'

'Oh yes there bloody is. I mean somebody should be because I never have. Had it I mean. Syphilis I mean. I mean it's not something you forget, is it?'

'All right, well, what were you being tested for then, Mr Dreghorn?' Daniel heard a note of triumph in her voice.

'Hepatitis, that's what. They thought I had hepatitis.'

'Ah now...' She looked through her notes again. 'I wonder...'

'Yes?'

'Well it's just a tick box you see and the two are side by side. Perhaps the wrong box has been ticked.'

Daniel's remaining patience evaporated like camel piss in the desert. 'This damned place. It's just the end. Nobody knows what...' He tailed off under the icy gaze of an irate professional.

'Mr Dreghorn, the abuse of staff on these premises is forbidden.'

'It's OK outside then, is it?' he muttered unwisely.

'Excuse me?' She pulled her shoulders firmly back, emphasising a Boadicea-like demeanour.

'I said it's a lovely day outside.' Daniel gestured to the window with its firmly closed blinds.

'I'm sorry, Mr Dreghorn, I don't have time for small talk. Do you wish a test or not?'

Daniel rolled up his sleeve and pushed his bare arm towards her. She wrapped a cuff around his upper arm, produced a syringe and proceeded to draw a sample.

'We'll fast-track it. Results should be available in two days,' she said. Then when the syringe was full, 'Do you inject?'

Daniel closed his eyes. 'Sometimes I think all I do is breathe.'

'I mean do you inject dru—'

'No, I flaming don't.' Daniel jumped to his feet. 'I don't. I never have, I don't even smoke and I only drink if there's an R in the month. Though right now if anyone offered me a line of coke I'd say lay it on me, pal.'

The nurse raised her hand. 'Please remain calm. I'll put you down as a potential user.'

At that point, Daniel let out a noise which he thought was a snort of derision but which the local paper would report as *a blood-curdling scream*. He then waved his arms about in a manner which, he had to admit to himself later, was rather excessive. This swept the nurse's coffee mug onto the floor along with her telephone and a bundle of papers. Daniel stared at the mess and the nurse rising from her chair.

'Sorry,' he said as his brain recognised the bleep-bleep of an alarm. She had hit a panic button probably designed to protect her from rapists and muggers.

'I'm sorry. It's a mistake,' he said as she retreated to the wall, lifted a stool and held it in front of her.

'Look, when will the results be ready?' He put a hand out towards her.

The nurse screamed.

'Right, well, I guess I'd better go.'

He backed up to the door and reached for the handle. 'OK, I'll see you later, I suppose, nurse.'

He pulled open the door to be faced with a scene of noise and much confusion. A large security guard confronted him.

'What's going on in there?' he demanded.

'She's had a turn, I think,' Daniel said. 'There's something wrong. Better get a doctor or something.'

The guard pushed past him and Daniel retreated towards the main door of the surgery building. Everyone was running in the direction of the nurse's room. The receptionist had gone. He thought of going back to see if the nurse was OK. He thought of jumping from a great height onto a hard surface. But he did neither. He slipped out of the front door, turned right and walked briskly away from the health centre as a police car wailed around the corner, blue lights screaming.

Twenty-Two

WHAT A SAD PLACE the world was, Daniel reflected as he stared at his coffee mug and once more picked up the letter that the grey man had thrust at him. Here he was, a decent, law-abiding citizen who wished no harm on anyone, except perhaps Farquharson and his cronies, and those loony bombers of course, and medical workers, although he didn't wish any actual harm on them. It had been a big misunderstanding back at the surgery, that was all. Soon he would have the major problem of retrieving his blood test results from that hellhole of idiots. For now, he had this. He read through the letter once more.

In essence, he would be given a package, board a specified train on a specified day and detrain at a specified station, leaving the package behind. Then they would release Lorraine. Simple. Bloody hell. Even in his brain's current semi-addled state, Daniel had not one shred of doubt he was being asked to plant a bomb on that train, a bomb that would undoubtedly kill people. Last time, at the university, it was different. He hadn't known. Perhaps he should have, but he hadn't, and no one had been hurt, well, not hurt much. This was another scenario entirely. He couldn't do it, he just couldn't.

But what would happen to Lorraine? Would they kill her? They were a bunch of lunatics for certain, but they all looked British, none of them had a Middle Eastern appearance, only a few of them had beards, which meant... What did it mean?

Was that good or bad for Lorraine? He had no idea. He slumped forward onto the table, resting his head on his folded arms.

The doorbell jangled. Daniel's head jerked upwards. He lurched sideways, toppled from his chair and collapsed in a heap on the floor.

'I'm coming,' he yelled as the bell continued to ring. Limping to the door, he yanked it open, ready to do battle with whoever lurked in the shadows. He stared, open-mouthed, at the bald-headed man with the red nose.

'Oh my god, it's you.'

'Indeed, Mr Dreghorn, indeed. May I come in?' said Inspector Dick, shouldering past a stunned Daniel.

After a glance to make sure no one had seen Dick enter his flat, Daniel pushed the door shut, his mind whirling. The inspector was already seated in an armchair and, with legs crossed and hands entwined over his belly, appeared relaxed and comfortable.

'I thought you were...'

Dick's face twitched. 'As you can see, I'm not.'

Daniel hesitated. He wanted to tell this intruder to take a hike, but this man was a policeman, a profession he did not wish to mix with at this moment, with bomb plots, dead Celias and dead taxi drivers cluttering his life. He reached over the table, casually plucked the grey man's letter from where it lay almost under the inspector's nose and stuffed it into his pocket.

'So... busy, are you? I mean, at work and so forth. Crime solving, and such like.'

'Busy, Daniel? Well no. Not right now.' His expression darkened. 'I'm on what they call sick leave.' He spat the words out as if someone had squeezed a lemon onto his tongue.

'Ah, so you're not really...' Daniel had intended to say Dick was not on duty but he was interrupted.

'No, I'm not in the least sick. Stress, they said, but it's that bastard Merrywick behind it. He's always wanted to be rid of me.'

'So, you're not really... I mean right now you're not on duty as it were, not a policeman at the moment.'

Dick cleared his throat, peered at his fingers for a few seconds, then attempted to prise some dirt from under his thumbnail. 'Once a copper, always a copper. I keep my eyes open.' He sniffed sharply. 'Take this latest disappearance for instance.'

'Would you like tea?' said Daniel, desperately.

Dick shook his head. 'A terrible business.'

'Coffee then?'

'It's bound to be murder, but they haven't found the body yet.'

'Oh, haven't they?'

'Naturally they will. They always do. Troublesome things to dispose of, bodies.'

'I know. I mean they must be, mustn't they? Heavy things,' he added hastily as Dick raised an eyebrow. 'I mean, what murder?'

'You haven't heard? It was mentioned on the local news last night. Celia Power, tragic. A fine woman.'

'I don't watch the news, boring.'

'She'll be in the canal, that's my guess.'

'No! I mean no, that's ridiculous.'

'Your average murderer is not that clever, Daniel. It's often unplanned. If, for instance, hypothetically you understand, the murder had been committed here, the canal might seem an excellent hiding place to an uneducated mind.'

Daniel stared at the inspector's impassive face. If that face had been a fragment of Egyptian papyrus retrieved from an ancient tomb, he would have learned more. What did the man know? Was he simply wittering on or had he somehow found out? If so, it was the end, probably. Was there any way out?

'The local force has their work cut out right now,' Dick continued.

'They do. I mean they do?'

'Yes. A body in a quarry. They're thinking suicide, but there again, who's to say it's not a contrived murder?'

Silence descended while Daniel fidgeted.

'I'll take that tea now,' the inspector said.

'What? Oh yes, right.'

Daniel turned to the kitchen, his mind yo-yoing between dread and despair. He popped a teabag into a mug and added water, then dunked the bag into another mug of water. What if he added something to the man's tea? Nothing lethal, a sedative of some kind, but that would just leave another body.

Back in the lounge, he handed Dick the mug and flopped into his chair. 'Look, I'm right in thinking that you are not acting as a policeman right now. Am I right? In thinking that?'

Dick took a long drink from his mug and licked his lips. 'On paper, correct. In reality, I have conducted a little investigation of my own.'

'But it's not official or anything?'

'No, but the results might be my pass back into the force.'

So that was it. He was the inspector's prop. Daniel's heart took the down elevator. He lifted his mug with hands he struggled to prevent shaking, took a sip of tea and spat it back into the cup. It was cold. Not just cold tea; he had forgotten to boil the water. He watched as the inspector took another mouthful with apparent enjoyment.

'I'll make you more tea, shall I?'

'But there is another way, Daniel.' Undeterred, the inspector continued. 'I need help, you see. With my boss, Merrywick.'

'Oh, right.'

'Alas, he is not all right. He is very wrong. An arsehole, a supercilious jackass, a cretin.'

'Standing for Parliament, is he?'

'What?'

'Sorry, nothing. You were saying?'

The large red spot on Dick's nose grew in intensity, seeming to pulse like a distress beacon.

'The man was glad to see me on the sick. Now he can do what he likes. The bastard has to go, he really must.'

Daniel glanced at the inspector who was once more sipping from his revolting mug of tea-coloured water. 'So... I guess you don't get on?'

Dick frowned. 'Let's not beat around the bush. You're in deep shit. I need your help and in return, I can offer you some assistance.'

Daniel's heart reached the sub-basement and stopped, or so it felt. He opened his mouth and closed it again. There seemed no appropriate comment. If only there was something to slip in the inspector's tea. 'I need to go to the pharmacy,' he said finally as his companion drained his mug and placed it back on the table.

'Are you with me, old son?' Dick extended a chubby hand in Daniel's direction.

A Great Pit opened underneath Daniel, a pit in which snakes writhed and did things that snakes did when no one was looking. He grasped the inspector's clammy hand. 'Do I have a choice?'

Dick ignored his question and sat back, rubbing his hands together. 'A good decision. I have a plan, you see.'

'So you won't need me.'

'We need to have the man investigated. Need to have him under suspicion. Mud sticks you see. Once they start digging, they'll find more. I'm sure of it.'

'You don't have a heart condition, do you by any chance?' Daniel muttered.

'Excellent. A sense of humour. How wonderful. Now what I plan is that a body will be found in Merrywick's garden. To be precise, a body buried in his greenhouse.'

'A body? You're mad.'

'Possible, but irrelevant right now. Body in greenhouse, tipoff, body discovered, eureka.'

This was ridiculous. The man was pitiful. 'Just one tiny detail; you're going to need a body? Yes?' Daniel folded his arms.

The inspector stared back at him, sighed and examined the ceiling for signs of dust or evidence of spiders' webs.

Then Daniel stopped breathing as the Great Pit which had given indications it might be closing, if slowly, suddenly yawned even wider and a snake jumped out and bit him on the nose. No. He couldn't mean? 'You don't mean?' he said.

The inspector nodded. 'In theory, it doesn't matter where the body comes from. In practice, even in your profession, I suspect they are not thick on the ground. Or even under the ground. Ha... ha...'

Daniel's stomach gave notice of potential evacuation. 'But... but I didn't, I haven't, I couldn't, I mean I shouldn't, it was only for... anyway, she'll be all... Oh my god.'

'I'll leave the details in your capable hands, my son. I'll supply you with more information in good time. I assure you that once back on the force I will do what I can for you. In the meantime...' He tapped his nose with his index finger. 'Must toddle.'

'Sorry, there's a box over there.' Daniel pointed to the pack of tissues on the shelf by the sitting-room door.

Dick glanced at the box, blinking rapidly. 'OK... I'll be in touch. Look after yourself, Daniel.'

The front door slammed behind the inspector. Oh, I will, Daniel thought. And you can go back to your cowpat.

Twenty-Three

DANIEL ENTERED THE SURGERY with some trepidation. He had allowed three days to elapse since his last appointment and the unfortunate misunderstanding with the nurse, but he was not looking forward to the return visit. To his relief, the large and hectoring receptionist had been replaced by a woman who looked almost normal, although what was normal in this hellhole he couldn't begin to guess.

His spirits lifted when she smiled at him as she ticked him off on her screen and invited him to take a seat in the waiting room.

'Have you worked here long?' he asked.

'Only a couple of days. I'm still finding my feet.'

Daniel nodded and stopped himself from making a comment. She would find out soon enough.

There were half a dozen other patients scattered about. He sat as far from anyone else as possible even though none of them looked as if they had any connection with the Allotment Society. He was also relieved to see the nurse's office door firmly shut, so he only had the doctor to worry about. His mobile announced a call. It was Alex.

'Hi mate, where've you been?'

Where had he been? Where had he not been? 'Alex, sorry. A lot happening right now. How're you coping?'

'Not too well. Sandra's left so things are tight.'

'Sandra... She was due to leave next week, wasn't she?'

'Yeah, but she's just sloped off. Never said a thing. Not even goodbye. We were kind of... sort of seeing each other.' There was a wistful sigh. 'So I guess it's over.'

Daniel resisted the temptation to tell Alex that he knew very well which part of Sandra he had been seeing and that he could have seen it himself if he had wanted. But instead, he said, 'Women, eh?'

'Yeah, we could really do with you back.'

'Daniel Dreghorn?'

Daniel looked up to see Dr Culshaw at the top of the waiting room and jumped to his feet. 'Got to go, Alex. I'll see you soon. Just got a few things to straighten out.' He cut the connection and followed Dr Culshaw into the surgery.

'Ah, Mr Dreghorn, do sit down. Sorry to keep you waiting. I've had to use Dr Crummey's office this morning. Just finding my way about.' He smiled. 'And how are you today?'

Coming from a doctor, Daniel knew that question should be treated with deep suspicion.

'Well, overall, I suppose, not too bad all things considered.'

'Excellent, excellent. It's the weather. Everyone feels better when the sun shines. In fact, we are better. It's been proved.' The doctor nodded sagely. 'Mind and body are interconnected. We're less busy here on a sunny day.'

'That's nice,' said Daniel, not sure where this was going. Was the doctor attempting to break bad news to him in a round-about way? Hell's teeth, perhaps there was something wrong with his head. A brain tumour. He had had a few headaches recently which he'd put down to too many whiskies, but what if it was much more than that?

'What... what do you mean, doctor?'

'Oh, people have more to do on a sunny day.'

'Yes, but...'

The doctor rubbed his palms together. 'Only two days to go and I'm away. Five-week cruise, wonderful, always wanted to do it.'

'But what about me, doctor?'

'Take a holiday. That's my advice. Doesn't have to be a cruise, just whatever you can afford.'

Daniel licked dry lips. 'What... you mean... a holiday? Like a... a last holiday?'

Culshaw shrugged. 'Last holiday? Well, it all depends, doesn't it? If that's how the dice fall. Well.'

'Oh my god.'

The doctor was humming to himself in a rather insensitive way and now picked up a photograph from his desk, a photograph of a middle-aged woman and two teenage girls.

'Are you married, Mr Dreghorn?' The sunny smile had left the doctor's face.

Unable to speak, Daniel shook his head.

'I am.' He pushed his bottom lip out and stared at the photograph. 'Don't let my experience put you off. It works for some people.' He slammed the photograph face down onto the desk.

'Deborah's taking the girls to Florida, you know. She doesn't like cruising. I'll be on my own. For five weeks.' He winked. 'Awful, isn't it?'

Daniel closed his eyes. What was going on? Was this the doctor's way of distracting him? Trying to make it easier for him? 'Please,' he said faintly. 'I need to know. What's wrong?'

'Hah. How long have you got? That's the question.' Mutely, Daniel nodded. 'How to explain a lifetime of marriage in a few minutes.' Culshaw sighed.

Daniel blinked. 'Marriage?'

The doctor buried his face in his hands. 'I'm sorry. I don't understand what came over me. I shouldn't have said those things.' He pulled his shoulders back, turned to his computer and pressed a few keys. 'Now, what can I do for you, Mr Dreghorn?'

Daniel's mouth opened and shut a few times. 'Well... I...'

'Ah, here we are. Is it your repeat blood test result?'

'Y... yes.'

The doctor peered at the screen for a moment and frowned. 'Tch, tch. Oh no, dear me.' He tapped something on the screen.

Daniel's heart rate soared. He clasped his hands together to stop them shaking.

'What... what is it?'

'It's filthy.'

'Filthy? I don't understand.'

'These screens are dust magnets. Static charge builds up. It's vital to clean them regularly. The thing's likely crawling with bugs. God knows what's in the keyboard. I shall have a word with Dr Crummey.' He wrinkled his nose. 'Crummey by name and Crummey by... never mind. Blood test, was it?'

'Yes,' Daniel said in a tiny voice.

'Well, I'm pleased to say it's all perfectly normal. Was there anything else?'

Daniel stared. 'Anything...'

The doctor raised his eyebrows. Daniel became aware that his mouth was hanging open and shut it quickly. 'You're telling me there's nothing wrong? I haven't got Heparitis... I mean...'

'Absolutely not. Just make sure you always use clean needles or, better still, don't use them at all, eh? I can refer you to a programme.' The doctor bent forward solicitously.

'But you told me before... I mean the first sample...'

'Ah yes. Bit of a bummer that. Don't quite know what happened. That's why we always double-check. The lab is investigating.'

'So, I'm OK?' Daniel found it difficult to fasten on the concept of OK.

167

'Oh yes. Fighting fit. Of course, we never know what's around the corner, do we? Take Deborah for instance...'

'No.' Daniel pushed his chair back. 'I mean... I don't mean Deborah; it's just I'd better go and not take up your time and so on. Oh, and thank you.' He offered his hand to the doctor who shook it gravely.

'Thank *you*, Mr Dreghorn for listening. You would make a good doctor. A good doctor always listens.'

But Daniel had already closed the door behind him. He floated to the reception desk. 'Life's wonderful,' he said to the receptionist. 'I haven't got it you know, but you really need to look for another job.'

⟫⟫ ⟪⟪

He sat that evening with a smile on his face, watching the evening news, whisky in one hand and a bag of lime and coriander-flavoured poppadums within reach of the other. But he wasn't watching the news, his mind still assimilating the fact that he did not have a nasty disease, and so a brief report on the suicide of a middle-aged man from Greenwich did not register.

Twenty-Four

It was a dark, damp night. An owl hooting somewhere among the trees to the side of the canal, quite unaware it was a cliché, made Daniel shiver as he heaved the wheelie bin along the towpath. Occasional lampposts scattered beside the path did little to help other than cast dense shadows in front and behind him.

He had thought never to return to the canal bank, at least not in this life. Come the day of reckoning – well, whatever. Yet here he was, feeling as conspicuous as a strawberry in a plate of custard. He stopped at the place, there was no question as to where the right place might be, and removed his body retrieval device from the bin. This comprised a butcher's hook bound tightly to a stout bamboo cane.

Pausing, he looked to right and left. This was the last moment when he could come up with an innocent explanation for his evening excursion, insanity being the obvious reason for taking a bin for its evening constitutional along the canal towpath. Now it was for real. No innocent explanation existed for hooking a dead body from the depths. He took a deep breath and plunged the bamboo into the black water.

It didn't take long before his hook snagged on something. He pulled on the rod and a moment later a shape broke surface. It wasn't the package he had expected. A quick flash of the torch he had brought with him showed a suitcase handle and a suitcase. He bent down, tugged it onto the bank, released the hook and cast once more. This time, a large and exceedingly heavy package surfaced. Feeling nauseous, he heaved it towards the bank and hauled it up and onto the towpath.

The parcel looked lumpy under the plastic wrapping. The outer covering more yellow than he remembered. Hardly surprising after the time it had spent immersed in filthy canal-water. He prodded it gingerly with his toe. It was reassuringly solid. He had had grave doubts about Celia's condition after several days' immersion, but she seemed to be in reasonable shape. After spreading a large piece of sheet plastic on the ground, he rolled Celia and her wrappings onto this and wrapped and tied her off again. Best to be doubly sure. Besides, the stink that wormed up his nostrils was one that should be contained. Job done, he sat back against the low wall bordering the towpath and tried to catch his breath. His body rested, but his mind didn't.

He had got away with it once: disposing of a body. He had been very lucky. What were the odds of getting away with it twice? Statistically, what was the chance of being caught while trundling a rubbish bin containing a dead body through city suburbs at one o'clock in the morning? He hadn't the faintest idea but felt sure it was proportional to the length of time he spent in the body's vicinity.

Jumping to his feet, he threw the bin lid open, grabbed Celia around what might have been her waist and heaved upwards. No result. The water-saturated package was far too heavy now it was out of the canal. He tried again and failed. A pinprick of panic opened and, like a black hole, began to swell as it consumed all about it. If he had to abandon Celia here, he would be in a position infinitely worse than he had been half an hour ago. Think.

Of course. It was simple.

He grabbed the bin by its handles, tipped it on its side with its open top next to one end of Celia and, with a fusillade of curses, pushed and pulled the body into the bin. Once the process started it became easier as the plastic sheet slid on the smooth sides of the bin. Then, with the body completely inside, he grabbed the bin's handle and heaved it upright. With leverage and good handholds, a much easier job than moving the body on its own. Slamming the lid shut, he surveyed his handiwork and smiled.

'Ahoy, matey.'

Heart thumping, Daniel whipped around, searching for the source of this piratical comment. A tiny man with a fluffy white beard stood a short way behind him, legs akimbo, arms folded.

'And what might ye be up to, matey? No good, I'll be bound.'

Daniel stood his ground, unable to move as his mind attempted to analyse the situation: pirate, canal, dead body, wheelie bin. His mind gave up and classified the encounter as unlikely but happened, so wait and see. That was what he did since no words he could find seemed adequate or relevant.

The man closed in on Daniel until he was within head-butt range, stared up at him and belched loudly. A stench of beer and partly digested chips pulsed up Daniel's nostrils. This pirate was pissed.

'Oh dear, sorry,' the pirate said. 'I mean oooh arrh.'

Daniel's fear of discovery had dissipated in the face of this spaced-out loony. A quick escape was his requirement. Still, he couldn't resist.

'Why are you talking funny?'

The man drew himself up to his full five feet nothing and said, 'Don't you know? This is international talk like a pirate day. International,' he added for emphasis. 'And naturally, us real pirates have to join in.'

Daniel nodded sagely. 'Of course. So where's your ship then?'

'My ship?' The man glanced around vaguely. 'Me ship be lying off shore awaiting me going back to it when I'm done with me piracy. But here's me cutlass.'

Daniel watched, amused, as the man rummaged inside his jacket, but jumped back with a yelp as the pirate produced a wicked, serrated bread knife and lunged towards him.

'Have at thee, varlet.'

Ignoring Daniel, who had toppled against the wheelie bin, the pirate pushed past him and slashed away at the invisible enemy.

'Cross swords with me, eh? Back here you scurvy, yellow dog. Have no fear, Captain, I defend you to the death.'

This last was shouted back to Daniel who raised his eyes to heaven and offered thanks to whoever was in charge of pissed-up pirates. As the man staggered away in pursuit of the scurvy yellow dog, Daniel tipped the bin backwards and began his long push into town.

The address in Camberley Street that the inspector had given him was roughly the same distance from the canal as Daniel's flat, although in a steeply upmarket direction but not in an uphill direction to his relief. Nevertheless, he arrived red-faced and sweating and paused at the head of the street to take stock.

Camberley Street was long, lined on both sides by de-tached and semi-detached houses, most with good-sized gardens. Number fifty-seven was a long push away. He tightened his grip on the bin and began. Until that moment the back streets that Daniel had used were almost deserted bar the odd taxi, so he was dismayed to hear a vehicle approaching from be-hind, doubly dismayed to hear it slow as it passed him, and more than trebly dismayed to see the yellow flash of a police patrol car and a pair of keen eyes appraise him from the passenger seat. He flicked his head in the opposite direction and held his breath, but the car sped up and disappeared around the bend at the end of the street. He stopped and wiped a film of sweat from his forehead, only partly caused by the effort involved in pushing Celia.

The house beside him was number twenty-one, so almost halfway there, but he had only pushed for a few seconds more when he heard another vehicle coming up behind him. His heart did a bungee jump as the car passed. A police car: the same police car. It had gone around the block. It pulled into the kerb just ahead of him.

Daniel slowed. What should he do? Speed up and ignore them? Abandon Celia and run? Fall down and pretend he was dead – he did have a heart condition after all. It would be their fault if he died. They would be reprimanded, demoted. It would serve them right. That fleeting thought made him smile as he drew level and the car's window slid open.

'Good evening, sir. Can I ask what you have in there?' A pair of gimlet eyes surveyed Daniel from a granite face.

'In here?' Daniel looked at the wheelie bin as if he had just noticed it. 'Well, it's… erm…' Later he would examine his reply and wonder whether it indicated Machiavellian subtlety or astonishing idiocy. For now, it surprised him as much as it did the policeman. 'It's… a dead body.'

The policeman let out a long sigh and opened the car door. He swung around and levered himself out of the seat. He was a big man, towering over Daniel by at least a foot and casting a wide shadow on the pavement.

'Sir,' he began. 'I assure you that I have as well developed a sense of humour as the next man.' From the man's expression, Daniel knew this statement contained an element of untruth. 'But I must warn you that my colleague and I have had a very tiring evening and also that wasting police time is a criminal offence. Do you understand?'

Daniel nodded, appalled at what he had said.

'So, I repeat my question, *sir*, just what are you doing with a wheelie bin at this time of the morning?'

Aha, thought Daniel, not quite a repeat of the question. If he could just keep his head.

'I'm only helping my neighbour out.' He gestured vaguely ahead. 'See, I've been away, hardly any rubbish, but... Jack's always got too much so I said he could fill mine. My bin. My wheelie bin here. So... I'm taking it round there.'

The policeman nodded and made a show of glancing at his watch. 'At two o'clock in the morning?'

'Good heavens, is that the time?' *No, Daniel no.* 'I mean I promised it to him yesterday, but I've been away like. Like I say. So, had to get it to him. Always keep my promises. That's me. Promise keeper-in-chief.'

The policeman raised his eyes skywards. 'We'd better not detain you, sir. You're obviously going to have a busy morning.'

'Thank you, officer, thank you and a good night to you too and I hope you have a... and a pleasant shift and... right I'll be going.'

With obvious effort, Daniel heaved the bin to its balance point and trundled down the road. He paused at a gateway, waiting for the car to pass. It cruised slowly towards him and braked. He turned into the open gateway and started down the drive, much relieved to hear the patrol car move away.

A dog barked in the house in front of him. Time to move on. He crept back to the road and peered right and left. The patrol car seemed to have gone. It couldn't be far to fifty-seven. He retrieved the bin and trundled along the pavement.

A tall iron gate and equally tall hedge barred the driveway of fifty-seven. Thankfully, the gate was unlocked, and he pushed his heavy burden down a curving path, pausing as he came within sight of the palatial residence at its end. *House is empty, my son, guaranteed.* It was a modern house, looking as if its room-count matched its street number. An outbuilding on the right might have contained an Olympic swimming pool. He gazed in awe; how could a chief inspector of police afford this pile? It must be worth millions. He shook his head. Forget that. He had a job to do.

Pushing the bin before him, he trudged along the brick path that led to the left of the building. There, as Dick had briefed him, stood the king-size greenhouse. It *'ll be unlocked, my son, guaranteed*. And it was. Now for the final act. All right. Do it. He slid the door open.

The greenhouse was in keeping with the rest of the house: BIG. A variety of beds and staging stretched about him. From a choice of tools at the back, he picked out a sturdy spade and started excavating in a bed of tomato plants close to the door-way. Half an hour of sweaty work left him with a body-sized hole. Returning to the bin parked outside, he heaved it through the door and tipped it forwards. It crashed to the ground but not in the planned trajectory, instead bashing against the door-frame and sending a shiver through the entire greenhouse structure. He watched, mouth open, as a glazed pane at about head height, gently tipped inwards, hesitated for a full five seconds, then gravitated earthwards, finally shattering on the paving with a sound fit to raise Celia from her big sleep.

Daniel's heart stopped, or so it seemed, as he froze in position. What if, in spite of Dick's assurance, there was someone in the house? What if those policemen were still nosing about? He waited more than minutes, jumping at every rustle and bark but eventually decided that his luck had held. He reached into the bin, seized the plastic sack and dragged Celia from her tempo-rary coffin. With great effort and much swearing, he lugged her to the graveside and rolled her in.

The hole wasn't deep enough.

In despair, he stared at the hole and the plastic package sticking above the surface. Of course it wasn't deep enough. How could he possibly have thought it was deep enough? He was an idiot.

An hour later, he lay on his back, sweat soaking through his shirt into the cool earth below, staring at the glasshouse ceiling and the stars above. If only a friendly alien would abduct him. They were welcome to a few experiments in return for a new life on planet Bingo-Bongo. Still... he turned his head sideways and looked with satisfaction at the slightly raised bed and the row of wilting tomato plants. Job done. His problems were over. Well, this one was at least. Feeling lightheaded, he struggled upright, closed the greenhouse door behind him and pushed the blessedly lightweight bin back up the path.

Daniel's head was down as he pushed the bin up the gentle slope leading to the gate. So he was unaware of the two figures who stood there, watching. Unaware until one of them spoke.

'Well, well. Good evening, sir. Again.'

This was some sort of nightmare, Daniel decided, staring at the two familiar faces lounging by the gate. All he had to do was get home, and now, just when he thought his luck was holding, the fates piss on him. How much had they seen? He looked from one expressionless face to the other and decided that the answer was nothing. If he had been spotted manoeuvring a body into a hole, he would be lying on the ground with handcuffs on his wrists and a knee in his back. So...

'Um... good evening. Warm, isn't it?' He smiled and rubbed a grimy hand across a dripping forehead.

The policeman stared down from a great height. His expression indicated he had caught sight of a many-legged thing crawling from under a stone. 'Thought you were leaving your bin here. Sir.'

'Yes... no... It's the wrong house. I couldn't see the number.'

The policeman raised an eyebrow. 'This number on the outside of the gate? The one that says fifty-seven in very large numbers?'

'That one, yes. Bit short-sighted you know. With vision and so on. Easy to miss.'

Daniel tugged open the gate. 'Well, mustn't keep you guys. You'll have detecting to do. Looking for criminals and such like.'

'Just a moment, chum.' The sergeant's hand closed around Daniel's upper arm, squeezing unnecessarily hard. 'I'd like to see what's inside that precious bin of yours now you've got rid of the dead body.'

The world seemed to lurch but then he heard the sergeant's companion snigger. It was a joke. They likely thought he had been robbing this house. No problem then. The bin was empty.

'Sure, no problem,' he said, reaching for the lid with his free hand. But then he hesitated. The bin was empty, yes. Celia was buried, but was any trace of her left inside? Poor Celia had been treated exceptionally roughly. Had any of her broken free from the package? And were there any of those bits lurking at the bottom of the bin? Hair, blood, a hand even?

'No problem,' he repeated, as two pairs of eyes bored into him. 'OK,' he added, as his fingers closed around the handle and pulled at a lid that seemed to be super-glued to the rim of the bin.

'Ahoy, landlubbers!'

Two law officers and a relieved suspect turned as one, searching for the greeting's origin. Only the suspect knew what he would see.

A white-haired pirate advanced erratically towards them, bread knife in hand. 'Fear not, Captain, I am at your side.'

'Bloody hell,' breathed the sergeant, dropping his grip on Daniel's arm.

'You verminous scum will wish you'd never tangled with battling Jim Blackheart.'

The knife slashed towards the policeman who abruptly came to life. 'Right, Brian, let's get him.' They separated and cautiously advanced. A radio crackled.

Daniel was the audience at a piratical circus ring as the policemen pincered towards a drunken, knife-wielding nutter. He retreated a few steps, pulling the bin behind him. This manoeuvre felt so good that he repeated it, and repeated it again, and again until he was running as fast as an empty wheelie bin allowed, which was very fast indeed. From behind him came a cacophony of shouts, screams and curses, but this was of no concern to Daniel as he raced for home, with peace and the prospect of relative sanity within his grasp.

›››››› ‹‹‹‹‹‹

Sometime later, back in his flat after a hot shower and change of clothes, he sat nursing a warm beer and wondering why he had switched his fridge off on leaving the flat instead of the kettle. But that was life: a succession of mistakes and unintended consequences.

What now? Well, he had done the inspector's bidding, and the body was in place. As a result, Dick had agreed to help him with the mess he was in. Just what form that help would take once Dick was reinstated, he couldn't begin to guess. Would Dick be reinstated? He seemed confident, but Daniel guessed his colleagues had partied past midnight, possibly until one o'clock, when the man had been kicked out. But those two policemen had seen him outside the inspector's house. They would remember that when a body turned up: remember that a suspicious character with a wheelie bin had been doing god knew what. Daniel shrugged. They didn't know who he was and anything else was the inspector's problem. And Farquharson? What would he think when Celia's body turned up? But as beer lubricated his torpid brain, Daniel decided he didn't care what Farquharson thought. There was just one problem remaining: Lorraine. He would need help with that.

Twenty-Five

THE CALL WOKE DANIEL from a dream. The dream had been an enjoyable one in which several young ladies had smiled at him, removed their clothes and were about to let him sample their strawberry truffles when a mad monk appeared and stamped his feet. Stamping feet morphed into a firm knock at his front door.

'Shit,' Daniel muttered as he heaved himself to his feet and grumbled to the door.

'Shit,' he muttered as he saw the middle-aged man in suit and tie who stood outside, briefcase in hand.

'Delivery for Daniel Dreghorn.'

He resisted the temptation to say Mr Dreghorn was not at home, remembering just in time that the vague plan that had been gestating required the presence of this particular package. Instead, he took the hefty briefcase from the man.

'You will be contacted with...'

'Final details,' Daniel finished the sentence

The man frowned. 'Expect a text.'

'I can't even say it,' he mouthed.

Something dark flashed in the man's eyes. 'This is a project dear to Number One's heart,' he snapped. 'Please treat it seriously.'

Daniel shrugged. 'Sure, yeah.'

'Be alert.' The man saluted smartly and was gone.

Pushing the door shut, Daniel returned to his seat and set the briefcase down carefully on the floor in front of him. He looked at it for some time, then dunked a tea-bag in a mug of hot water and stared some more at the briefcase. He opened a can of Guinness and continued to stare. Finally, he reached over and tried the lock. It was, of course, locked.

He sat back and mulled over the possible suggestion of the hint of a plan that had formed in his mind. He nodded to himself, may even have talked to himself and, as he did so, some interesting possibilities crystallised.

—»»» «««—

'One like this,' Daniel said, showing the assistant the photograph he had taken.

Rodney Emhurst Ltd was an old-fashioned leather goods shop: leather goods in the strictly non-fetish sense of the expression. The type of shop that is over-supplied with assistants and under-whelmed by customers. The window display had given Daniel hope that he would find what he needed.

The assistant stared at the photograph for a long time. He then stared at Daniel, who remembered that the shirt he had picked up had a rather frayed collar.

'You wish one exactly the same, sir?'

'Exactly the same, please.'

'We do have a high-quality own brand.'

Daniel sighed. Why did people never listen to him? Perhaps it was a body language thing. He straightened his slumped shoulders.

'I would like this case, thank you. Assuming you have one.'

'Oh yes, we have it.' The assistant paused and coughed. 'You do realise this is a Mulberry Lucian?'

'I don't care if it's a raspberry tart. This is what I want, OK?'

'Of course, of course, sir. Just a moment, please.' The assistant hurried away, disappearing through a door at the back of the shop.

Daniel wandered around the displays of shiny leather cases and handbags on glass shelves. A prickling on the nape of his neck made him swivel around to find the assistant and an older man both staring at him from the doorway. The assistant hurried forward.

'Here we are, sir, as you ordered.' He held up a shiny cardboard box.

Daniel followed him to the counter and watched as the case was unpacked, uncomfortably aware that he was still being eyed by the older man.

'Excuse me, but is that a shoplifter over there?' He nodded towards the man in the doorway.

The assistant's face reddened. He whispered, 'Sir, that is the manager, Mr Doombs.'

'Well, tell him from me, he looks like a shoplifter.'

'Here is your case. Would you like to check it, sir?'

Daniel looked at the gleaming leather briefcase sitting on the counter. It was identical to the one in his flat.

'Yeah, it'll do.'

'I'll just pack it up for you.'

'No problem. I'll just take it as it is.'

The assistant blinked several times. 'As it is? But...'

'There's a handle, isn't there? Easier to carry, right?'

For a moment, it looked as if the assistant would argue, but he turned away and started punching numbers into his till. 'Would you like some leather treatment, sir? We highly recommend...'

'No, no, it's fine.'

'I recommend it to retain the leather's suppleness. Otherwise...'

'I said it's fine. I'm not keeping it long.'

With a shake of his head, the assistant returned to the till. 'How will you be paying, sir?'

Daniel glanced in his wallet. Two twenties, that was all. Best not to use up all his spare cash. 'Better be credit card.'

'Fine, sir. If you will just place your card in the slot. That will be eight hundred and forty-nine pounds and ninety-nine pence.'

To Daniel, the world around him slowed. He seemed to watch from a great distance as a hand, presumably his own and definitely holding his credit card, crawled towards the gaping maw of the card reader.

'Forty-nine pounds?' he heard a voice say.

'And ninety-nine pence. Yes, sir.'

There had been another number. Had he heard correctly? It couldn't be. The last briefcase he had bought was from Lidl's stocktaking sale and had cost him nine ninety-nine. It had been an attractive pastel-green shade and had lasted for months.

His card was nearing the slot. Did he really need this case? Perhaps an own brand would do. There might be a case looking almost the same. But having identical cases was a crucial part of his plan. If they weren't mistaken for each other, it would all fall apart. Lives depended on him. With a start, he realised his card was in the slot.

'If you could just enter your PIN, sir.'

What credit did he have left? He had a lot owing on this card but there must be some. But how much? Hundreds, yes, but was it enough? The decision was taken from him as he watched a finger type his PIN into the keypad. Hell, how did they know? At this moment, he couldn't even remember his PIN.

'Thank you, sir. There's your receipt, and here's your brief-case. The guarantee and owner's manual are inside. A quality item. It will give you many years of pleasure. If I may be bold, sir, a very discerning choice.' The assistant shook Daniel's free hand and guided him towards the door. 'Should there be any problems, we offer a free aftercare and advice service.'

The roar of rush-hour traffic clicked Daniel's brain back into gear as he stood outside the shop, briefcase in hand. He turned to stare back through the plate-glass door and watched, blankly, as the manager and assistant high-fived. The manager caught his eye and abruptly turned away, adjusting his fuchsia-tinted tie.

Twenty-Six

DANIEL PEERED AT THE two cases as they sat side by side on his kitchen table. There was no question that they were identical. Perhaps the bomb case had a few scuff marks, but he could easily duplicate that. He smiled as he thought of the salesman's reaction should he find his shiny Mulberry whatsit being buffed by a piece of sandpaper. The weight was wrong of course. The new case would need supplementing, but he had already rescued several bricks from the back court. In the meantime, he needed food to fortify him for the evening.

A rifle through the sparse contents of his fridge and cupboard produced a few slices of bread long past their sell-by date, some blue brie that may or may not have been blue when he bought it, several cans of Stella and an unopened jar of Marmite. He looked at the feast for a full minute before admitting defeat and cracking open a can. As he drank, his phone warbled, announcing a text.

The message was clear. *Contact will call with instructions–one hour–be there.* This was it. If his plan was to work, he had to move. He rummaged through his wallet for the card he had looked out earlier and keyed in the taxi company's number.

'Hi, I'm looking for Beezer?'

'Beezer the geezer here. Where to, mate?'

'I need your help, actually.'

'What?'

'Need your help. You gave me a ride before.'

'Not with you, mate. Before what?'

Daniel took a deep breath. 'It was a few weeks ago. You helped me follow a car.'

There was silence for a moment, followed by a low whistle. 'Hey... yeah... right, I remember. MI you know what. With you now, squire. You just tell me what and when.'

'OK, I need you at an address I'll give. Just wait outside until I join you and then we need to follow someone.'

'No problemo, partner. You've come to the right guy. Not a word to nobody, that right?'

'Spot on Beezer. Mum's the word.'

'Mum? Mum,' Beezer repeated. 'Sure, I'll remember.'

Daniel spelt out his address, slowly, to avoid mistakes.

Ten minutes later, he heard squealing brakes and glanced outside to see a taxi sitting on the far side of the road, engine idling. He nodded to himself and ticked the first point on his mental list.

The next fifty minutes allowed him to finish the two cans and institute an unsuccessful search for a third, a search interrupted by his doorbell. The same unsmiling face greeted him on the doorstep, and a small box was thrust into his hands.

'Your device.'

'Thanks,' Daniel said and stared at the man. 'It might never happen.'

'It had better,' the man snapped back and turned away.

Daniel dropped the package on the floor, picked up the bomb briefcase, pushed the door so that a crack remained and watched the man disappear downstairs. He threw on his jacket, pulled the door shut noisily behind him and crept to the head of the stairs. He could clearly hear feet descending and followed them downstairs as quietly as he could.

Once outside, as the delivery man slipped into his Volvo, Daniel scampered across the road to where Beezer waited. His accomplice bounded out, pulled open a rear door and saluted smartly as Daniel slipped inside.

'Where to, guv?'

'That car, quick.' Daniel gestured at the Volvo's disappearing taillights.

'Yes,' Beezer mouthed, clenched his fist and threw himself behind the wheel.

The taxi's wheels spun as it raced towards the top of the road and screeched left. 'Don't you worry, squire, he'll not lose me.'

Daniel stared anxiously through the windscreen at the forest of tail lights ahead. Were they following the right car?

'Are you sure...?' he began.

'I'm on it,' Beezer interrupted. 'The one in front of the one in front, that's your man. Don't want to be seen, see.'

Daniel sat back. There was nothing he could do. Several silent minutes passed as the taxi weaved through busy traffic.

'Do a lot of this, do you, squire?'

'Too bloody much,' Daniel muttered.

'Know what you mean. Get the picture.' Beezer winked into the driver's mirror. 'No routine in your job, every day different.'

'Yeah, well.' He sighed and resigned himself to playing the MI5 card.

Five minutes had passed, but they had passed very slowly for Daniel, as he watched the Volvo turn into the gateway of a dark, Victorian mansion. Beezer cut the taxi's engine as they passed the gate and coasted to a halt. From what he had seen of the house as they drifted past, he was now certain that this was the place where he had previously met Number One.

'This will count towards my application, right?'

'Application?' Daniel watched the upper floor where a light had just come on.

'Yeah, took you up on your suggestion.'

'Right.' He was debating whether to stay where he was, relatively safe, or take his chance at creeping up to the house while it was occupied. A quick escape might be needed. Would Beezer wait for him? Hold on, what had the man said? 'My suggestion?'

'Yeah, to apply, to your lot. The university.' He mimed air quotes. 'Did it online.'

Daniel stared at Beezer. He didn't want to know but felt he had to ask. 'Ah... where did you apply?'

'Like you said. Coatdyke University. Filled in the form. Said I'd work anywhere. Gave you as a reference.'

'Oh, bloody...'

'What?'

'Nothing, nothing.' Daniel shook his head. This was a distraction. 'I need to get in there. Will you wait for me here?'

'Sure, squire. No problemo. Better wait a mo though. Your guy's coming back.'

Daniel glanced behind and sure enough, the courier had appeared at the gateway. The man stopped and glanced towards the taxi. Daniel ducked below the level of the rear window and prayed. What could he say if caught here? Nothing, he would likely be dead. He hunkered down, prayed that he couldn't be seen and that the growing pressure in his bladder was psychosomatic.

Time passed. Beezer started whistling to himself; it sounded like the funeral march. Daniel sweated. Eventually, he hissed, 'What's happening?'

Beezer half-turned. 'What's that, squire? Can't hear you.'

'I said, what's he doing?'

'That guy? Oh, he's gone. Left a couple of minutes ago?'

'Shit.' Daniel struggled upright and turned around. The car had disappeared. 'Why didn't you...' He stared into Beezer's wide eyes. 'Oh, never mind. I'm going into that house.' He pushed open the taxi's door.

'Need any help, squire?'

'Just wait for me, OK?' Daniel muttered, grabbed his briefcase and headed for the top of the drive.

As he crept towards the building, keeping to the shadows, he realised that he hadn't a clue how to get inside. Burglary was a new addition to his litany of crimes. Perhaps there would be an open window. But a quick circuit of the house, several bruises and two sopping wet feet later, he had to admit that all the windows were tightly shut.

Stepping to the nearest window, he gave the frame a hard thump, more in frustration than hope. He didn't expect it to spring open and it didn't. He clenched his teeth and clenched his buttocks, debating whether this would be a good time and place to relieve himself.

'Wouldn't do that if I were you, squire.'

Daniel whipped around, his heart making an urgent bid to escape through his chest, and gaped at Beezer. 'I told you to wait.'

The man shrugged. 'Probably alarmed, see.' He pointed at the window and stepped forward, a lumpy toolbag in his hand. 'You want in here, right?'

Daniel nodded.

Beezer peered at the window and shone a powerful torch around the inside of the frame. 'Thought so.' He nodded. 'Just a cheapo magnet system. Soon be in.'

He produced what looked like a large bar magnet from his toolbox and held it against the window frame, then forced a flat chisel underneath and levered upwards. The window lurched open and Beezer blu-tacked a smaller magnet to the contact, stood back, folded his arms and winked.

Daniel decided questions were best left for later. He slipped one leg over the sill, then the other.

'You'll need this, squire.' Beezer pressed his torch into Daniel's hand.

He took the torch gratefully, turned away, and briefcase clutched to his chest, headed into the darkness.

Twenty-Seven

ATTEMPTING TO ORIENTATE HIMSELF, Daniel flashed the torch around the room. Cooker, fridge and a smell of frying: clearly the kitchen. A door in the corner led to a wide hallway. Dim light filtered through a large, glazed front entrance. The place smelt of money and dusty carpet. An upright clock ticked lugubriously in an alcove near the stairs. Apart from the clock, there was total silence save for his thudding heart.

The courier had gone upstairs, so that was where he had to be, but first he crept towards the door on the right of the stairway. It opened soundlessly, and a rapid sweep of the torch confirmed that this was the room where Number One had interviewed him. It would do. Skirting several armchairs and tables, he made his way to the wide bay window where a chunky settee sat. He shoved the briefcase under the settee as far as his arm would reach. Completely invisible. Now he had to, he simply had to.

The room was vast, walls lined with old portraits and expensive-looking antique furniture, but everywhere a feeling of dust and neglect. Nowhere here, then. But wait, this was a Victorian house. All the furnishings looked original, or at least in period. Now, didn't the Victorians have...?

Yes. To the left, set in a discrete corner, was a bow-fronted sideboard with two wide and deep drawers. He pulled the bottom one open and congratulated himself on a piece of smart detective work. The commode's decorated ceramic bowl was set into a plain, wooden shelf. There wasn't a moment to spare. With torch gripped between his teeth, Daniel aimed as best he could in the wavering light, trying hard to keep the burnished walnut exterior dry, and nearly succeeding. A linen antimacassar from a nearby chair served to mop up a few errant drips. Job done, he spread the slightly damp fabric over the chair back. With the well-known equation, *empty bladder equals clear head*, helping his concentration, he closed the door behind him and continued the quest.

Heart beating faster, he mounted the broad stairway to reach the first landing. Mysterious doorways spread on either side each firmly shut in the wavering torchlight. The light he had seen from outside had been on the next floor so he ignored the mysteries and carried on upwards. Again, a corridor stretched to left and right and there, from under the third door along, seeped a sliver of yellow light: a light that snapped off as Daniel's foot creaked on the landing. It had to be Lorraine, but was there anyone with her? No. If any of the plonkers were around, they would have been out here waving guns, not skulking in a room.

He knocked cautiously on the door. 'Lorraine? Is that you? It's me, Daniel.'

There was no reply, no sound at all from inside the room, and of course the door was locked. 'Lorrie, I've come to rescue you. Don't worry, I'll get you out.'

How to get through a locked door? The frame was strong and solid, not original, probably reinforced. A shoulder charge would do no good. That point had been proved in many movies. Something more was required. Torchlight picked out lots of pictures, a bookcase and books and several sturdy chairs. Just the job.

He dragged a chair to the door, lined the back up with the lock and took a trial swing. The result on the door was nil, but his heart rate headed into the stratosphere as a quickly stifled scream came from within. Well, there was no doubt now. 'Lorraine. I'll be with you in a minute. Don't worry. Stay clear of the door.'

With renewed strength, he swung the chair again and again. On the fourth swing, there was a crack as the wood around the lock splintered and Daniel's momentum carried him into darkness.

⟫⟫ ⟪⟪

What a lot of pretty lights. He stared at the night sky above him. The universe was huge and so many, many stars: red, blue, green, magnolia with sparkles. And all moving so fast, circling around and around a central core. Perhaps this was the opposite of the big bang: the infamous big crunch, where it all ends and everything spirals down into a singularity that disappears up its own analysis. Mind you that didn't explain why his hands were tied behind his back, or why there was a knee pressing on his throat.

The stars had gone and now he saw the light. It came from a gaudy and probably expensive chandelier that floated above him attached to the ceiling of a room that was presumably the one he had broken into some time ago. He attempted to turn his head, but the knee got in the way.

It wasn't his own knee he realised. That would be surreal and mean he was either dreaming or dead. No, this knee had another owner. The owner spoke.

'Who the fuck are you?'

Now, Daniel's brief experience of life had taught him that the answer to seemingly simple and innocent questions such as this could, in certain circumstances, be of great importance. He firmly believed this to be one of those circumstances. He tried to think through a range of answers but hadn't got very far before

193

a head lurched into his field of view, eclipsing the chandelier. A head surrounded by a hairy halo.

'Lorraine?' he croaked.

The knee pressed harder into his Adam's apple. Not Lorraine, then.

'Come on, you heap of crap. I know you're one of them, but why the hell d'you have to break in? Lost the key or something?'

Daniel tried to say, 'I can't speak,' but as he really couldn't, what came out was a noise like a frog on heat.

The knee was removed from his throat causing a sudden inrush of air to his lungs and a rush of oxygen to his brain. The room snapped into focus. He watched as a young woman got to her feet, kicked him none too gently on the buttocks, and took a seat somewhere above him. There was a sharp intake of breath.

'Aw Jeez! You?' Then a moment's pause before she continued. 'Right, give.'

Daniel stared at the woman. 'My god. Sandra? It's you.'

'I'm waiting.'

'It's me. Daniel. From Coatdyke.'

'I can see that now. I've got working eyes. I want to know why you're keeping me here, arsehole.'

'I'm not one of them,' Daniel croaked.

'You can do better than that.' Her expression told him he had to do better.

'Came to rescue you.'

'Yeah, right.'

'No, really. I mean I thought you were Lorraine, my girlfriend. She was kidnapped. I thought she was here. They told me they had her.'

Sandra frowned at him. 'You know you sound so pathetic that I almost believe you.'

'It's true. Every word.'

'Daniel! Fucking hell.'

'Ah.. yes?'

She was staring at him rather oddly.

'They kept telling me that a Daniel was working for them and that he only had to deliver and everything would be OK. I kept telling them I didn't know any Daniel, and he didn't know me. They laughed in my face. Never thought about you for a second. Days they've kept me here. Threatened me. Bastards.'

Daniel's mind whirled so fast it was in danger of overheating. Lorraine wasn't here. The loonies were holding Sandra thinking she was Lorraine. So, she wasn't kidnapped. They had no hold over him. but... where was she? He was almost worse off now. At least before he had thought he knew where she was being kept.

'Do you think you could maybe...?' He rolled to one side to remind her he was tied, very uncomfortably tied.

She frowned, 'Oh, all right. I suppose so.'

Daniel made encouraging noises but closed his eyes tight when she produced a large knife and sliced rather cavalierly through the rope tying his hands. He staggered upright and then collapsed into a chair, massaging swollen wrists.

Sandra sat nearby, biting her thumbnail. 'Well, I guess you've saved me.'

'Looks like it.' He grimaced. Pain had returned with circulation, and he didn't enjoy it.

She extended a hand towards him. 'I owe you.'

They shook formally. Wait a moment. He glanced at her hand then lifted the other one. 'You've got all your fingers.'

She stared at him as if his head had rotated on its axis. 'Of course I've got all my fingers, dummy.'

'It's just that they sent me a photograph and a... thing.'

'A thing?'

'Yeah, a finger. In a bag. At least that's what I thought.'

'They took my photograph with a newspaper but no finger, look.' She held up both hands.

'Yeah, that photograph. How could...' How closely had he looked at the photograph? He hadn't wanted to see it, not really. And the thing in the bag? Well, it wasn't Lorraine's finger, and it wasn't Sandra's. Someone else? Or something that looked like a finger? Crap. That was it. A sausage or an animal bit. They had fooled him and fooled themselves by mistaking his colleague for his girlfriend.

'I can't believe you've done this for me, Daniel.'

'What? Well, actually...' He hesitated. It was perhaps not wise to emphasise that he had not done this for *her* at all. 'We should go right now. They could come back.'

'Oh my god. Come on.' She raised the knife still grasped in her fist. 'They'll not get me a second time.'

Daniel led the way back to the kitchen. At the window, he switched his torch off and listened. 'OK, it's all clear. You go first.' But Sandra was already through the gap and heading for the shelter of the bushes.

He took a last look around and slid a leg over the windowsill. Once out, he pulled the sash down and turned to the darkness. There was a muffled scream and then silence.

'Sandra?' His legs wobbled. 'Is that you?'

Had one of the allotment men returned? He wanted to run and not stop until he reached his flat but caution prevailed.

There was another voice, pleading. 'No, no...'

He took a breath and plunged into the bushes. Sandra was on her knees, beside the prone figure of a man, with her knife pressed dangerously into his throat.

'Don't worry, I've got the bastard,' she hissed. 'One move chum and you're pedigree dog meat.'

Daniel stared at Beezer's popping eyes. 'No, Sandra, he's a friend.'

'A friend? He tried to jump me.'

'No,' Beezer gurgled, swallowing in an attempt to keep his throat from contacting the tip of the knife. 'I never.'

'Damn right you never. You never got the chance. I ought to—'

'Sandra, he helped me. He's a taxi driver. He'll take us back.' Daniel was growing worried that she seemed determined to make use of the knife. A vision of a bloodied corpse floated in front of him. He did not want another corpse in his life.

She glared at him through narrowed eyes. 'Oh yes?'

'Honestly,' Daniel raised his hands.

Sandra stood up. 'Well Mister Taxi Driver, you are very lucky.'

Shakily, Beezer got to his feet and retreated a few steps. 'Is this a test?' he muttered to Daniel.

Daniel shook his head as Sandra said, 'What's this creature on about?'

'Tell you later. Come on, we've got to move.' He turned away and strode down the drive.

They sat in Beezer's cab in silence, heading for Daniel's flat. What was he going to do? Get Sandra back to her parents of course, but what then? He didn't want to be a hero with his picture plastered over the papers. Right now he needed a low profile, preferably a flat one.

'Your Dad will be glad to have you back, I suppose?' he said.

She sniffed and waved a hand. 'He'll make a show of it, that's for sure. It'll be a big production. He's a policeman, a head one, everything he does is for his career.'

Suspicion prickled on Daniel's neck. No, it was impossible. What was her second name? He must have seen it somewhere, but she had always been Sandra in the labs. He cleared his throat. 'What was your second name again?'

'Merrywick, of course.'

Yes, it was inevitable. Nausea grabbed his stomach and gave it a shake. It was him, it had to be: Dick's boss. Sandra's father was Dick's boss. The complications in his life were sprouting complications. He needed to get out of this. Right now, going back to his flat didn't seem the best plan as he preferred that neither Sandra nor her father knew where he lived. Traffic was light, but they were still five minutes away. He leant forward. 'Thanks, Beezer, that's great, anywhere here.'

Beezer's head swivelled around. 'What?'

Winking desperately, Daniel mouthed, 'Just stop here at my flat, thanks. Right here.'

'Yeah, OK,' Beezer muttered. He appeared to have lost confidence since his run-in with Sandra.

The cab pulled into the side and Daniel ushered Sandra out, but before he could slam the door Beezer tugged at his sleeve.

'Did I pass?' he muttered, puppy-dog eyes blinking.

Daniel gave another wink and a thumbs-up before banging the door shut and watched as an obviously relieved Beezer disappeared into the night.

Sandra stood, hands on hips, frowning. 'I thought you lived in a flat?'

'Yes. I mean...' He glanced around the short street of detached houses. 'That is, I call it a flat. It's not a flat as such. More of a house you would call it. Don't like to show off, see.'

'You're strange,' she said. 'Well? Where are we going?'

'Where are we going?' Daniel echoed, head swivelling from side to side. 'Here, right here. This is it.' He pointed to the left. The houses all looked much the same, some with lights on, most not. He had chosen an unlit detached house with an enormous hedge.

'All I want to do is sit down.'

'Of course,' Daniel said, leading the way down the drive. 'I'll make you tea or something.'

They paused by the front door as he made a show of fumbling in his pocket. 'Oh dear, I've forgotten my door key.'

'Christ, Daniel...'

'Don't worry. You just wait here. I've got the other key. I'll go around the back and let you in.'

'It's OK, I'll come with you.'

'No!' Daniel grabbed her arm before she could move. 'It's... I mean there's a lot of stuff back there. You might trip over something.'

'Oh, all right but hurry up will you?' she snapped.

He strode confidently along the path at the front of the house and turned the corner. Once out of Sandra's sight, he scuttled to the rear of the property and surveyed the inky-black garden. At the back, he could make out the outline of a tall fence behind a barricade of leafy vegetable plots and bean poles. That was the best choice. Going right or left meant he would have to return to the street at some point and possibly difficult explanations.

Unfortunately for Daniel, the owners of this house were not the tidiest of gardeners, as he discovered when his scurrying feet were introduced to a latticework of bamboo poles lying in wait behind the greenhouse. He barely had time to lift his hands in defence as a bed of broccoli rose up and smashed him in the face.

'Daniel? That you?'

Sandra's plaintive call woke him from a stupor. His first instinct was to run and run very fast, but the small part of his brain still functional reminded him that he was lying flat, at least partly hidden by a greenhouse, and the garden was very dark. Intelligence won, and he lay prone and silent.

He heard Sandra knocking at the back door and winced as an upstairs light clicked on and a curtain twitched.

'I'm going around the front again, Daniel. Please let me in.'

The curtains closed, and another light came on. This could get complicated, too complicated. Daniel struggled to his feet, untangled himself from broccoli and bamboo and made a dash for the rear fence. It was above head height but with the strength of panic, he reached for the top of the solid panel and hauled himself up. There was no time for the subtleties of philosophical questions such as – *I wonder what's on the other side?* Instead, with a muttered prayer to any deity who might have had a spare moment to listen, he hurled himself over the fence.

Twenty-Eight

DANIEL FLOATED IN BATH-WATER, staring at whorls of steam wafting around the bathroom ceiling. Scalding water eased his joints, numbing the pain in his back and his muscles and his legs. There wasn't a single part of him that didn't hurt. Some of the purple bruises on his thighs appeared to have developed their own deeper-coloured bruises. He tried to let the tension and worry ease from his mind, but the traumatic events of the last few hours kept playing over and over in his head.

For instance, who would have thought the rear fence of that garden bordered a deep railway cutting? At first, he had felt he was free-falling and that his end had come. He wasn't much happier to find he was rolling around and around and down and down a grassy embankment. Finally, he came to rest with his head in contact with cool metal and somehow still alive. He had only just become aware of being alive and of the cool metal, when the lights of the late-running and unusually busy 11.15 to Glasgow Central flooded his dark-adjusted pupils. As he had not the faintest idea where he was in relation to the rails, that he could now see his skin turning bright pink was the result of a fifty-fifty chance as he threw himself off the track instead of onto it.

Daniel closed his eyes as sweat formed on his forehead, only in part due to the water's temperature. Still, here he was, he reflected as he towelled himself dry and admired his rich crop of bruises in the mirror — alive. It was more than many people could say, the dead ones that is.

At least he had left Sandra behind. He was sorry for her. She had been through a kidnapping. Mind you, she had tried to asphyxiate him with a knee on his Adam's apple, but that was understandable in the circumstances and he didn't wish her any harm. She would find her way home safely for certain, the chief point being she didn't know where he lived. He shook his head. Her father was Dick's former boss, the man in whose garden he had planted Celia. He hadn't seen that coming. But right now it wasn't important. It was four o'clock in the morning and he needed sleep.

He woke with a bang, the bang of something dropping through his letterbox. A groan escaped his lips. Movement was painful. The postman came about midday so thankfully he had had a decent sleep. He moved his hands around and was pleased to find he had made it into his bed before falling asleep. But the bedside clock said eight; the post was early. In fact, he couldn't remember when he had last received any post. Only four hours of sleep, it wasn't enough. No one could survive on four hours sleep. His tongue was rough as sandpaper, and every joint complained as he levered himself upwards and swung out of bed. Hobbling to the kitchen, he switched on the kettle, switched it off, filled it, and switched it on again before struggling to the front door to retrieve a brown envelope.

No stamp, no address. From the Allotment Society for certain. He threw it onto the kitchen table, knowing precisely what it contained and prepared a cup of instant. Did he want to open that envelope? Did he need to? he wondered, sipping his coffee and staring at the package. After all, they had no hold over him now. They didn't have Lorraine. But what might they do on discovering that he had released their captive? They would not be happy gardeners.

He reached over and ripped the envelope open, fished a sheet of paper from it and read:

Tuesday 17th 16.30 Central to Westerton. Initiate 16.52. Initiation code: Channel 5, guide, mute.

Good luck

Daniel dropped the paper as if it had burst into flames. Indeed perhaps it might for added authenticity. But no, it lay, inert, on the table, challenging him. Would his plan work? Did he have to do anything?

He had to put it aside for now. His priority was Lorraine. What was he going to do? She had been missing for ten days, ten very eventful days, so eventful that he had pushed her disappearance from the front of his mind on occasion. Now he knew the nutters didn't have her, so where was she?

He should report it to the police, but that was not an option as he had to keep well clear of the police. Perhaps he should ask Dick for help. That could be the answer. It was the answer, he decided with increasing certainty. The policeman would know what to do. He might have contacts. He might well be insane, but that didn't mean he didn't have contacts.

Feeling pleased with himself, he popped a slice of bread in the toaster and pulled open the sitting-room blinds. Outside, birds sang and did things that appeared to be enjoyable. A couple wandered past holding hands and almost smiling at what might have been a joke. Above the grey clouds, no doubt the sun shone just waiting for a chance to warm the earth. Daniel examined the strange feeling that threatened to overwhelm him and decided it was optimism. Something he hadn't known for many weeks. And so it was that he was smiling when his mobile beeped to signal a text.

He picked it up, but before he read the message, it announced an incoming call from a withheld number.

'Hello,' he said, still feeling the after-effects of the dose of optimism that had washed over him.

'No need for names, my boy. This must be private.'

'Professor?' A small cloud coalesced over Daniel's head.

'Please, Daniel, I said no... Oh bother.' There was a pause during which Daniel stared at the ceiling.

'Right, OK, ah... Dennis, yes Dennis, it is imperative that we meet to discuss events. Do you understand me, Dennis?'

'Yes, professor, I understand.' A light drizzle fell from the cloud.

'Please, Dan... Dennis, this must be anonymous, understand? We meet this afternoon at... our place of learning, understand? Ring me three times when you are close and we shall pass each other accidentally in the ah... just outside the entrance of the place where we learn... things. Understand?'

Daniel watched his personal cloud begin a relentless precipitation. 'Professor you're...'

'What?'

Daniel breathed hard. 'You're wittering, that's what.'

'Watering? Well... In any case, this afternoon, understand?'

'Yes!' Daniel stabbed the hang-up button as hard as he could and stood for a moment trying to soothe his anger and his throbbing finger.

What did the man want? He had disposed of a body for him, what more could he possibly ask? Whatever it was, the idiot would not get it! He grabbed his cold toast and slapped a slab of hard butter onto it. An attempt to spread it left him with a heap of toast bits and a knife in his fist that he would dearly have loved to use on Farquharson. Instead, he took several deep breaths and opened the local paper that had been lying behind his door last night. A picture of a man in the lower corner of page two caused him to pause; he knew that face. Who was it? He scanned the brief paragraph. The man was a postman who stood accused of dumping much of his delivery round in a skip. That was him. It was his local postman. A new man whom Daniel had seen a few times grumping heavily up the stairs. Now wait—when *had* he last received a letter?

Indignation seized him. It was weeks since his letterbox had last rattled other than with personal deliveries from crazed horticulturists. OK, he never did get many letters, but there hadn't even been junk. This man had skipped his junk mail, and that wasn't right. His fists tightened. It was his prerogative to decide what to skip. He would complain and demand compensation.

Only nine o'clock and the day was not going well. What now? Wait, there had been a text, hadn't there? Just before the professor's call. He pulled out his mobile, checked the last text, and his day suddenly went from just bad to why-did-I-get-up-this-morning bad.

Must meet discuss progress re op dragon 11 am train station Dick.

Daniel shook his head. Operation dragon? Where had he dredged that from? But he would have to meet the man again. His hopes of finding Lorraine rested on those hunched shoulders and plucked nose.

⤜⤜⤜ ⤛⤛⤛

The station was little used. Once an hour a dirty diesel rumbled its way into central Glasgow, and once an hour another diesel dawdled back, disgorged a few complaining passengers, and repeated the cycle.

Daniel sat on a cold metal bench, designed, by means of its strangely curved back, to provide great discomfort to the weary traveller, and watched a crisp packet waltz across the deserted platform. Eleven AM? Well, the time now was twenty past eleven, and his patience was running low. He jumped as a hand touched his shoulder and spun around to see Inspector Dick with a finger to his lips.

'Sorry to startle you, squire. Just checking out the vicinity. We're all clear.' He sidled around the bench and slouched onto it, uncomfortably close to Daniel.

'Got to be sure we're not seen together, not obviously together. Knew this would be a good place for a talk.'

Daniel stared over the Inspector's left shoulder at the glass eye of a security camera and wondered if he should mention it but decided not to ruin the man's trust in himself.

'Hear you did a grand job, squire.' Dick tilted the brim of his hat up slightly and turned to stare at Daniel.

'They nearly caught me,' he said, indignation bubbling.

'Ah, but they didn't, eh?'

'Two cops were prowling around. They saw me coming out of that house.'

The Inspector squeezed his lips together, frowned, scratched his nose, and shrugged. 'It won't matter. They're friends of mine.' He mouthed the word *friends* instead of saying it.

'What? You've talked to them?'

Dick tapped his nose and looked as if he was attempting to cross his eyes. 'Let's just say there isn't a problem, OK?'

Had he really talked to them, or was he trying to prevent his protégé from worrying? 'All right, all right, so there isn't a problem. So the police force is even more corrupt than I thought.'

Dick frowned and tutted at this slur on his colleagues but spoiled the effect by winking. 'Everything is in hand. Merrywick's bread has been buttered, and he's heading for the slicer. There's a strange thing though, his daughter.'

Daniel bit his lip. 'What about his daughter?'

'Well, it turns out she had been abducted. No one knew anything about it and just last night she appears unexpectedly, claiming some wanker rescued her. Merrywick's over the moon, but he'll soon be down to earth.' Dick chuckled. 'Wouldn't have any knowledge about that I suppose? By any chance?'

Daniel shrugged. 'How could I possibly?'

'OK... So, I wanted to say that I'll be able to render some assistance to yourself. That is in relation to your situational position.' A strange expression formed on Dick's face as if the lemon he thought he'd swallowed had turned out to be a peach. 'When I get my job back.'

'Great, but there's something else.'

'Is there?' Dick asked, one of his eyelids flickering.

'Yes. It's my girlfriend. She's... well, she's missing.' Daniel realised that he was very limited in what he could tell the man about Lorraine's disappearance. He certainly could say nothing about his belief for the last fortnight that the mad gardeners were responsible.

'And?'

'Well, I just wondered if, with your resources, you might be able to help me find her. Possibly.'

'We'll see,' Dick snapped and pulled himself to his feet. The meeting was over.

'I'm really desperate to find her.'

'Yes, yes.' He brushed the seat of his trousers. 'I'll see what I can do.'

The man would do exactly nothing, Daniel thought bitterly, as the Inspector sauntered along the platform. Dick had blackmailed him into shuffling the dead around and now the job was done he was being abandoned. Why had he ever expected help there?

He got up, tired and depressed. What now? How would he find Lorraine? Practical matters first; he glanced around and located the station toilet. It was a small and smelly room with two urinals against an outside wall and frosted windows at head height above. He took a cautious sniff and wrinkled his nose.

Unzipping his flies with one hand, he reached up with the other and pushed open one of the small window panes. Glancing left, he saw Dick stroll from the station entrance and descend the steps en route to the car park. Then he stopped and appeared to do a double-take. In the car park was a police car with two officers emerging. They took a direct line for Dick who did not look as if he was expecting to meet his ex-colleagues for tea and crumpets. Instead, he stepped backwards and might have been intending to run, but another policeman was behind him and had a firm grip on his arm.

Daniel jerked back from the window. Dick was being arrested. Gooseflesh crawled on his neck. What did this mean for him? He peered outside again to see the man led away to the police car with much loud protesting. Shit, now they might come for him. Had his meeting with Dick been monitored? He was trapped in here. He glanced at the door and watched, horrified, as it swung open.

A wide and bulky man filled the doorway, cutting out most of the light. The man advanced into the room, seeming to fill the small toilet as he lumbered towards Daniel who shrank to one side, attempting to disguise himself as a pattern of green and white tiles. The man paused beside him, glanced slowly down and then up, and his face cracked into a smile.

'Nice one,' he wheezed through an asthmatic chest, then with a nod and wink he turned to the urinal.

Daniel rapidly backed towards the toilet door but with a sudden flash of intuition glanced downwards to see his willy poking out from his flies. With a scarlet face, he tugged his zip up and stumbled onto the platform.

He hurried to the exit, cursing himself with every curse he knew, but paused and drew breath before leaving the station. OK, that man hadn't been a policeman but were they waiting outside ready to grab him?

It seemed not. The police car had gone, a couple stood smoking on the right of the steps, a woman bumped a wheeled case up towards him, nothing suspicious. He headed down the steps, eyes flicking left and right, trying to look inconspicuous. OK, time for a quick lunch before his next meeting.

Twenty-Nine

DANIEL HAD SPENT FORTY minutes in the pizzeria mulling over, between mouthfuls of marinara, what Dick's arrest meant for him. Was Dick going to drag him into proceedings? Would the man just keep quiet? Why did they suspect him, anyway? He came to no useful conclusions but enjoyed the pizza.

Now, as he wandered towards the main university entrance, he reflected on how long it was since his last visit to the lab. Hell's teeth, he worked here. He was paid to be here but it must be ten days since he had put in an appearance. It was two pm and students milled about doing whatever it was students did. Several members of staff whom he didn't recognise huddled in a corner puffing at cigarettes. Daniel stood uncertainly in the middle of the square as people jostled past him. The professor's instructions had been typically vague.

'Follow me,' a voice hissed.

Daniel turned as he felt a light touch on his shoulder and wasn't surprised to see Farquharson's back weaving away from him through the crowd. He fell in step a short way behind and followed to the teaching block where Farquharson paused, looked right and left, before pushing inside. They took a twisted route through the department's corridors before exiting at the rear. Daniel swore under his breath. What did the idiot think he was doing? This was crazy. Nobody was following them.

The professor hurried on like a man with no time to waste, heading directly for the physical education building. Five minutes later he paused at a door marked *closed for refurbishment* and pushed inside. It was the changing room for the fitness suite.

Farquharson turned to face Daniel, took several wheezy breaths, and said, 'There, that should do it.'

Playing at spies had never been Daniel's favourite game. 'Do we really need all this creeping about?'

'Distasteful, my boy, I know, but events are forced upon us. We must react appropriately. Please, have a seat.' He indicated the long bench occupying one wall of the room, and Daniel lowered himself onto the edge ready for escape.

Farquharson folded his arms. 'Now, dear boy, what was it you wanted to discuss?'

Daniel failed to suppress a sigh. 'It was you who wanted to see *me.*'

No trace of embarrassment showed on Farquharson's face. 'Yes, yes, of course, that's what I meant.' He paused. 'Um... yes... Indeed, first of all, congratulations on a job well done. Celia has completely disappeared. There has been nothing in the newspapers. I don't know how you do it.' He placed a finger on his lips as Daniel attempted to interrupt. 'And I have no wish to know, let me make that clear. But you have done wonders.'

Daniel was not at all sure how the man would feel when Celia's body turned up in a greenhouse. Should he comment on this possibility?

'Well...'

The professor held up a hand. 'Enough for now. We were overtaken by events and had to act, but now we must return to the original problem.'

Original problem? What the hell was the original problem? Daniel's brain clunked into gear and began sifting possibilities.

'I refer to the investigation launched by my friends on the Senate.'

'Ah.'

Farquharson raised an eyebrow. 'I'm sorry. Am I boring you?'

'I didn't yawn. But surely that's all over,' *please god be over.*

'Far from it. So-called evidence is being heard as we speak.'

'So-called?'

'Quite so.'

'I mean what evidence?'

The professor coughed. 'Evidence of a sensitive nature.' He nodded gravely. '*Sensitive.*'

Daniel swallowed, attempting to quell the nausea spreading from his gut. *Surely the old goat wouldn't resurrect...*

'That is why I would like you to urgently continue the good work which you started so long ago: the investigation of the committee chairman.'

Daniel mumbled, and Farquharson frowned.

'I'm sorry, did you say good luck?'

'No, I didn't.' Daniel folded his arms.

'I seem to remember a suspicion of criminal activity. Some sort of secret society?'

A great weight bore down on Daniel's head. 'No! No, that was a mistake. A big mistake. A huge mistake. I got it wrong. It wasn't Reynolds.'

The professor tutted through his teeth. 'Unfortunate. Most unfortunate. Still, shoulder to the wheel now, eh? Soon be there. I know he's up to something. We just have to discover what.'

'*We* have to discover?'

'Exactly, my boy. Now that the err... distraction of my little problem vis-à-vis Celia has been put to bed, we can move on.' He glanced over his shoulder at the blank wall behind him as if he thought a gremlin might materialise from it and lowered his voice. 'The man is an art lover. An obsessive art lover. My feeling is that a look at his paintings might yield dividends for our little project. Take a camera.'

Daniel blinked several times as he tried to get to the meaning of the professor's words. 'So, I march up to his house and ask to have a viewing of his art collection. And he says, *oh yes do come in, you'll be wanting to take some photographs, the best ones are over there. Would you like a coffee while you work?* And I say...'

'Daniel, Daniel.' Farquharson shook his head. 'Your sense of humour is always welcome. I do appreciate an ironic commentary, however, the matter is urgent. You may have to use more unconventional means.'

'I can't go housebreaking.' Daniel's voice notched into a high register.

'Good heavens, no. Perish the thought.' The professor winked broadly and nodded.

'No, no, I mean really.'

'Don't worry, my boy, you can borrow my kit.'

Daniel leapt to his feet. 'I don't want your bloody...'

Frowning, the professor put a finger to his lips.

'I heard a noise,' he whispered. 'We are no longer alone.'

He crossed to the changing room door and paused with a hand on the lock, then with a quick twist of the wrist he yanked it open. A tall grey-haired man stood there; a startled expression quickly wiped from his stern face.

He coughed. 'Ah, Farquharson, so this is where you're hiding.' He glanced in Daniel's direction and wrinkled his nose.

'Reynolds, how delightful.' Farquharson smiled and extended a hand which was pointedly ignored. 'This is my colleague, Mr Dreghorn.' He swept an arm towards Daniel. 'And this is professor Reynolds, committee chairman.'

Reynolds gave the briefest of nods and continued to address Farquharson. 'The committee is waiting for you. You were reminded of the meeting time only yesterday by e-mail.'

'Good heavens, waiting for me? E-mail is so unreliable I find. Thank god you were able to find me, Reynolds.' He raised an eyebrow.

Daniel stared at Reynolds. So this was the man he should have followed. Why the hell couldn't Farquharson have shown him a photograph instead of a verbal description and then this whole sorry mess might never have happened. Farquharson and Reynolds were leaving, the professor scribbling a note on a scrap of paper.

'Here, dear boy, this is what you need. Good luck now.'

He shoved the paper into Daniel's hand and patted him on the arm. The door swung shut, and they were gone.

Daniel straightened out the crumpled ball in his palm.

My office, shelves on right of window, behind the collected works of Ovid.

Was there no end to this? He wanted to scream. But the bugger still had him by the shorties. He had to go through with it.

Thirty

DANIEL DREW HIS SHOULDERS back and stepped smartly towards the station entrance. *Walk confident, feel confident,* someone had once told him. Whoever said it was an idiot he decided as he slowed and his feet dragged on the approach to the ticket barrier. A cautious glance left and right confirmed his suspicion: people were watching. On the right, a railway employee, or at least a man dressed in railway uniform, scratched his armpit and stared at him with a feigned expression of boredom. To the left, a middle-aged man in a tweed jacket looked meaningfully at the briefcase Daniel held.

His heart did a fair impression of learning the can-can as he fished his ticket from a jacket pocket and shoved it into the slot. But why the hell was he so worried? The briefcase in his hand contained two house bricks. OK, a few people thought it contained a bomb, but that was their problem. You cannot be arrested for carrying around house bricks. House brick carriers do not end up in Guantanamo Bay. *Are you totally confident of that, Daniel?* a voice piped up as the barrier flashed red and his ticket spat back at him.

Sweat gathered on his neck as he pulled the ticket out and stared at it. He glanced hesitantly towards the railwayman. Shit! The guy was striding towards him. With shaking fingers, Daniel fumbled the ticket back into the slot, bending it in the process.

'Excuse me, sir.'

Shit, shit. Another try in the slot hopelessly mangled the flimsy card.

'Excuse me? Can I see that ticket?'

The man towered over him, a powerfully built giant with broad shoulders and a squashed nose. The briefcase in Daniel's left hand had become noticeably heavier, pulling him down, unbalancing him. Should he just drop the case and run? He fixed a smile on his face.

'Sorry. What was that?'

'I said, I need to see your ticket.' The voice was deep and resonant. The fingers of the man's right hand flexed constantly as if practising some obscene torture. Escape was impossible. He was toast.

'OK, here you are. It's only bricks, actually.' Daniel handed over the ticket, relieved now that this business was at an end. He would tell the police everything, every last crazy detail. They would lock him up in a mental hospital for sure. The man stared closely at Daniel's ticket.

'OK, just come with me,' he announced.

Daniel meekly followed man-mountain the length of the barrier. They stopped at a gate near the end. The man produced a key and unlocked it.

'It's only bricks,' Daniel tried for what he knew might be the last time.

His executioner turned and stared. 'Yes... well...' He cleared his throat. 'These ticket readers are crap, son, forever breaking down. Have a good journey.'

Daniel found himself on the other side of the barrier as the man strode rapidly away. With that, his train was called.

He was going nuts, Daniel decided, settling into his seat as the train whined up to speed. Paranoia, that's what it was. Nobody was after him, not right now, and HE DID NOT HAVE A BOMB. He wanted to shout it out to his half-dozen fellow passengers but resisted. He would leave the suitcase on the train and go home; nothing could be simpler. When the allotment people discovered that the train had not blown up, they would be disappointed, but could hardly blame him for a faulty bomb. He had done his bit. More than that, he had saved lives.

By the time the conductor passed, Daniel had summoned up enough self-assurance to smile at the man as he presented the mangled card. Now was the time to do it, as soon as the conductor left the carriage. Now, before the next stop.

He stood up and gripped the briefcase handle firmly. Making his way to the toilet at the end of the carriage, he stabbed at the button and the door hissed open. It was a wheelchair-accessible compartment and huge, but there was nowhere to hide a briefcase. Anyone entering would see it. Did that matter? Possibly. He flushed the loo, left the compartment and returned to his seat.

Next plan, leave it and go. He placed the case between his legs and pushed it back under the seat as far as it would slide. Done. He got up and strolled through the connecting doors to the adjoining compartment. Easy. Simple. He sat down and took a deep breath. Get off at the next stop. Job done. A long sigh escaped his lips and his eyes closed.

'Excuse me?' A female voice. A hand squeezed his shoulder.

Perhaps if he kept his eyes shut, the voice might go away.

'Excuse me, is this yours?'

Daniel opened his eyes, knowing exactly what he would see, and he wasn't disappointed. A plump, middle-aged lady with blonde hair hovered uncertainly beside him, clutching a Mulberry Lucian briefcase. Fate had pissed on him again.

He dredged up an approximation to a smile. 'What?'

'Sorry to disturb you but is this case yours?' She pushed the briefcase towards him.

Daniel scratched his head, glanced at the case. 'No, no. Not mine. Never seen it before, sorry.'

'Oh.' Crestfallen, she turned the case over in her hand. 'I'm sure I saw you with it earlier.'

'Not to worry. We all make mistakes. There are people around who look quite like me. It must have been one of them.'

The woman remained standing beside him, biting her lip. 'You sure it's not yours?'

'Absolutely. How could I forget a nice case like that? Thanks for thinking of me.'

'It's just been abandoned under a seat,' she said, indignantly.

'Well, better just put it back in case the owner... you know. I wouldn't worry about it if I were you.'

She turned away, muttering to herself. Daniel glanced at his watch. Five minutes to his stop. Just five minutes. He could survive that.

Four minutes later the woman was back and at the head of a procession of other passengers all jostling past his seat. 'What's going... bloody... nonsense... typical...' filtered back to him as the group grumbled through to the next carriage. Bringing up the rear was a panic-stricken conductor.

'Everyone through to the front carriage, please. Now. There's a fault. Everyone to the front, please.'

Daniel leapt up. 'What's going on?' He caught the man's elbow as he passed.

'There's an electrical fault. Train terminates at the next station. We have to stop short. Only the front carriage will be at the platform. Please move.'

'An electrical fault? Where?'

'Never mind. It's technical. You must move.'

'Oh, technical is it? Too complicated for my little brain? Well, let me tell you...' Daniel stopped. Crap. It wasn't a fault. It was a bomb alert. That stupid woman had reported his briefcase to the conductor. 'It's a bomb isn't it?'

'Bomb? God no. Please don't say that to the other passengers. We don't want panic.'

Daniel swallowed hard, shut his mouth and moved ahead of the guard into the adjoining carriage. What now?

Confusion met them at the station. Half a dozen police cars, blue lights panicking, flashed their message of flap and fluster. Dozens of people running in circles answered the call. Passengers were herded into the tiny station waiting room while the empty train was reversed a considerable distance down the track. A minute later, two Land Rovers skidded onto the platform, Army Bomb Disposal painted on their side.

Daniel found the woman who had approached him with his case staring reproachfully at him. 'It's my daughter's birthday,' she said.

An apology came to his lips, but he swallowed it back before it escaped. That would be to admit guilt in some way. He was guilty of nothing. 'That's nice,' he muttered.

The passengers were kept for an hour and briefly interviewed one by one

What was the purpose of his journey?

'Leisure.'

Had he seen anything suspicious?

'No.'

Had he seen this briefcase – photograph of Mulberry Lucian?

It was always best to stick to the truth where possible. 'Well, I saw a blonde woman carrying one very like it.'

Sometimes your body tells you what it needs. Daniel retrieved a half-price box of expired mint chocolates from under his bed

and slumped on the sofa. As he nibbled, he realised perhaps he had not lost those nutcases after all. The first thing he would have to do was destroy the remote detonator, but when the bomb didn't detonate, what would they do? A defective bomb wasn't his responsibility, but would that stop them blaming him? Would the whole episode make the national news? A bomb alert triggered by an abandoned briefcase containing bricks. They would not be happy gardeners.

After a dinner of mint chocolates and beer, Daniel settled down to the evening news.

***

The doorbell rang and Daniel groaned. This would not be good. It was never good when his doorbell rang. What disaster was waiting for him now? He put down his half-empty glass and plodded towards the door. He opened it a fraction and peered through the gap.

'Oh,' he said. 'It's you.'

Sandra Merrywick stood outside.

'Ten-ten, Danny. Can I come in? I need to talk to you.'

'But how did you find...' his voice trailed away.

'You're in the phone book, dumbbell.'

'Ah... Look, sorry about the other night.'

'That's OK. No worries. But I'd like to come in. It's draughty out here.'

No worries? That was remarkably understanding in the circumstances. He stared at her for a long moment.

'Daniel?' she snapped.

'Right, right.' He pulled the door wide and she marched past into the sitting-room. He closed the door behind her.

She stood in the middle of the room, head nodding as if in approval.

'What was it you…' Daniel began but stopped. He had noticed what Sandra had trailed in with her: a bulky suitcase.

'This is a nice flat, Danny.'

'It's a bit small.' He had no idea why Sandra was here, but this seemed the right response.

She turned to face him and snapped her suitcase handle home. 'It's fine. Two bedrooms, you told me, right?'

'Yes, I mean no… wait…' He could not recall telling her any such thing. They had never discussed his flat.

Sandra's shoulders slumped, and she stared at the floor. 'I need somewhere to crash, Danny. I'm homeless.'

His eyes closed for a moment as the world seemed to spin just a little faster. 'But you're not homeless. Your parents, your father.'

Sandra stamped her foot. 'He's become impossible. He even blames me for being kidnapped. It's embarrassed him, he says. Embarrassed! What do you think of that?'

'Well… it seems a little unfair.'

'So, I've left and now I've nowhere to stay.'

'Look, really, I'm sorry… but…'

'I'm not looking for charity. I'll pay rent.' Her eyes opened wide.

'It's not that, it's…'

'It's what? You don't like me?'

'No, no, that's nothing to do… I mean it's not about like or dislike.' What was he supposed to say? 'You're… fine. But I thought you and Alex were, you know…'

'Were what?'

'Um, seeing each other.'

'Oh, you mean having sex?'

'Yes, that. So maybe you could stay with him.'

'Didn't work. Weren't compatible. We split. Couldn't ask him.'

'But—'

'Would you like a cup of tea?' she said brightly.

'Tea?'

'Good, I'll put the kettle on.' She disappeared into the kitchen, leaving Daniel staring at a suitcase.

Half an hour later, he lay back, bemused, watching Sandra stretched out on his sofa and idly channel hopping. All his arguments had come to nought.

Lorraine: *Well she's not here now is she? And anyway, I only want the spare room.*

Flat's too small: *I won't be under your feet. I'll be out most evenings. I'll wait until you're done before I have breakfast if you want. You won't know I'm here. No problem.*

Lorraine II: *I'm not after you, Danny. My new boyfriend lives at home with his parents, that's all. He's looking for work. We can't afford to move in together.*

Lorraine III: *she can't be that unreasonable. You'll have more money coming in. She'll be cool about it.*

Daniel was not at all sure that Lorraine would be either reasonable or cool about a female sharing the flat, but it was true she wasn't here right now. He heard himself agreeing that Sandra could stay for a few days until she *sorted herself out*.

Thirty-One

DANIEL SPREAD MARMALADE ON his breakfast toast and bit off a mouthful. Sandra occupied the bathroom. Last night she had unpacked without fuss and made herself comfortable in his spare bedroom. Perhaps it would all work out. When Lorraine returned, what harm could a paying lodger be? *If* she returned, a small and disagreeable voice muttered in his ear, but he was saved from replying as Sandra appeared at the bathroom door.

'There's tea in the pot,' he said. 'Would you like some toast?'

She beamed a smile in his direction. 'Love it, thanks.'

He headed into the kitchen as she poured a cup for herself and settled onto the sofa.

When he returned, toast in hand, she had switched on the TV and was trying to change channels.

'You need new batteries, Daniel. This thing's not working.'

Perhaps that was his problem: he needed new batteries. If only your life was fixable with a fresh set of double A's. 'Here, let me see,' he said, taking the remote from her, then blinked several times as he stared at the device, mouth suddenly dry. This couldn't be happening again.

'Well, have you got new batteries? I don't want to watch this rubbish.'

'Uh,' he said and then 'mmh,' as he began to breathe too quickly. 'Err Sandra... what did you...? I mean did you press anything... at all?'

She stared at him. 'Of course I pressed it. I'm trying to change channels. It must be flat.'

Daniel turned the remote over and over in his hand. 'I don't suppose you remember what you pressed... um?'

'Don't be silly. What does it matter? I was trying to get BBC1, but then I pressed everything, trying to make it work. Nothing does, so it needs a new battery. End of story.'

He sat in silence for a moment, staring at the remote the bomb man had given him. Sandra might have stumbled on the combination, she might not.

'It's the wrong one.' He reached down and under the cushion beside her. 'Look, here's the remote.'

She took it from him, shaking her head. 'And how was I supposed to know that?'

As the channel changed, Daniel sank back into the chair, his appetite for toast evaporated. He should have destroyed that controller instead of leaving it about. What had happened? No way of knowing. Perhaps nothing. The briefcase, the one containing what he assumed was an actual bomb, was in Number One's mansion. Now... if it had gone off... heck. People might be dead and his fingerprints would be everywhere. The news droned on in front of him. MPs, famine, plague, China, war... all so predictable, only the details changed.

Newsflash! Daniel leant forward.

'Reports are reaching us of a gas explosion in a detached house in Gatston. No more details are available at the moment. We'll bring you more information as soon as possible.'

That was it. His stomach lurched and then lurched again. Gas explosion? Not that, he was certain.

Sandra stood and switched off the TV. 'Gas is so dangerous, don't you think? Electric's much safer.'

What could he do? Nothing, absolutely nothing.

'Daniel? Are you awake?'

'Gas. How do they know it's gas?'

'I'm going out now.'

'Could have been anything.'

She frowned at him. 'I hope you're not always like this.'

'It might have been gas.' Daniel looked up as the front door slammed shut. Sandra must have gone out. OK, there was one thing he had to do.

⤞⤝

He shouldn't have come here. He recognised that immediately as he took in the emergency vehicles, blue lights winking, the flurry of policemen and others in bunny suits, and that not very much of the house had been left standing. Daniel stood with a small crowd of onlookers behind a length of shiny striped police tape.

The ruin that teetered before him was unrecognisable as the splendid Victorian mansion he had so recently quit in the company of Sandra Merrywick.

'What the heck happened here, son?' There was an elderly man beside him.

'Gas explosion... I believe. That is... I heard.' No one here would have any idea about his relationship to this building. Even so, discussing it made him nervous.

'Excuse me, gentlemen.'

Daniel jumped and whirled about. There was a uniformed policeman at his elbow.

The policeman raised an eyebrow. 'Do either of you two gentlemen have an interest in this property?'

Daniel opened his mouth to reply.

'He does,' said the elderly man, pointing at Daniel.

'What?' He stared at the man. 'What are you talking about?'

'You said you lived here.'

225

'I did not.' Daniel's voice rose indignantly.

'You said it was a gas leak what blew yon up.'

'Yes. So?'

'Gents, please.' The policeman waved a placatory hand. 'This is merely an enquiry. No need for arguments.' He turned to Daniel. 'So, can you explain exactly? Do you own the house, rent a room?'

'Don't be ridiculous. How could I afford a place like that?' He felt his face growing red.

'So you rented then.' The policeman was writing on his pad.

'Told you so,' said the old man.

'No, no, no. This is crazy.' Daniel had a premonition of something terrible about to happen. What had possessed him to come here? 'I have nothing to do with this house. I was just passing.'

'I see, sir. And where do you live?'

'I... I...' He lived five miles away. It was obvious where this would go. *And what were you doing here, sir?*

'I... I'm in Camberley Street... fifty-seven.' Then he cursed himself. Camberley Street was where Sandra Merrywick lived. It was only a few blocks away. That was good, but why had he given that exact number? That was stupid.

The policeman frowned. 'Camberley Street. Now why does that ring a bell?'

'I didn't hear anything,' said Daniel, desperation closing in on his brain like smog. 'Did you hear anything?' he looked at the old man.

'Tinnitus,' the man said. 'Hear bells all the time. Like being in a bloody churchyard.'

'Have you seen a doctor?'

'What? Where?' The man peered behind Daniel, eyes narrowed. 'Bloody quacks. Should be shot the lot of them.'

The policeman pulled his shoulders back. 'Now just a minute, what's going on here?'

Daniel pointed. 'This poor man needs a doctor.'

'You what?' shouted the old man.

At that moment, the policeman's radio crackled to life. 'You two just wait here. I have some more questions.' He turned away and mumbled into his lapel.

Daniel manoeuvred himself behind the old man.

'Bloody quacks, bloody policeman, bloody... ow.'

Daniel had given the man a not too gentle prod in the back of the right knee. The leg folded, and the man tumbled to the road.

'Help,' Daniel bawled. 'Need help here.'

Several of the men in white suits ran towards him. The policeman was on his knees beside the man who was mumbling, '... bloody... bloody...'

Daniel raced towards the white suits, waving his arms and shouting, 'Over here.' They passed him. He kept running. Glanced over his shoulder. Speeded up. Past the smoking ruin, turned right, left, right again. After a couple of minutes, he paused by a wooden fence and leant back, panting hard. He could hear no sound of pursuit.

'Bugger,' he said to no one in particular. What were the allotment people going to think of that? Only two hours ago he had thought that his coming evening expedition might be the potential disaster of the day. What would be next?

Thirty-Two

SOMEWHERE AN OWL HOOTED; a bird that seemed to be the background to Daniel's recent life. At least it sounded like an owl, although it could have been a passing bird imitator. The former was of no concern; the latter most certainly was, as he tried to blend in, chameleon-like, to the colours and contours of a Georgian front door with brass accoutrements. He realised that in this endeavour, as in so much of his life, he had failed.

Farquharson had given him a long and detailed demonstration on the use of his tools. So long and detailed that Daniel's attention had wandered before the end to other matters, such as the economic crisis and whether the E. Coli on the piece of expired chicken breast in his fridge had multiplied sufficiently to kill him or just subject him to a mild tummy upset when he had it for dinner that night. Now, with a bright street light behind him and the passing of the occasional bird imitator, he wished he had given the professor every second of his attention.

The very fine Georgian door belonged to professor Reynolds, who he had watched being picked up in a shiny Lexus just fifteen minutes previously. Farquharson had assured him that there would be no one else in the house, and for some reason, which now escaped him, Daniel had believed this.

He glanced once more over his shoulder, checking for pedestrians, then selected yet another of the slim, surgical-steel, toothed blades and inserted it into the lock. This time, the blade turned smoothly, and the door clicked open. Mightily relieved and mightily terrified, Daniel stepped into the darkness and shut the door behind him.

As Farquharson had suggested, he closed his eyes and counted to five to allow dark adaptation to take effect. On opening them, he found enough light filtering through the skylight above him to reveal a broad lobby with three doors on each side and a staircase ahead. At the foot of the stairs, a tall and probably very expensive grandfather clock ticked away the seconds of his life.

Some heavily framed pictures hung on the walls, but the light was too dim to make out detail. *Mostly in the dining room, on the right*, Farquharson had said. Daniel took the doorknob in his sweating hand and turned. The room he entered was curtained and completely dark until his searching fingers found the switch by the door. He winced as light flooded in.

A long and wide room, palatial being the word that jumped into his mind. An enormous dining table that would have seated twenty occupied the centre. Antique-looking dressers and desks bordered the walls, and above stretching to near the high ceiling, paintings crowded the wall. Unbelievable. He shook his head. He knew more about the surface of the moon than he did about art and artists, but he was sure that these things weren't reproductions. This stuff was... expensive. How did someone on a university salary afford all this? But then that was Farquharson's question.

OK, photographs. He pulled out his pocket Nikon, zoomed in on the nearest picture, and pressed the button. He had taken about twenty when a voice from near the open door said, 'Hello.'

Daniel froze, his eye focussed on the display on the camera's screen. But his brain didn't freeze. It went into overdrive. In a microsecond, it had decided: female voice, small voice, young girl's voice, neutral tone, not frightened, therefore possibly not too much to worry about. But then, his brain had always been stronger on observation than deduction. He pressed the button on the camera, fixed the corners of his mouth upwards and turned towards the source of the greeting.

A little girl stood in the doorway, wearing a pink 'hello kitty' nightdress. She might have been seven or eight. Wide, unblinking eyes regarded him from beneath a frizz of curly blonde hair. She stood with arms folded, a book clutched protectively to her chest.

'Hello,' Daniel said.

They both stared at each other for several seconds.

'That one's by Nasmyth,' said the girl.

Daniel turned to look at the painting he had just photographed. 'It's nice,' he said.

'It's my favourite,' the girl replied. 'Uncle doesn't like it. He's going to give it to me when he dies.'

'Lovely,' said Daniel. 'I mean lovely that you will have this lovely painting. That's lovely,' he added for emphasis.

'I'm Mandy,' the girl said. 'Who are you?'

'I'm...' Daniel paused. Who the hell was he? Certainly not Daniel Dreghorn. 'I'm...' He glanced at his hand. 'I'm the photographer.'

The girl stared at him with saucer eyes until he was forced to look away. Finally, she said, 'It's very small.'

Daniel considered pointing out she wasn't the first female to make that observation but instead said, 'This is my practise camera. I don't want to waste my big one.'

The girl took a step back in the doorway. 'Are you a burglar?' she whispered.

'Good heavens, no.' Panic rose, like boiling milk in a saucepan. The last thing he wanted was this little girl screaming for help. 'Your uncle hired me to photograph his collection.'

'Mummy says that all men are bastards.'

Daniel, whose knowledge of the subtleties of conversing with precocious eight-year-old girls wearing hello kitty pyjamas was on a par with his knowledge of Renaissance motets, said, 'Um.'

'She says she didn't, but I heard her say it to Aunty Sally.'

'Um... right.'

'What's a bastard?'

Daniel stared at her and his eyes focussed on the book she was holding. Relieved, he recognised a familiar wizarding cover. 'I've read that one, it's the one where they get lost in the maze and it all closes in and starts moving about and Harry's friend gets killed and..' He paused, seeing the frown on Mandy's face.

'What maze?' she said.

He cringed. 'Ah, you haven't finished. At least, now that I think about it, that's another book I'm talking about. A different book completely. Different author. I read a lot. I get mixed up.'

'This isn't the book I'm reading,' Mandy said, looking down at the book still clutched in front of her. 'I was just tidying up when I heard you burglaring.'

'Ah, but now you know I'm not, eh?' Daniel said, waving his camera. 'Well, I guess I'd better get on. Your uncle will want his photographs.' He turned back to the art gallery and raised the camera to his eye, praying that the girl would simply return to her room.

She didn't. Instead, she said, 'I'm going to get Mummy.'

Daniel cursed. Of course, of course, of course. A girl her age wouldn't be here on her own. Why hadn't he thought of that?

'No!'

Mandy withdrew a step.

'Sorry, I mean... no. Let's not disturb Mummy. She might not like it.'

Her head nodded. 'She gets cross when you wake her.'

'Exactly, exactly. We don't want a cross Mummy, now do we? Goodness no.'

'Will you get me a biscuit?'

'A... biscuit?'

Mandy's saucer eyes fixed on him. 'Yes, a biscuit. Don't they have biscuits on your planet?'

'What?' Daniel shook his head.

'That's what Mummy says when people don't know what she's talking about. Because if you were an alien you might never have seen a biscuit. The kitchen's through here.' With that, she disappeared.

'Wait.' Daniel scurried after the girl. Oh the indignity: black-mailed by an eight-year-old to feed her sugar addiction.

The kitchen had a floor area, he estimated, larger than that of his entire flat. There was a lot of stainless steel and bright lights and leafy plants.

'It's in there,' she said, pointing to a cupboard high up and well out of her reach.

'I'll give you this and then you can go back to bed, right?'

Mandy nodded enthusiastically as Daniel reached up and pulled the cupboard open. Inside, sitting full square on a white plate, was an enormous chocolate cake of the Bavarian forest variety, protected by a transparent cover.

He turned back. 'Sorry, there are no biscuits here. Must be another cupboard.'

Wide green eyes stared up at him. 'I said cake.'

Daniel frowned. 'You distinctly said biscuits.'

'Said cake.' There was a pause and then she sighed. 'I suppose I'll have to get Mummy.'

Daniel groaned. 'Wait, wait. Yes, of course, cake.' He reached up, retrieved the plate, and planted it in front of the putative politician.

While Mandy started excavating with a large spoon, Daniel crept back to the dining room, well aware now of the sleeping mummy lurking upstairs. It took only a few moments to snap the remainder of the pictures. Now what? *Run*, of course. This very sensible suggestion was stymied by a scream from the region of the kitchen that could only be described as blood-curdling, or at the very least, blood-thickening.

He pocketed his camera and dashed to the kitchen to find Mandy standing at the work surface, spoon in hand and a large chocolate cake lying by her feet, upside down. In fact, strictly speaking, the cake was on her feet rather than by them.

'Fell on the floor,' Mandy wailed.

'Shush, please,' Daniel muttered, bending down to pick up the cake. 'It's fine, look,' he said, scraping the lump of mashed chocolate and cream onto another plate.

'Can't eat that. It's been on the floor. It's got germs.'

'Please, not so loud.' Daniel waved his arms around. 'We don't want to wake poor Mummy, do we? Look.' He poked a finger into the revolting mush and licked off the mess. 'It's delicious, see,' he said, trying not to screw up his face.

They both froze in place as a door slammed upstairs.

'It's Mummy. You've made an awful mess,' Mandy said, staring at the chocolate-covered floor.

Daniel cast about, desperately seeking an exit strategy. There was none.

Footsteps on the stairs. 'Mandy? Are you down here?' An irritable female voice from behind the door.

'You'd better hide,' Mandy said. 'You can use that cupboard.' She pointed towards a tall cabinet next to the upright freezer. 'It's OK, I won't tell,' she added with a wide smile.

Was there an alternative? Could he bluff his way out somehow? Caught at midnight with this woman's young daughter, in the kitchen with a messy chocolate cake and a camera? Daniel pulled the cupboard door open and slipped inside with a brush and an upright vacuum cleaner. He heard the kitchen door open.

'Mandy? What on earth... What are you *doing*?'

'Was hungry,' Mandy mumbled.

'I'll give you hungry. You get back to your bed right now, young lady. How on earth did you reach that cake, anyway?'

'The man done it.'

Daniel held his breath. Women, you could trust them as far as you could throw them.

'You'll clear up this mess first thing in the morning. Now off to bed.'

'But the man done it. He should clear it up.'

'Man, what man?'

'He's hiding in that cupboard.'

Daniel prepared for fight or flight as his heart went into overdrive. Perhaps he would have another heart attack. That might well be the best option, he conceded.

'Young *lady*. I have had just about *enough* of your imaginary friends. Now get up those stairs.'

'But...'

'Up!'

'But...'

'This instant.'

'You'll be *sorry*,' Mandy yelled.

The kitchen door slammed and small feet pattered upstairs. An exasperated grunt escaped Mandy's mother and then silence.

Please go, he thought in the darkness. I'll clear up the mess, promise. A floorboard creaked, and a shadow fell across the crack of light visible under the door of Daniel's cramped prison.

No, please no. He offered up a prayer to any gods who might be listening. Could he hold the door shut? But there was nothing on this side to grasp. OK, he would run for it. Just rush past the woman and out while trying to hide his face. She might not see him well enough to give a description. And then he heard a muttered, 'Oh come *on*,' from Mandy's mother, and a second later the lights went out.

Safe. He wilted against the back of the cupboard and attempted to kick-start his lungs and heart which seemed to have ceased operation several minutes ago. Once equilibrium of a sort had returned, he pushed open the door and peered out. Soft moonlight bathed the silent kitchen. The blackmailer and her mother had gone. Time to leave.

He made his way through the dark hallway to the front door, eased it open a fraction and squinted through the gap. No one in sight. With a deep sigh, he stepped outside, closed the door quietly and headed down the steps to pavement level. He turned right.

'Well, well,' said a throaty voice, and a hand descended on Daniel's shoulder.

Initial panic turned to resignation as he recognised the voice. 'You,' he said.

'Me,' agreed Inspector Dick.

'What do you want?' Daniel pulled his shoulder free. 'Have you been watching me?'

'Just keeping an eye out for you, old son.'

'Wish you wouldn't,' he snapped and walked away.

The inspector matched pace beside him, whistling tunelessly to himself. 'You sound stressed. Too many irons in the fire?'

Stressed? Damn right he was stressed. 'Anyway, I thought they arrested you.'

Dick shrugged. 'Just a formality and Merrywick's reign will soon be over in any case. The body will be found today.'

'Shit.'

'For Merrywick, yes. Just keep your head down, old son.'

Daniel stopped walking. 'What about those two cops outside Merrywick's place? They saw me.'

Dick waved this minor matter away. 'I told you already. Don't be concerned. It's fixed. They don't know you. You've no record. We're safe. And other evidence will point to Merrywick too.'

'Other evidence?'

Dick tapped the side of his nose as if trying to clear a blockage. 'Other evidence.'

There was just too much happening. Daniel had a sudden urge to lie down in the street. 'Well, mustn't keep you,' he said.

The inspector raised a hand in salute. 'As the French say, a bean toe.' He turned away.

Daniel stared after the inspector for a moment, trying to figure out this cryptic remark, then shrugged and set off for home.

He let himself into his flat as silently as possible in case any insomniac neighbours were counting woolly ungulates. Slipping out of his clothes, he slid into a blessedly cool bed and tried to calm his throbbing brain.

Thirty-Three

DANIEL WOKE WITH A start. 'Lorraine?' he muttered, rolling over to the far side of the bed. But of course, there was no Lorraine. An eyelid cranked open Eleven o'clock! He had slept in His eyes closed again, preparing for more sleep. There was a noise. He sat up and his torpid brain spun up to half speed. It was the fridge. Someone had opened his fridge door.

Lorraine? Could it be? Or was there a burglar out there? Someone intent on relieving him of ninety grams of dodgy brie and half a litre of milk. It seemed unlikely. He swung his legs out of bed, tiptoed to the door and opened it a crack. A female figure sat at the breakfast table.

'Bugger,' he muttered, recognising the broad shoulders and blonde hair. He pulled the door wide. 'It's you,' he said.

Sandra turned, 'Good morning, Daniel.' Her gaze lowered. 'Is this how you greet all your guests?'

Daniel retreated into the bedroom and pulled on some clothes. This would not work.

'It's not going to work,' he said to Sandra as he dropped onto a chair by the dining table.

She stared at him, jaws working on a mouthful of coco-pops. 'It's fine. Don't get your knickers knotted. Told you I'll not be here long. Just need somewhere to doss down for a while.'

Daniel removed a coco-pop from his sweatshirt and thought of Lorraine returning unexpectedly right now to find him tête-à-tête with Sandra. He thought of Sandra's father, about to find something unexpected in the greenhouse.

Perhaps mistaking his hesitation, Sandra went on, 'Don't worry. I'm not going to jump into bed with *you*. I told you I've got a boyfriend now. He's cool about me sharing with...' She paused and looked away. Her cheeks reddened noticeably.

'What did you tell him?' he said, warily.

'Well... just that I was sharing with a nice old couple.'

Daniel winced.

'Come on, it's almost true. You'll be old sometime. Don't worry so much. I know there's nothing between us; you know there's nothing between us. It's just convenient, that's all. Here's a week's rent.' She reached into an inside pocket and slapped a bundle of notes onto the table between them.

Maybe she was right and he did worry too much. Compared with his other problems, this was nothing. What would be would happen anyway. Oh to hell with it. He picked up the money.

After seeing Sandra out, he left his flat and headed for the university. When had he last done any work there? His life had become so complicated and confusing that he couldn't remember. He had a job there, he worked there, at least until he could persuade Farquharson to release him. How did the lab manage without him? Likely very well was the answer that batted back from whoever he was having his internal conversation with.

Farquharson had to be the first stop. Those photographs he'd taken had to be passed on. Then? The lab... perhaps. Check up on Alex? He headed upstairs to the professor's office, tapped once and peered cautiously around the door. The female mastodon who had greeted him last time was absent. He knocked on the inner door and pushed it open.

Farquharson's swivel chair faced away from him, but he could see the top of the man's head sticking up above the parapet. Likely he had dozed off staring through the office window. What *did* the old fool actually do all day?

'Professor, I've got what you wanted,' he announced.

The chair twirled around sharply. 'Excellent, Mr Dreghorn. Just place it down here,' said an unfamiliar, gravelly voice.

Daniel stared, horrified, at the stick-like figure before him. 'Professor Reynolds!'

Reynolds nodded, sat back and placed his hands behind his head as Daniel stood by the desk, unable to move. What was going on here?

'You had something for me?' he asked, mildly, raising an eyebrow.

'Yes, no professor Farquharson. Where is... I mean...' Daniel stopped and took a deep breath.

'Farquharson has taken a short sabbatical.' Reynolds spat the name out as if it left a particularly sour taste on his tongue.

'But...'

'A sabbatical that may be extended should circumstance warrant. In the meantime, I have stepped in to fill the professor's shoes. At some personal inconvenience, I may add.'

Daniel's shoulders drooped. 'Very good of you,' he mumbled, desperately wondering how to get out of this situation.

Reynolds' eyebrows drew closer together. 'So if you have anything for Farquharson... Any outstanding business...'

'No, no. Really. It can wait. I mean it's nothing. There is nothing.' Daniel's hand turned the camera in his pocket over and over.

Reynolds sprang to his feet and in an instant was beside him, towering overhead like a stork with its beady eye fixed on the minnow beneath, breath whistling through his nose. A whiff of peppermint, or perhaps sulphur, wafted down on the breeze.

'Any business you have with Farquharson is now my business, Mr Dreghorn. So, anything you have for him, any reports, papers, notebooks or photographs… must be handed to me for appraisal.'

Daniel winced as Reynolds lingered on the word *photographs* and felt sure that the man must have noticed. What did he know? What did he think he knew? Had Mandy blabbed and described the strange man with the camera?

Reynolds took a step forwards. Daniel took a step backwards and pulled his shoulders up. The man couldn't know anything for sure. 'There's absolutely nothing, sir. Nothing at all. I have to be going now. Busy in the lab, work… and so on.'

A wide smile cracked Reynolds' face. 'Of course, Dreghorn, I don't wish to hold things up. How is your *job*, by the way?'

Daniel gave a non-committal gesture meant to indicate that everything everywhere was totally pukka and reversed out of the office.

He stumbled downstairs, fearful and depressed. Farquharson had gone. Reynolds knew about the photographs and knew that Daniel had broken into his house. It wasn't good, not good at all. He stood in the gloom of the admin block's entrance, looking out on a dull, damp day. What now? Look in on the lab? If Reynolds had his way, he might not have a job for much longer. Well, Reynolds and Farquharson could stuff their job. He had another one to go to just as soon as this mess was sorted.

He turned away from the university buildings and headed towards his flat. A couple of minutes later, an elderly woman with grey, shoulder-length hair fell in step beside him. She wore a dark suit and green tights along with a pair of unflattering, round-lensed glasses.

Daniel sighed a long sigh. 'Hello, professor.'

The woman frowned and coughed. 'Daniel,' she said petulantly. 'You recognised me.'

He raised his eyes skywards. 'Yes, professor, I recognised you.'

'I was trying for the incommunicado look. I felt I was doing well. I like to blend in as a woman,' Farquharson said, slipping an arm through Daniel's. 'I'm always comfortable as a woman. What do you think? Do I make a good woman?'

Daniel's stomach turned over as the professor pulled him closer. 'I'm sure you'll make somebody very happy,' he muttered, staring at the obvious wig, the too-tight suit and the bright, gaudy tights.

Farquharson seemed not to hear, carried away in the moment, smiling at passing pedestrians, whistling tunelessly as he perhaps imagined elderly women did.

'To your abode, Daniel. Avanti,' he cried.

Thirty-Four

DANIEL SLUMPED BACK IN his chair, staring at Farquharson who sat, glass in hand, green-tighted legs splayed in front of him. The early evening news played in the background.

The professor raised his glass. 'Good sherry, Daniel. A connoisseur's choice, if I may say so.'

Mechanically, Daniel lifted his beer in salute, wondering if the supermarket's wine buyer had got it right for once.

'Things are looking good for us, my boy.' Farquharson tapped the camera that sat in his lap.

'Well, that's just wonderful,' he muttered.

'Yes, isn't it?'

To Daniel, Farquharson sounded bright and happy, like a man on a roll rather than a man in green tights.

Farquharson continued, 'We have confirmation here that the creature Reynolds is involved in large-scale art theft, as I have long suspected. Now all we need is evidence. Hard evidence.'

'More sherry?' Daniel stared straight ahead, wishing that the professor would keep his knees together.

'Yes, thank you. We need one of those paintings.'

'I'll get you one while I top up my glass.'

'Excellent, Daniel, although I think a little more preparation may be required.'

In the kitchen, he poured more sherry into Farquharson's glass. No way would he get involved in any continuation of the idiot's mad fantasies. As he returned, glasses in hand, his eye caught the TV where white-suited figures buzzed about a white tent like flies around a... Daniel froze as he recognised the house behind them. It was Merrywick's place. They had found the body.

'Dreadful business, eh?' Farquharson shook his head. 'It seems they've arrested a senior policeman on suspicion. Can no one be trusted these days? I'll have that sherry, thanks.'

Daniel handed over the sherry and sank back in the armchair. Well, that was always what was intended. There would have been an anonymous tip-off. Dick would be pleased. He grabbed the remote and upped the volume.

... this morning at nine-thirty. The body has been taken for forensic examination but the BBC believes that from materials found on the body police have provisionally identified it as that of Joseph Svenkowski, an underworld figure who disappeared last year after being implicated in a jewellery robbery.

Feeling suddenly cold, Daniel stared at the screen. More was being said, but he didn't hear it. Joseph Svenkowski, a man. Had Celia changed sex? Had she been a man all along? Don't be stupid. What then? He could think of only one explanation: he had fished the wrong body out of the canal. Another body had been dumped in the water, lying there for god knew how long until he had pulled it out. Disgusting, awful, but did it matter? It probably made no difference to Dick what body was found in Merrywick's greenhouse. In fact perhaps a criminal's body was better as it raised the possibility of many complex motives. And the big plus point – Celia was still in the canal, and long may she continue to be.

Farquharson was watching him keenly, head nodding back and forth.

'You are a busy man, my boy. Wheels always turning, eh?'

'What? No, I...' He paused, realising that to deny anything meant he understood the professor's implication. 'Work's not been too bad recently.'

'So I see.' He raised a hand. 'But let us return to the matter of the paintings. We only need one.'

It was almost a relief to turn away from thoughts of decomposing bodies. 'Only one, well that's good. So I don't have to steal two paintings.'

'Exactly, my boy.' The professor placed his empty glass on the table. 'This one here should do. Good sherry by the way. Did I say?'

He handed the camera over with the display zoomed in on one of the paintings.

'A particularly fine Raeburn, if I am not mistaken. Stolen from Huntly Hall eighteen months ago. That should do it.'

'Professor.' Daniel pulled himself upright and pushed his chin forward. It was time to put a stop to this nonsense. 'I am not, repeat not, going to get involved in another of your crazy schemes.'

Farquharson sniffed. 'I must point out that technically it is part of the same scheme.'

'That's not the point.' Daniel wanted to jump up and down and shout but was saved from this as his front door opened.

'Hi, Daniel. Forgot my...' Sandra paused in the doorway as she spotted the professor. 'Oh, sorry. Daniel, who is...'

Daniel was on his feet, gesturing towards Farquharson. 'This is my...' He paused, staring at Farquharson's nauseating, hairy, green-clad legs, his prim skirt, his slightly askew wig. 'My boss, professor Farquharson.'

Farquharson rose to his feet, a smile cracking through the layers of make-up plastering his face. He wriggled his skirt down towards his knees and extended a hand.

Sandra stood transfixed, staring at the ghastly apparition in front of her.

Daniel raised both hands to his head and squeezed. Come on. Come on. 'He's... he's... in a play. Rehearsing for a play.'

'What?' Sandra and Farquharson said together, both turning to stare at him.

'Yes, a play.' He nodded vigorously. 'About women... and men... and things.'

'Ah, yes.' The professor winked in Daniel's direction. 'A play. In fact, it's a farce. My dear, your ah... friend here has most courteously agreed to help me in certain aspects of my performance. I am required to don dress of a feminine nature for this part and alas I have no one to advise me on the correctness or otherwise of my attire.'

Sandra, at last, tentatively shook Farquharson's hand. 'Well, he's not doing a very good...' She paused. 'That is... Look, Daniel, sorry professor, must rush. I forgot my phone. I'll just collect it and leave you to whatever it is you're doing.' She smiled vaguely and picked up her mobile from the kitchen table.

As she opened the front door, she stopped, turned back and stared once more at the tableaux that faced her. 'Right,' she said, blinking rapidly. 'OK... see you, Daniel... professor.' The door closed behind her.

Farquharson cleared his throat. 'Well, well, Daniel. A comely young lady if I may say so. I wonder if she would be prepared to...'

'No,' Daniel snapped. 'She wouldn't.'

'I only mean that...'

'No.'

The professor shrugged. 'You know best. Let's return to the little task at hand.'

'Little task! Stealing a painting?'

'Exactly. I'm glad we are in agreement. After all, compared with other matters...' Farquharson let his gaze wander to the television screen where a reporter conducted an interview. 'This will seem a straightforward matter for you.' He raised an eyebrow.

Daniel collapsed back into his chair, covering his eyes with one hand. When would this nightmare end? He had no idea. How would it end? That was much easier – disaster.

Thirty-Five

DANIEL WATCHED WITH GROWING unease as Reynolds descended the steps in front of his townhouse and glanced first right, then left. He appeared nervous, constantly checking in all directions before opening his car door. It was a chilly night, but the shivering that afflicted Daniel had little to do with the temperature.

As Reynolds Jag purred down the street and out of sight, Daniel headed for the lane to the left of the row of townhouses, the central and largest of which Reynolds occupied. There were no high walls here, just picket fences, and it took him only minutes to reach the rear door of the property, Farquharson's tools in hand. After his earlier practice, it was remarkably easy to gain entry to what appeared, in the light of his shaded torch, to be a large utility room. The door at the far end led to the kitchen where he had been blackmailed by an eight-year-old and almost discovered by her mother. Well, that wouldn't happen again. This visit would be over in the least possible time.

He crept through to the dining room and turned his torch from the photograph in his hand to the display wall with its three tiers of paintings. *Fourth from the left*. Daniel stared blankly at the seascape that hung there. That wasn't right. He looked back at the photograph. It was the correct position but the wrong picture. Daniel's heart, which until then had been having an easy time of it, started thumping. Reynolds had moved the painting, perhaps taken it away. Was he expecting Daniel's visit? Surely not likely.

To hell with it. Daniel strode to the doorway, hit the light switch, and stared once more at the amassed paintings. Hah! Relief flooded in like a spring tide. The painting had been moved. It was there, top row second from the right. He stared up at the possible Raeburn. It stared back, mocking him, well out of reach above his head. He looked, and blinked, and looked some more. How the hell?

In front of him was a pillow-soft sofa – no. Behind him, the dining table – a possibility, and dining chairs – maybe. He thought it through. Move heavy sofa. Drag table to wall. Place chair on board. Climb up. Reach up. Daniel winced as he saw himself overbalance and crash onto the dining table. No, there was a better, safer solution.

He returned to the utility room where he had entered the house. The external door hung open. Surely he had closed it? He pushed it until the lock clicked shut. Now, he was sure he had seen one earlier, and there it was – a stepladder.

Back in the dining room, and with much effort, he heaved the sofa out of the way and opened out the stepladder into an A-shape. Only another minute or two and this would be over. He climbed the ladder cautiously, testing each rung for stability, until on the second from top he was level with the painting. He put one hand out and nudged the frame. For a moment, he wondered if the thing was screwed to the wall, museum-like. But no, it hung conventionally from cord. He took a deep breath and, holding his balance, placed his hands on either side of the frame.

He froze at a guttural chuckle from below. The chuckler spoke. 'I wouldn't do that if I were you, mate.'

This was the end. There was no way out of this one. Maintaining his position, because he knew that if he didn't, he would fall off the ladder, so violent was the trembling in his arms, Daniel's gaze lowered to floor level and took in a bald, thin-faced man with a smirk.

'It's alarmed, see. Soon as that sucker comes off the wall, the balloon goes up.'

What could he say? What plausible reason could there be for breaking into a house, climbing up a ladder and attempting to remove a painting? Through a constricted throat, Daniel croaked. 'I was just... just... dusting.'

'Dusting, hah. Dusting? That's a good one. Must remember that. OK, look, you carry on. I've got to get moving.' The speaker produced a craft knife from his pocket and stepped to the nearest painting.

Daniel watched as the man slid the knife along the top edge of the frame, slit it from one side to the other and repeated the operation on the other three sides. The canvas was then deftly removed and rolled into a tube. The man moved to the next painting.

'Err...' Daniel said, as his brain tried to assimilate and concluded that all was not as he had first thought.

It took only a few seconds for another painting to end up in the same condition as the first.

'Look...' Daniel said.

The man glanced up and frowned. 'Best not hang about, mate. Quick in quick out, that's my motto. The girlfriends not so happy though, eh?' He let out a coarse laugh.

Daniel remained on the ladder, still holding on to either side of his painting. It seemed to him that the ladder wobbled alarmingly, although it may have been only his legs. There was no doubt. This man was a burglar, stealing those paintings. 'Look, I don't think you should do that.'

'What?' The man paused as he started on the fourth canvas. 'Listen, chum, no sweat, right? There's plenty here for both of us. I don't want no aggro. Take what you like and split.'

'No. You don't understand. I'm not a burglar.'

'Me neither, mate. Fiscal redistribution, that's me. Take from the rich and give to the poor: poor me.' He continued cutting the canvas.

'You're going to damage the paintings. Some of these are important.' The ladder trembled and Daniel clung closer to the wall.

The man stopped and sighed. 'You know. I'm getting tired of you, my friend. Just shut it. Two more and I'm out. You can do what you like.' He looked critically up at Daniel. 'But I would go careful with that. Alarm, remember?'

'What?' Daniel snatched his hands away, and the ladder swayed backwards. He tried to lean forward and grabbed for the frame again. He caught it but the ladder gave up the fight, flew from under his feet and...

>>>> <<<<

Daniel woke with a tight band of pain around his chest. Something heavy lay on top of him. In a panic, he pushed upright, fighting whatever pinned him down. It was the Raeburn he realised as he sat up. He still held the painting, and he had been lying on the sofa. It must have saved him when he tumbled from the ladder. Thanking all the deities he could muster, he got to his feet. Burglar Bill had disappeared. A plus point. He had the Raeburn. That made plus two. And the burglar alarm, if there was one, had not triggered, plus three. Feeling much relieved and realising that his next priority involved a rapid exit, he turned towards the door. That was when he saw the red light flashing from a box in the top corner of the room. Did it mean...? If it did, that was a minus ten at least.

With the painting under his arm, he hurried to the back door and listened. There was no sound inside or out. He yanked open the door, stepped out and into the arms of a broad and meaty policeman.

Thirty-Six

DANIEL STARED AT THE green-painted wall that faced him. There wasn't much else to stare at in a police station cell. The thin mattress he sat on did nothing to protect his bum from the hard boards below. He sincerely hoped he did not have to spend a night in this hellish box.

The first interview had not gone well. His instinct was to tell everything: every tiny detail of how he ended up in this mess. This was soon overtaken by the realisation that he was in deep shit and careful thought was required. There were many things he did not want the police to know: his involvement with Celia's disappearance and subsequent resurrection as an underworld character — a dead underworld character, his inadvertent planting of explosives for another. Either of these might be a more serious issue than the theft of one painting. So he had stalled, much to the disgust of both the interviewing officer and his police-appointed solicitor. Even to Daniel, his statement seemed evasive and contradictory. And they were charging him with the theft of six paintings. They had not believed his description of a thief busy below while Daniel balanced at the top of a ladder. The injustice was staggering.

He stood up and paced the room. Three paces in one direction, then three in the other. This was his first experience of a police cell and he would make certain it was his last. They had fingerprinted him, taken a saliva sample, taken his shoelaces.

Fingerprinted! He stopped pacing as an awful truth ambushed him. His one consolation with his previous escapades was that he had never been in trouble with the law. He had no fingerprints or DNA on file, so he couldn't be found from traces left behind. Now that had changed. There must be all sorts of trace evidence sloshing around. This was very, very bad. He sat down. At that moment, a key turned in the lock.

The door swung open and a police constable stood outside holding a tray.

'Hungry?' he asked.

Daniel grimaced. 'Not really.' But he accepted the plastic-wrapped sandwich and bottle of orange juice on the tray.

As the constable reversed out of the cell, there was an indistinct shout from above.

'That you, Sarge?' the constable shouted back, but got no reply and, frowning, pulled the door shut and locked it.

Daniel unwrapped the sandwich and bit into it. The growl from his stomach said that perhaps he was hungry. Was that another shout? He stopped chewing and listened. Something was going on upstairs. Probably some drunk having the crap beaten out of him for resisting arrest. That happened. He had read about it, although there had been no evidence of thumbscrews and gloved fists so far in his case. He finished the sandwich and lay back on the hard bed to contemplate the disastrous turn his life had taken.

More noise. Right outside the cell door this time. Daniel pulled himself up as the heavy door unlocked and slammed back against the wall. He stared in disbelief as a gaggle of men pushed through the doorway, shouting and gesticulating. The gaggle resolved itself into four burly men. No, three burly men and a thinner, older individual who seemed in charge.

'Up,' the older man yelled at Daniel.

The meaning was not - *can you please get to your feet my dear friend just as soon as you feel able, thank you*. No, it meant up and now. But Daniel did not get up. He sat tight and stared. He stared at very big, black guns, directed at him by the three larger men. His mouth opened in an attempt to speak, but he could think of nothing sensible to say. Instead of something sensible, he said, 'Would you like a drink?' and held out his soft drink bottle to the older man with a hand that had developed a tremor.

'On your feet, idiot,' the man shouted as one of his companions seized Daniel by the collar and yanked him upright.

'What's going on?' he felt obliged to say, although he did not expect an explanation. His expectations were fulfilled as they bundled him through the cell door and into the narrow corridor. With much pushing and shoving and noise the party of five staggered upstairs and tumbled into the police office. Staring at the sight that met him, Daniel's mood changed from panic to horror.

Two more men with large guns stood by the door that led to the street. On the floor, the police sergeant, the inspector and the constable who had brought him the tray lay handcuffed and bound. Daniel opened his mouth, but no words escaped.

The police constable turned his head and saw Daniel for the first time.

'Bastard,' he spat. 'We'll get you for this. You'll not get...' His words stopped as a boot lashed out and caught him in the ribs.

Daniel's mouth hung open. 'No, no, no. It's not... I'm not...' But the constable's attention was elsewhere and a violent shove propelled him towards the entrance.

Five bodies formed an intimate huddle beside the door and the leader peered out. 'Clear,' he snapped and multiple hands shoved Daniel forward, through the opening and into bright sunlight.

A capacious minivan with blacked-out windows sat by the kerb, engine running, driver at the wheel. One of the men yanked the rear door wide and Daniel sprawled on the back seat.

As the door banged shut, the leader shouted 'Go!'

'Go!' echoed a second voice.

'Go!' repeated a third.

The driver went.

Daniel passed out.

Or that was what he thought had happened as violent braking jolted him awake. Perhaps he'd been drugged or knocked unconscious but he could remember no sudden blows or stabbings with needles, but then amnesia could be the result of either he reasoned as he lay on the rear seat of the unoccupied van. He raised his head cautiously until his eyes were level with the side window.

Outside, there was movement. A huddle of men conversed in low voices, hands and arms occasionally flailed in emphasis of some point or other. In the background, a traditionally styled bungalow. Around the driveway where the van sat, the thick foliage of an overgrown garden. Escape, Daniel thought.

As the psychic vibrations of the word transmitted through the ether, there was a shout from somewhere and, as one, the group turned and headed towards him. Not escape then, as the van's door flew open, and he was ripped from his seat. The next few minutes blurred as rough hands dragged him not too gently across the grass, into the house, through a door and tipped him onto the carpeted floor of a large room.

He lay there for what would have been for a moth a substantial part of its lifetime, with eyes shut, testing out all the bodily functions he remembered. Most appeared to be in working order. Then he opened his eyes because someone had kicked his bum.

'Welcome,' said the man Daniel knew as Number One. 'I hope you are comfortable.'

There was a ripple of laughter from somewhere and Daniel twisted a stiff neck to see half a dozen men, who might or might not be the ones who had spirited him away from the police station, standing in a semicircle.

'You are a hard man to catch. Get him up.'

Two of the men grabbed Daniel by his arms and deposited him in a chair facing Number One across a broad desk.

Number One's face was impassive, but the thumb and forefinger of his right hand rubbed together rapidly in a way that said his mind was not at ease.

'Ah... hello,' said Daniel. 'How're things?'

'Hello?'

'Yes. Hello. Just wondered...'

'You fail in your mission. You destroy my headquarters, spring our captive from captivity and then you come here and all you can say to me is *hello*?' Number one's voice had risen considerably.

'Well, I wouldn't say I exactly came... not as...'

'I plucked you from obscurity.'

'Well...'

'I gave you a mission. A mission central to our great cause.' Murmurs of agreement came from behind Daniel. 'You have betrayed us.'

'That's a bit...'

'Yes? A bit what?'

Daniel grew a little in confidence. These people were certainly mad, but also rather stupid. 'Well, a bit strong, I was going to say. I mean, it's all been a big mistake when you look at things.'

'Is that so?' Number one sat back, arms folded.

'Yes, I mean the whole business. I shouldn't have been there in the first place, wouldn't have been if I hadn't followed the wrong guy and that wasn't my fault. Stupid Farquharson didn't give me the right description. So, there I was and there you were and I thought we were talking fertiliser, which we were, in a sort of way, if you know what I mean. Know what I mean? Ha, ha. I mean, the Allotment Society? What idiot dreamed up that?'

Daniel stopped. The moment the words were out he knew, just knew for certain, that it was the wrong thing to say. It would antagonise and you do not antagonise mad and stupid people, but really, the Allotment Society? 'The Allotment Society,' he said, attempting to turn a snigger into a snort but only succeeding in splattering snot onto the polished desk.

'Oops, sorry.' He rubbed the mess with his shirt sleeve.

Number one appeared oblivious to the nasal excretions on his desk. 'The Allotment Society was dreamed up by my trusted confidante, The Surgeon.' He nodded to someone behind Daniel. An enormous mountain of a man appeared beside Number One. Gnarled hands hung at the end of tree-like arms.

'Surgeon?' Daniel said in a small voice.

'Show him the tools of your trade, Surgeon,' said Number One.

A sliver of a smile cracked across The Surgeon's craggy face and he turned away for a moment and then a huge axe clattered onto the desk in front of Daniel.

He stared at the axe for several seconds. He took in the thick but beautifully polished and shaped wooden handle and the gleaming steel edge of the blade, which reflected sunlight in a pleasing way, but most of all he stared at the brown stains that splattered the rest of the blade and lower handle. 'Ah...' he said.

'We have taken a leaf from the book of our Eastern cousins. When we meet betrayal, we believe in retribution, Mr

Dreghorn, appropriate retribution.' A murmur of approval spread around the room.

Daniel shook his head, trying to clear his fogged brain. They were mad as hatters, every one. This couldn't be happening. It really couldn't.

'You can't be serious,' he said.

'On the contrary, sir. Our dedication and seriousness, as you call it, has never been questioned. Are you right or left-handed?'

'What?'

'Are you right or left-handed?' Number one spoke slowly, enunciating each word.

The surgeon's fingers delicately stroked the haft of the axe down and towards the gleaming edge, a hint of a smile on the man's lips.

Daniel hesitated. His mind refused to assimilate what his heart told him was about to happen. He was right-handed, but what was the significance of the question?

'I'm...' he paused.

'Yes?'

'Well...' What was he supposed to say? 'Actually... left-handed.'

'Good. Then let us proceed.' He stood up. 'Prepare the patient, Surgeon.'

Before Daniel could react, the man-mountain grabbed him by the neck, dragged him towards the corner of the room and forced his right arm onto a rough wooden table.

'Left,' Daniel yelled. 'I said I was left-handed.'

Number one raised a hand for silence. 'Exactly. Therefore, we shall remove your right hand. We have no wish to cripple you for life. We are not barbarians.'

Daniel peered at his right arm held fast to the table and at The Surgeon who was brushing the blade of the axe along his cheek as if shaving. 'No, no, I got it wrong. I'm right-handed. You confused me. You can't do this.'

Number one smiled. 'We are wasting time.' He nodded to The Surgeon. 'Continue,' he said.

Daniel watched as a black curtain seemed to descend around him, raised voices receded into the distance, and he fell into darkness.

Thirty-Seven

Inspector Dick watched from his car as four unknown men bundled Daniel into the rear of a minivan. They could have been undercover officers, but he thought that unlikely. Thank goodness he had kept an eye on his friend. It was a surprise that the man had been caught housebreaking. But what the hell, we all have off days. Parking outside the station, he had taken time to weigh his options. Dreghorn might, for instance, discuss aspects of their relationship which were better left in an undiscussed state. It would be preferable if he could be released without charge. Now here he was, leaving abruptly in the back of a van and apparently not all that willingly. Intrigued, Dick started his car and followed.

They had driven for thirty minutes. Exceedingly fast at first, but at a more leisurely pace now. Brake lights flashed ahead, and the van turned into a driveway and disappeared from view. Dick pulled to the side and waited. After a few moments, he heaved himself out of the driver's seat and lumbered towards the drive. A high brick wall surrounded the house, broken only by the driveway and a set of black iron gates, thankfully open. He peered around the corner of the gatepost and down the drive but saw only bushes as the road curved sharply to the left. Even the house was out of sight from this angle. He leaned back against the wall. What to do?

He was already breathless. At times of stress, his asthma took over. Who were those people who had Dreghorn? They did not look happy with their lot. They could right now be interrogating the man who might blab all sorts of nonsense. He did not want any of his ex-colleagues involved here. There was only one choice. A deep breath, then he faced the driveway and marched forward.

⋙ ⋘

The house soon came in sight, a sprawling thirties bungalow. The van was parked, rear door open, immediately beside the pillared portico of the house. To the right, a black Audi sat close to a brick-built garage. He paused and glanced about. There was nobody visible, not a soul. Keeping in the shade of the bushes, he worked his way around to the gravel turning circle in front of the main door. There was movement in the room on the left where a man stood with his back to the window, shifting from side to side, his attention focused on what was happening within.

Dick crouched down and shuffled forward across the crunching gravel, swearing as his knees creaked and protested. He struggled over a flowerbed until he was directly underneath the window, then dropped onto hands and knees. Something was happening all right. Voices were raised. One of them could be Dreghorn's. Difficult to be certain. Surely there had to be someone watching? He inched towards the three steps leading up to the black and shiny front door. His hand touched the handle and turned. The door opened a fraction, and Dick stepped back, ready to run. His heart thumped and his breath rasped in a constricted throat, but no one came to investigate. Now he heard those voices again, shouting.

Dick was acutely aware that he was defenceless, with no back-up. Then a scream came from the house. A scream of terror. It had to be Dreghorn. Wracked with indecision, he turned towards the van. Could there be help available there? He tiptoed to the rear and peered inside, recoiling at the stink of sick, or worse, that wormed up his nostrils. And then he smiled. There, discarded at the back of the van, was exactly what he needed.

He grabbed it, turned back to the house, pushed open the front door and squinted into the hallway. Deserted. The door to the left must lead to the room he had crouched under. More muffled voices, shouting, arguing. Right. Dick rotated each shoulder blade several times and strode forward.

Thirty-Eight

WHEN DANIEL WOKE FROM his faint, it was to find that he was seated at the table with his arm strapped to a flat board and a rag stuffed in his mouth. A tourniquet was being tightened around his forearm. The Surgeon stepped towards him, eyes bright, face flushed. The crowd pressed forward.

'Wait,' Daniel gasped, words muffled by what tasted like someone's underpants. 'I meant to tell you...'

But the occupants of the room, including Daniel, would never find out what he might have told them, for at that moment the door crashed open, someone bellowed 'Police. Down,' and a burst of gunfire deafened them as plaster fell from the ceiling in a shower of dust.

Daniel looked on as allotment people dropped to the floor in seeming total silence. As his hearing returned and dust cleared, he stared in disbelief at the podgy figure in the doorway. It was Inspector Dick who stood there, blinking and coughing, and waving a very large automatic weapon. A weapon which seemed in control of him rather than the other way about.

Dick gestured at him but as Daniel watched, a dark shadow came into view behind his rescuer, raised a hand holding something long and heavy-looking, and whacked Dick on the head.

⤜⤜⤜ ⟫⟫⟫

Daniel nudged the inspector with his toe, none too gently, and watched as the man groaned and stirred.

Dick grunted and sat up. 'My head,' he moaned and clasped both hands to the back of his skull.

'Yes, it's still there. Good job there's not much inside to get damaged.'

Dick appeared not to hear this comment. 'What happened? Where are we?'

'You made an arse of it. We're in the cellar.'

'God, my head.'

'Somebody clouted you. They tied me up and threw us in here. Now get this tape off my wrists.' He shuffled over to the inspector who started to unwind the parcel tape from around Daniel's wrists.

'They didn't tie me up?'

'Blistering insight.'

'What?' Dick frowned.

'But of course, you're a detective. You get paid for these observations.'

'Just a minute. What's got into you, Dreghorn?'

'What's got into me? An hour ago, I was going to have my hand chopped off. Then you come charging in with a machine gun. So I'm saved and then you cock up and we're here and I'm screwed and wondering what they're going to do now. That's what's got into me.'

'Oh my god. We have to get out of here.' Dick scrambled at Daniel's feet, unwinding the remains of the tape.

'Well, good luck with that.'

Daniel stretched and massaged his aching wrists and ankles.

From the floor, Dick surveyed the bare brick walls, absence of windows and massive wooden door of their prison. 'Crap,' he said and buried his head in his hands.

The room was no bigger than a medium-sized kitchen, the floor of roughly smoothed cement. A bare energy-saving bulb hung from the middle of the ceiling. Well, at least they were environmentally conscious. They would probably have saved his blood and sprinkled it onto the compost heap.

He got to his feet and walked the perimeter of his prison walls. There had been plenty of time to survey all the points of interest while he waited for Dick to wake. But maybe, just maybe, there was something he had missed. Five seconds later, back at his starting point, he knew there was nothing to miss. They were completely in the hands of these nutters.

He kicked the door hard, producing only a sharp pain which told him a toenail had probably broken. He grabbed the handle and pushed and heaved... and turned... and the door opened towards him so suddenly that he tumbled backwards onto the inspector.

When they had disentangled, they both stared at the open door and the darkness and mystery beyond.

'What did you do?' said Dick, in an awed voice.

'Nothing. It wasn't locked.' Daniel's thoughts tumbled over and over. Had they forgotten to lock it? Was the door faulty? Was this some crazy test? Was there an axeman waiting behind the gaping door? 'Come on,' he said. 'You can go first. I'll watch your back.'

Inspector Dick, whose imagination seemed less highly developed than Daniel's, struggled upright and poked his head through the gap. 'Nobody here,' he said.

Daniel struggled for control of his thumping heart. 'OK, let's go.' He stepped past Dick and into a short passageway. Ahead, a flight of about twelve wooden steps led up to another door. It would be locked for sure. He climbed the steps slowly, unwilling to reach the final disappointment. Placing his ear close to the door, he listened for a few seconds then took the handle, held his breath, and pressed down. The door swung outwards and he breathed again.

The inspector wheezed along behind him as he peered left into a broad and eerily deserted foyer with several closed doors. He took a step forward. The entrance door to the house, through which he had been dragged so recently, was tantalisingly close.

Dick pushed past him. 'They've scarpered. Right, sunshine, time to go.'

This had to be a trap. But why? What would be the point? Had they simply been abandoned?

Outside, it appeared that they had. The van stood with its back door wide open, but the car was gone. Out on the road, Dick's car waited for them. Daniel paused, looking right and left.

'I can't believe this. They've gone. Just left us.'

Dick fumbled in a pocket for his keys. 'What, you wanted to go with them?'

'No, I mean why leave us? They had us both in that cellar. They could have killed us.'

Dick shrugged. 'They knew I was police. We were on to them. Probably thought I'd called it in. Who gives a stuff? We're out. Just have to sort out the mess.'

They drove in silence for five minutes before Dick pulled into a lay-by. He sat for several seconds, drumming his fingers on the wheel, then turned to Daniel.

'OK, squire, here's how it is. I rescued you. Fired a few bullets in the air. They ran for it. I got you out. Fair?'

Daniel thought for a moment. It was nearly true. 'OK, but your people think I was with those nutters. That they broke me out of that cell.'

Dick shrugged. 'I'll tell them you weren't.' Then he paused briefly and scratched the stubble on his chin. 'You weren't were you?'

'No. What do you mean? Of course not.'

'OK, OK. Don't wet yourself. Didn't think you were. That lot are smart.'

Daniel began to protest but thought better of it. He needed this man on his side.

'And excellent work with that body, squire. Svenkowski, eh? That was a touch of class. Pure bloody genius. Gold medal territory that.'

Daniel nodded and said nothing.

Thirty-Nine

Two days later............

'My boy, you have excelled yourself.'

Farquharson beamed. A two-hundred-watt grin split his crinkled face, and Daniel all but ducked as the light hit him.

He sat in the professor's office, coffee in one hand, chocolate digestive in the other. 'Thank you,' he said through a spray of crumbs.

'I don't know how you did it. And I don't want to know,' he added, as Daniel opened his mouth again. 'The less I know, the more I know, in a manner of speaking. Suffice to add that Reynold's arrest has been a grievous shock to the entire university.' He nodded gravely. 'Who would have thought that our academic bosom was nurturing such a viper as he? Thank goodness his life of crime is ended, succumbing to the investigations of a master.' He treated Daniel to a very large wink.

'So, he really had stolen that painting?'

'That and many more in his collection. Oh, I don't suppose he stole them himself, but he either commissioned their theft or was a willing and knowing participant in their subsequent sale. So that is the end of Reynolds and his so-called ethics committee. Ethics, hah.' The professor made a one-fingered gesture and blew a very loud raspberry.

'Professor, I was going to ask...' Daniel paused as Farquharson raised a hand.

'No need to ask, my boy. Consider it done. A transfer of funds will be made to your bank account today. Your help has been incalculable.'

God, not more money. 'No, that wasn't...' But then Daniel stopped. Damn it. The man owed him. All the problems he had surmounted were Farquharson's doing. Why shouldn't he take his money? And Reynolds was a crook. It wasn't all in the Prof's sordid imaginings. 'Well... er... thanks.'

Farquharson raised his thumb. 'That tame policeman of yours proved a godsend, did he not?'

'Dick.'

'What?' Farquharson blinked rapidly.

'Inspector Dick.'

'Yes of course. Him. How did you get him to say that he had commissioned you to look at Reynolds's paintings?'

'It suited him, that was all.'

'Indeed. Perhaps I should offer him a little cash settlement for his expenses.'

'No! Please no. Let's leave that. I'll see to it myself.'

'Ah yes. Of course.' Farquharson gave a knowing wink. 'More appropriate. I'll advance you a little extra.'

'Oh... fine.' Daniel rubbed his forehead. All he ever wanted was a quiet life. It wasn't a great ambition. Surely it was attainable?

A long silence followed while Farquharson moved papers on his desk from one pile to another and then back again. Finally, Daniel coughed.

'Was there anything else, professor?'

'What? Ah no. That is... no.'

'I'll be going then.' Much relieved, Daniel headed for the door.

'Ah, Daniel, my boy.'

269

He stopped with his hand grasping the handle and turned to see Farquharson nervously rubbing his palms together.

'Yes?' Daniel said, trying to keep the frustration from his voice.

'You're a man of the world.'

What now? 'Possibly.'

Farquharson cleared his throat. 'I have a new friend, a young lady, well, younger than me.'

'Congratulations,' said Daniel, dryly.

'It's just that she herself has a friend, a female friend whom I'm sure would like you. She's a little older than you, naturally, but these days it's of no consequence. I wondered if some evening we might all get together for tea and... things.'

Daniel's stomach turned over. He knew exactly what Farquharson was suggesting, and tea would play little part in it. Wrinkly sex with Farquharson's two crones. He fought to keep down nausea. 'Er... thank you, but no... my girlfriend, you know, she wouldn't... well, you know... don't you?'

'She could come too,' the professor said. 'But maybe not,' he went on, perhaps seeing Daniel's nauseated expression. 'Anyway, the offer is there. A bientot mon ami.'

Daniel pulled the office door open and lurched out, trying to quell his desire to puke.

~~>>>> <<<<~~

Back home, he poured himself a large whisky. Incorrigible, that was the word for the man, although what he had suggested was fairly tame. On the Farquharson scale of perversion, it warranted no more than a two, perhaps a three at the most. The man had no morals. Then why was it he seemed to have such a good time? Oh well, that question was too deep. He downed the whisky and felt better.

Inspector Dick had also been grateful, although not to the extent of offering him money. Merrywick had resigned after the finding of the body in his greenhouse. Naturally, he denied all knowledge but resigned to save the force from embarrassment while he tried to clear his name. Dick believed he would be shoe-horned into the job and had been lauded for his heroism in rescuing Daniel from the mad gardeners who, it seemed, had disappeared into their own fertiliser. He had assured Daniel that there would be no further problem with the matter of two dead bodies. Fingerprints? DNA? Dick had tapped the side of his nose and winked.

There was only one problem left: Lorraine. Daniel sighed and placed his glass on the table. He had come to accept that perhaps she had really left him.

Forty

DANIEL SLEPT WELL THAT night and woke with a contented sigh and a long stretch. At last, life had calmed down. There was less stuff going on. Life stuff was much overrated, at least the stuff he had been subjected to lately. Thinking to get up in half an hour, he stretched and turned over towards the centre of the bed. It was then that his arm fell around the body beside him.

For a fraction of a second, his mind blanked. A body. There was a dead body in his bed. And then he screamed and tumbled onto the floor, knocking over his bedside cabinet and everything on it. At that, the dead body screamed and leapt out of bed, staggering against the bedroom door.

'What? What's going on?' the body shouted.

Daniel stared at the questioner, too shocked to move.

'Daniel, what are you doing? Is there something wrong? Is there somebody in the house?'

He gawped at Lorraine, quite unable to move or speak.

'Why did you shout like that?' A frown creased her forehead.

'Y... you,' he stuttered, finally.

'I thought you'd be pleased to see me?'

'I... it's you.'

'Well, duh,' she pouted. 'I know I'm a day early, but I didn't think that would be a problem.'

He shook his head and found that it wouldn't stop shaking. 'No, no, no, it's not but, where... when did you... I mean...' He raised his hands helplessly.

Lorraine folded her arms. 'Daniel, I know I'm back early, but why is it such a problem?'

'A day?' Daniel squealed. 'A day early?'

'A day. Yes, a day. I told you I wouldn't be able to phone. There's no mobile reception at Altnahara and you didn't answer your landline.'

'I've... well, I've been out a lot. But where have you been all this time?'

'I told you, at my girlfriend's, near Altnahara. I took some leave. She and her partner have this little croft, miles from anywhere. It's like the Good Life. They keep hens and pigs. No internet. It was wonderful, well, for a short time. I told you I was going there.'

'You did?'

Lorraine frowned. 'Yes, Daniel, I did. After you left hospital.'

After he left hospital? That was when life had gone down the toilet. Could he have forgotten? Or just not been listening? Either was possible.

'It's true that I went away rather suddenly, but your behaviour was disturbing, Daniel. I needed time to... well, to get myself together. Decide what I wanted. And I have decided.' She smiled, reached forward and her hand squeezed his elbow.

'But I didn't know. I thought...'

'Yes, OK. I shouldn't have gone like that, with no warning. I know that was wrong. But I sent you a postcard immediately after I arrived and then a long letter. What was it you thought?'

'Bugger!' The postman. That damned postman who had skipped his letters.

'What?'

'Sorry, I mean... I thought... I thought...' What the hell had he thought? What could he tell Lorraine of the quagmire he had struggled through? 'You mean you've been at your friend's ever since you left me? You haven't been kidna... kidding me about it?'

'Kidding? Daniel, what on earth do you mean? You're making no sense. My friends have invited me back to stay anytime.' She sniffed and turned away, searching in a drawer for underwear.

Daniel watched while she pulled her nightshirt over her head, balanced on one leg and stepped into a pair of blue knickers. 'Ah, ye... s,' he said as his body nudged him, reminding him of what it had been missing for the last few weeks.

'What do you mean, yes?' she snapped. 'You want me to go back?'

'Oh no, that's not...'

'And you can put that away right now.' She pointed at his crotch. 'I'm very disappointed with you, Daniel.'

'Oh, OK, sorry.' He adjusted his pyjama bottoms into a more discrete arrangement. 'It's just it's all been a shock. You coming back like this. I didn't know... I mean I did know... with your letter and postcard and everything, but there again I didn't *know* if you see what I mean.'

'No, Daniel, I don't see what you mean,' she said, pulling on a shirt and jeans. 'I hope we're not going to end up as we were. I'm going to brush my teeth. Excuse me.'

Daniel moved aside as she swept past him and into the bathroom. This was unbelievable, he thought, pulling on his own clothes. He sat on the edge of the bed and stared into space.

A few minutes later, Lorraine appeared at the door and beckoned him over. She put a hand on his shoulder and kissed him on the forehead.

'Let's start again, Danny. OK?'

'Absolutely!' His mood brightened in an instant. 'Absolutely. I'll just brush my teeth too.'

She smiled. 'You do that. I'm making some toast. I'll do you a slice.'

Daniel mechanically brushed his teeth and watched his reflection in the mirror as foam ran down his chin.

Lorraine had never been kidnapped, not even a little, and so those idiot allotment people never did have a hold over him. He had been sucked into this whole charade for no reason at all. Of course, Sandra Merrywick *had* been kidnapped, and he had liberated her. That was a good thing, wasn't it? Mmmmh came a non-committal answer somewhere deep inside his brain's right hemisphere.

Sandra? He stopped brushing. Sandra! Lorraine was unaware of the new lodger. Right now asleep, please god, in the spare room was another female. A female that his female knew nothing about. How might that play out?

Hi Danny. I've just found an attractive blonde, curvy girl in the spare room. I've got to go to work now. Have fun while I'm gone. I'll bring something back for dinner.

Well, it was possible, in a parallel universe where life was sweet and spaghetti grew on trees. He listened: silence from beyond the door. That was probably a good sign. He rinsed his mouth, opened the bathroom door a crack and peeked through the gap. Lorraine stood by the table, spreading marmalade on toast. Definitely a good sign.

He fixed a smile on his face and stepped into the room. 'Hi, Lorrie,' he said, brightly.

She looked up. 'What's wrong now?'

'Wrong? Nothing's wrong. Everything's right.'

'You sound funny,' she said, crunching a slice of toast and marmalade.

'Do I? Strange that. Anyway, thanks for the toast.' He lifted his piece and attacked it, trying to dispose of it as quickly as possible. 'I suppose you'll need to get to work soon,' he said indistinctly.

'What? Danny, that's disgusting. I can see the food in your mouth.'

For a moment, Daniel felt he was going to choke. He gulped down a mouthful of tea and did. When he had recovered and dabbed the mess from his shirt, it was to see Lorraine's frowning face.

'Sorry about that. I was just saying you'll have to go now. I mean, I suppose you'll have to go. Or you'll be late,' he added, noting her changing expressions. 'I wouldn't want to keep you back.'

There was silence in the flat. Not a single dropping pin could be heard. Silence, apart from... Had he imagined it? Of course he had. It couldn't be real. Just for a second, right on the limit of his auditory sensitivity, he had heard gentle snoring. Snoring that seemed to be increasing in volume. He repainted the smile on his face, turned to Lorraine who was rising to her feet, mouth opening.

As she spoke, Daniel heard her words slow, lengthen and deepen in timbre as if time itself was slowing to a halt and, like an iron age man frozen in a glacier, he might remain forever in this moment.

'Daniel,' she said. 'What... is...... that......... noise...................................'

Forty-One

DANIEL SKIPPED ALONG THE pavement, whistling a tune to himself. Everything was fine. He was fine, Sandra was fine, Lorraine was fine, life was fine. Lorraine had been absolutely cool about a lodger – *great idea, Danny* – the fact that the lodger was blonde, female and curvy seemed to matter not. After all, it was clear she had been sleeping in the spare room. He squinted into the sun shining from a cloudless sky, possibly niggling at an incipient melanoma on his nose, but what the hell.

'It's all fine,' he announced to the dour, elderly man patrolling the school crossing, lollipop board in hand. But he didn't wait to hear the response. He turned the corner and waltzed into the florists. A young woman behind the counter beamed a radiant smile in his direction.

'Isn't it a lovely day?' she said. 'How can I help you?'

He returned her smile. 'It's a beautiful day. I'd like a nice bunch of flowers. Something bright. For my girlfriend.'

'Of course. Let me show you.' She came around the counter. 'Actually,' she smiled shyly, 'the manager's on his lunch break and I've not been here very long, but I know we have these very nice ready-made bouquets. Just over here.'

Daniel could have sworn a drop of cold water fell on his head. A big fat drop that splattered onto his crown and trickled down through his hair. He glanced up. There was no damp patch on the ceiling, but the chilly feeling continued to trickle from the nape of his neck and down his spine. There was something he should have remembered.

The young woman had several bunches in her arms. 'Would any of these do? I'd love to get flowers like these.'

'Um,' said Daniel, as his eyes roved around a suddenly familiar shop. How had he forgotten this place?

'Of course, you can have a bouquet made to order.'

The walls were closing in – he was sure of it. The windows had those metal roller blinds. Were they shutting ever so slowly? The front door beckoned. Was it already locked?

'You said the manager was out for lunch. I'll come back another time when he's here. No offence. I'm sure you're perfectly competent and all.' He edged toward the entrance.

'Oh, he's due back any second. In fact, he's a little late,' she said, glancing at her watch. 'He's not usually late, so if you could just wait a minute, I'm sure he'll be here.'

Daniel turned towards her. 'Ah no, unfortunately. There are things you know. Stuff I have to. Appointments and so on. I'll come back when...' His voice trailed off as the door latch clicked open behind him and footsteps entered the shop.

'Ah, that's him now. Hello Mr Shazar.' She gave a cheery wave over Daniel's shoulder. 'Customer for you.'

Daniel stood frozen to the spot, his back still to the door. He fumbled in his pocket for his mobile but it wasn't there. He could have dialled 999, reported a crime about to happen, or called for an ambulance. It was well known that the earlier treatment started the better. A rapid scan of the floor revealed no trapdoors he could drop through.

His expression must have changed, for the assistant was no longer smiling. 'Sir? Mr Shazar here will see to you.' Her forehead creased. 'Are you all right?'

Daniel grabbed the baton and sprinted with it. 'I'm going to be sick.' He covered his mouth with his hand. 'Sorry... toilet...'

'Oh yes, this way, through here, please.' The assistant threw open a door behind her and urged Daniel inside. 'On the left.'

He stumbled into a tiny toilet cubicle, slammed the door and locked it. Taking deep breaths, he tried to slow his racing heart before it left him far behind. He was trapped. Shazar would be outside, baseball bat in hand, ready for some sport.

With an ear pressed against damp gloss paint, he listened intently. A low murmur trickled through. They must both be talking in the shop, so nobody watching. Fingers trembling, he slid the bolt back, cracked the door open and peered through the gap. Clear. To the right was the doorway through to the front shop, to the left shelves lined the corridor and at the end another door which just might lead to escape.

Holding his breath, he crept towards the rear exit and reached for the handle. If only his luck would hold.

'Mr Dreghorn, sir?'

The voice came from behind. He grabbed the handle, twisted it, pushed it, pulled it. Locked. Slowly he turned about, hands rising to protect his face from assault and stared in wonder at the smiling man in front of him.

'This way, please. You have taken a wrong turning.' Mr Shazar pulled open the door to the shop and ushered Daniel through. 'Are you feeling better, sir?'

Daniel hesitated in the middle of the floor as Mr Shazar and his assistant watched him solicitously. 'I'm... um... fine, thank you. Look... about the money, the flowers...'

Mr Shazar interrupted, hands flapping. 'Please, no need. Everything is fine. Your friend explained when he settled the bill.'

'Friend... bill...?'

'Yes, Mr F. Carson he has said is his name. He is a good friend, I think.'

Farquharson. Well, sometimes things just work out right. 'Oh yes. A great friend.'

'He settled your bill and explained your... problem.' He shifted uncomfortably.

Daniel struggled to absorb this dramatic about-turn in circumstances. 'Bill... problem?'

'Yes, sir. Your mother's illness, your stay in the ah... in the hospital. But now you have been released and I hope everything is good in your life.'

Well Quentin, for once you're a star, Daniel thought. But what hospital? Best take it no further. 'Yes, yes. He told me he'd settled the bill. Look, I'll be back later for the flowers. Just remembered something I've got to do... left the oven on.' Daniel reversed towards the door.

'But, sir.'

'Sorry, back later. The postman... big delivery.' The door shut behind him. He was free.

Forty-Two

DANIEL SAT IN FARQUHARSON'S outer office watching Miss Kylie Timpson filing her nails. Petite, with coal-black hair and a chest quite out of proportion to the rest of her body, she giggled and announced, 'He's such a sweetie-pie don't you think?'

Oh well. At least Farquharson's life was getting back to normal. He searched the girl's face for any trace of irony but found none. 'Well, I suppose he's been called worse.'

She pouted. 'Sweetie-pie's not a worse thing, it's a good thing. He's a dear old man. He reminds me of my grandpa.'

Should he try to warn her about her grandpa look-alike? No, no, no, no. 'No,' he said. 'I mean, got about a bit, did he, your grandpa?'

'He was in the merchant navy. Travelled all over.'

Daniel didn't want a long conversation with Farquharson's squeeze. He glanced at his watch. 'Do you think he's free now?'

'Oh, he's dead.'

'What?'

'Grandpa. He's dead.'

'Oh, yeah. Right. I mean sorry. I meant is Farquharson free?'

She pressed a button on the box at her desk. 'Quentie, are you free now?'

Quentie! Daniel's stomach tried for the backflip. Indistinct words crackled from the speaker.

'Naughty,' said Kylie. 'It's Mr Dreghorn to see you about something.'

She turned towards Daniel. 'You can go in now, he says. He mentioned a rock?' She looked puzzled.

'He has a granite fetish,' he said, knocking on Farquharson's door. 'You should ask him about his Silurian schist.' He left Kylie scribbling on her pad and pushed open the door.

'My boy!' Farquharson stood in front of his desk, arms wide and advancing. Both hands wound around Daniel's shoulders and pulled him tight. Their bodies squashed together. Arms by his side, teeth clenched, Daniel tried to suppress the gag reflex.

Farquharson released his grip and stepped back. Apparently moved, he produced a large green handkerchief and dabbed at moist eyes.

'Where would I be without you, Daniel?'

'Honestly, professor, I have no idea.'

'Exactly. I would be lost in the nether jungle, cast from the bosom of our alma mater, gnashing my teeth in the outer darkness while evil triumphed in the light.'

He took a seat by Farquharson's desk without being asked. 'I suppose that means you would have lost your job?'

'That too. Most certainly. And now the beast Reynolds has gone, dismissed while investigation continues into the art theft. All is well.' He dropped into his chair, opened his hands wide. 'What can I do for you, my dear friend? You have need of more funds?'

'No, I do not have need for more funds.' Daniel fished in his pocket and produced a rather crumpled envelope. 'I came to give you this. It's my resignation letter.' He placed the crumpled envelope on Farquharson's desk.

Farquharson stared at the letter for several seconds, then bent forward and picked it up by the corner, holding it between thumb and forefinger as if closer contact might transmit some deadly infection. He made no attempt to open it but took a deep breath and replaced it on his desk.

He regarded Daniel with watery eyes. 'I knew this moment would come, my dear boy. But that doesn't make it any easier.'

Daniel folded his arms and concentrated on the cord of the window blind behind Farquharson's head.

'This is a sad day,' Farquharson continued. 'A sad day for us both. We are like a couple you and I: a couple breaking asunder after a long and happy marriage, a fruitful marriage, a marriage of like minds, a marriage of equals.'

Daniel looked at the ceiling and kept his mouth shut.

'Can I dissuade you, my boy? How can I change the course you have set for your life's voyage? How can I deflect the trade winds that are blowing you from my bosom?'

'Sorry, professor. My mind's made up. I have another job offer which I have accepted.'

'A higher remuneration?'

'Money's not the issue.'

'It's not?' Farquharson's brow furrowed. 'I see. Well, what else could we offer you? A car with the job?'

'No, professor.' Daniel shook his head.

Farquharson rubbed his chin. 'I'm sure we could find something for a young, red-blooded, heterosexual male such as yourself.'

'No.'

'But—'

'You already tried that.'

'Did I? Ah.' He tapped his teeth with his pen. 'You are heterosexual, aren't you?'

'Yes I am. Definitely.'

'Thought so. I can usually tell. I myself, as you may know, have always believed in keeping doors open lest opportunity comes knocking.'

'Revolving doors,' Daniel muttered.

'Sorry?'

'I have a girlfriend.'

Farquharson appeared puzzled, as if the presence of a girl-friend was irrelevant. He lowered his voice. 'The little tryst I suggested to you earlier was a mistake. It would not have been suitable to your tastes. Now the young lady next door, Kylie is her name, seems very accommodating. We go for a meal tomor-row evening. I would be delighted if you could join us. I'm sure something could be arranged.'

'No. I'm leaving,' Daniel said, his voice so firm that it sur-prised him. 'Nothing will persuade me to stay.'

'But who can replace you? I will be bereft.'

'Alex is quite capable of replacing me in the lab, although he's not good at break-ins or dealing with psychopaths.'

'Your colleague? Yes, yes indeed.' Farquharson closed his eyes, tapped his fingertips together. 'And where are you going, may I ask?'

Daniel hesitated. Should he reveal anything? Yet to say noth-ing seemed rude. It was likely he would find out in any case. 'It's a pharmaceutical company, Thompson's Tablets.'

Farquharson's fingers stopped tapping. 'Thompson's Tablets? How quaint. What do they make?'

'Well, tablets I suppose. You can tell by the name.'

'So, you are leaving our hallowed walls to prostrate before the god of mammon.'

Hallowed walls. Should he laugh aloud at that? 'If that means I'm going to move to a job where I don't get chased by maniacs and nearly get bits of me chopped off then, yes,' he said.

Farquharson stroked his chin. 'I think you exaggerate, my boy. But no matter, I can see your mind is made up.'

He got to his feet and extended a scrawny hand. 'I wish you well in your future. Rocks like you are hard to find in today's shifting sands. May you prosper and live long.'

Daniel stood and shook Farquharson's hand almost warmly. He had expected some last-minute trickery from the old reprobate. Why, he could just about believe there was a tear in the fossil's eye. 'I suppose I should say thank you, for... well... everything.'

'You are most welcome, my boy. And don't hesitate to let me know if you need a reference.'

'I will. Well... thank you, professor.'

As the office door closed behind him and he made his way downstairs, Daniel reflected that perhaps the randy old goat wasn't such a bad sort after all. In the end, he had accepted the resignation with good grace. After all, there was nothing wrong with trying to persuade him to stay. It was quite natural, as he had given the man a lot of help.

And now – a new life. A life in which Farquharson and his shenanigans would take not the tiniest part. He threw open the outer door and stepped into the sunlight.

The office door closed and Farquharson resumed his seat. He stretched and yawned. It was a shame. He felt sure that leaving the university was the wrong move for Dreghorn. The young were so wimpish nowadays, taking fright at the slightest obstacle placed in their path. Dreghorn was made for academic life. He drummed his fingers on the desktop while he worked out the best approach. Then he picked up his telephone and dialled. After a few seconds, the call was answered.

'Is that Thompson's Tablets?'

'Excellent. By the way, my dear, you have a lovely voice...'

'You're welcome. A credit to your organisation...'

'Oh yes, I'd like to speak to Tommy Thompson, please...'

'Who? Oh, just say it's QF here, concerning a personnel matter. He knows who I am.' He allowed himself a smile. 'We go back a long way.'

If you enjoyed The Allotment Society try the first in the Dreghorn series A Clear Solution

Scanning the code below will take you to the listing on Amazon or you can order direct from the author at

www.ericmcfarlane.co.uk

SCAN ME

Printed in Dunstable, United Kingdom